MW01223826

DIVINE
Elemental

A Novel

Raywat Deonandan

We acknowledge the support of the Canada Council for the Arts for our publishing program. We also acknowledge support from the Ontario Arts Council.

Cover design by David Drummond

Edited by Charles Anthony Stuart

Author photo by Tine De Marez

National Library of Canada Cataloguing in Publication

Deonandan, Raywat S. (Raywat Shanker), 1967-
Divine elemental / Raywat Deonandan.

ISBN 1-894770-08-0

I. Title.

PS8557.E583D59 2003 C813'.54 C2003-905672-4

Printed in Canada by Coach House Printing

TSAR Publications
P. O. Box 6996, Station A
Toronto, Ontario M5W 1X7
Canada

www.tsarbooks.com

For Phanindra, Bhashkar, Abhi and Kalowatie

Contents

1

The Tale of Tomamu Nomei

The story of Kalya's great-great-grandfather was well known in certain villages in Bihar. Narinder Lal had been a zamindar, after all, and the undeserved mystique of a great landowner transcends the passage of time, changes of governments, and revolutions of most kinds.

Kalya nuzzled the crook of her Ajee's elbow, the familiar and calming scent of baby powder filling her nostrils. The serenity of the halcyon womb was forever unattainable, but a close simulation could be found in her grandmother's warm embrace at late twilight, as the fireside spat random embers and dessicated leaves rustled in the early evening breezes.

The tale was a familiar one, of course, but it was always welcome—more so now that it was being told here in a Bihari village, with proper Indian constellations looming above them and the evening air vibrant with enchanting subcontinental smells. The setting was like a dream, its etherealness softened by the dulling hues of descending night. Ajee spoke rhythmically while rocking backwards and forwards, occasionally slapping her knee to mark the cadence.

Like Indian music, which revels in melody but has never discovered harmony, Ajee's voice was a tuneful solo but it carried great affection and presence. For Kalya's benefit, she spoke in English, though sometimes sighing under her breath in Hindi or in the tribal language Mahali. She spoke of Narinder Lal, zamindar of a Bihar village called Whell, many years before Independence. Like all landlords of the type, he was wealthy for a village man, accepting payments, honourable and otherwise, from the farmers who, by his grace, were productive on his lands.

It was into this miasma of feudal exchange, the story went, that the foreign woman arrived. She was paler than most northerners, but small of bone and lithe of hand. In the Himalayan region there was much interaction with the Mongoloid races, and many Indians had acquired sage epicanthic folds through generations of interbreeding; this woman could have been one of them. She had the softly slitted eyes of the people of Sindh, and her milk-white skin suggested legends of divine beauty.

As the tale had suffered through many years of retelling and enhancement, it was not truly known how the woman had arrived, nor where exactly her first appearance was noted. But it was generally agreed that she had deliberately made her way to the estate of Narinder Lal. As Ajee told it, the moon was but a sliver and the sky cloudless that night. The air was warm, with an occasional chilling gust that swirled the dead leaves, and caused the passing women to pull their saris tightly around them. But as it was a temperate time just prior to the monsoons, there were philanderers aplenty lazily roaming the estate, each entranced by the silent beauty that shuffled by them, but none courageous enough to approach her.

The woman walked delicately, with short steps hindered by the tightness of her long and foreign sari. She gripped the folds of cloth about her hips and kept her eyes downward, yet she progressed with noble intent up the estate's great walk and directly to the front door.

Old Ajee paused to reshape her grey hair into a ponytail. Kalya took the opportunity to snuggle into Ajee's side. The sun had fully set, and her older cousin, Subodh, was beckoning them to return to the tent, but Ajee waved him away. The boys could never appreciate the placidity of such experiences; this was for Kalya.

"Was it Tomamu Nomei, Ajee?" Kalya asked.

"Mmm, yes. That's what we know now."

Tomamu Nomei rapped softly against the pine door. She was greeted by the servant, who frowned and hesitated, but who nonetheless wordlessly beckoned the visitor inside. Balls of dust wafted out the open door, embarrassing the sloppy servant, who harrumphed dutifully as if to blame Tomamu for the shoddiness of his own cleaning.

Narinder Lal's wife and children were away from the village, possibly visiting relatives. So the grand home was dark and silent, lonely but for the scurrying of the servant and the occasional turning of the heavy pages of Tennyson's *The Lady of Shalott*, the half-deaf Narinder Lal's favourite Western verse. There was complete silence when Lal's gaze slowly lifted from the yellowed pages to the delicate figure framed in the hallway.

The wordless moment was palpable, thick with the flow of biochemical fogs that spread from their bodies and mingled in between. A man not old, but well beyond youth, Lal felt his manhood stir beneath his lungi, yet Tomamu's face could not be seen from the hallway's darkness. Her femininity was betrayed only by her scent and by the ghostly figure she made against flickering candlelight.

Ajee paused then, and looked abruptly at the expectant Kalya. The girl was only eleven, but Ajee knew that America aged them faster. Had she been allowed to grow up here in India, among her histories, she would possibly be betrothed by now, and but a few summers from real womanhood. Yet she would have been protected by the harshness that was always lurking beyond the perimeter.

"You know what big people do, child . . . when they're alone?" she asked.

"Yes, Ajee. It's okay." Kalya sighed inwardly, anticipating the censored version of the tale, with few if any references to the male lingam and female yoni. Hollywood movies were more graphic, but nothing titillated better than a slyly told story of ancient and phantasmic seduction.

In the tale, Tomamu Nomei stepped forward into the heart of the candlelight, revealing her phantom beauty to Lal's intensifying gaze. He, of course, was overcome by physical desire. He lunged to his feet, paused for a moment to allow Tomamu's womanly form to be consumed fully by his widening eyes, then took her forcefully into his arms. He buried his face into her neck and sunk rapidly to her heaving breasts, tasting the sweet beads of perspiration that settled there, and sucking in her odour, breathing deeper with each intake, as if drawing recklessly from an opium pipe.

Tomamu offered no resistance, cupping Lal's shoulder blades in her soft palms. In Ajee's version, Tomamu whispered barely audible words of seduction into Lal's unhearing ear. Though his brain remained too distracted to decode the soft words, his soul heard them loudly and was enchanted by them. She spoke special words that remain unknown to most mortal men—words of power and control, words that are howled by wild beasts in the depths of deep-hued forests and recited with fear and diligence by healers and priests.

So, as Narinder Lal tasted of Tomamu Nomei's fleshly delights, she consumed his will.

Lal's wife and children weren't expected to return from their journey for some months and Tomamu was well entrenched in the Lal estate long before then. She occupied the home with queenly dictate, gesturing her orders to the servants, and commissioning a greater monetary fealty from the farmers who used the Lal lands. No one seemed to mind; she commanded such charm and allure that the farmers eagerly lined up to pay her their dues. Not since the last great festival had these men bathed so thoroughly or oiled their hair so fastidiously.

The Lal family coffers grew rich from Tomamu's ministrations. But Narinder Lal himself seemed oblivious to his new wealth. His life consisted of devouring Tennyson by day and his mistress by night. It is not known if he had had other illicit lovers prior to the enchantress. But surely no man before had been so utterly consumed by an extramarital dalliance as was Lal by Tomamu. In her he saw the Lady of Shalott, or Helen of Troy, a terrible beauty who could cause great kingdoms to fall. On her first arrival, she had intruded upon his reading of Tennyson, so it was understandable that he was fixated upon those words whenever bathed in her pheremonal cloud.

On a moonless night prior to his wife's return, Lal drew Tomamu to his bed and took her beneath him, carefully peeling back the white silks in which he had bid her dress. "Lying, robed in snowy white. That loosely flew to left and right . . ."

"Yaar," she cooed

". . . the leaves upon her falling light. . ."

"Tomorrow your wife returns. You must deny her," she sang into his deaf ear.

". . . thro' the noises of the night. . ." She took his earlobe between her lips and tongued the little hairs that cowered there. Surely, it was a serpentine tongue that must have proceeded into his aural canal and through to his brain, slathering his unconscious mind with her reptilian saliva.

On that night, for the first time, Narinder succeeded in completing his recitation of a whole Tennysonian stanza: ". . . she floated down to Camelot."

When Mrs Lal returned from her travels the next morning with her three small children, she found her personal belongings packed, and servants waiting by a lorry. Ajee's version did not relate Mrs Lal's reactions or emotions, merely that she was ushered away while her children were suffered to stay. Kalya bristled at this, sensing that something was being held from her. Surely, a dispossessed wife would have ranted and flung herself upon such an intruder. Surely, she would have gathered her children to her bosom, refusing to leave them under the shadow of a mysterious and diabolical woman. And surely, she would have rushed to her father and brothers, gathering an army for the recapture of her rural estate.

But no. For the sake of the tale, Mrs Lal obeyed her husband and fled the village wordlessly, leaving her distressed but silent children standing on the walk-up, perplexed as to the status of the new woman of the house. "But she did not leave completely silently," Ajee added. "No, child. When the lorry passed the village outskirts, Mrs Lal turned her head back to her former home and spat a curse. She spoke to God and asked that Tomamu Nomei's descendants be hunted like the animals they were. For that is what Tomamu was, you know, an animal taken human form."

Kalya swallowed hard and poked her head out from under Ajee's armpit. The night was too dark for the trees of the forest to be made out with certainty. But the glow of the fire illuminated well the canvas sides of the tents. Aside from this, the blackness was total, for the stars and slivered moon were masked by clouds. But the soundscape was imperfectly silent, with the wind beating the tops of trees, the fireside embers snapping now and again, and the occasional howl of a distant monkey slicing through the stillness.

Daddy had said many times that there was nothing in the dark that was not there in the light. But Daddy did not know everything. It was from the darkness that such creatures as Tomamu Nomei emerge. In the light, perhaps, their powers wane, but persist. In the dark, they are born and thrive.

"It was not long," Ajee said, "before Tomamu was pregnant with Lal's child."

Though burdened with child, she did not seem to grow larger, only more alluring. Lal took the news without care, concerned only for his own physiological responses to his Lady's inhuman chemical fog. Her ministrations upon him continued nightly, never waning in intensity or novelty. And her management of the family finances continued to solidify, until the estate became the only nexus of wealth in the region.

Narinder Lal's children lived these months nervously, their mother being absent and their father distracted. Essentially raised by servants, they went to school by day, and cowered back to their rooms at night. Never did they hear Tomamu speak, and rarely were they in her company. In truth, she seemed only to speak to Lal, and to the occasional vassal farmer who attempted to plead indolence to her call for greater rent. Even then, her words were soft but compelling.

The children did not fear Tomamu. They simply felt like strangers in their own home. The eldest, Jagdip, was approaching his teens, and therefore would soon be expected to adopt some of his father's managerial duties. Yet he had not spoken with his father in months and was now unsure of his place.

Kalya had been raised on Western fairy tales. These semi-dark accounts of abandoned children were familiar to her, and she could sense the next phase of the story: the revolt of the children against their oppressors, aided by a *deus ex machina* such as fairies or talking mice. Surely, she thought, the mother was in secret contact with her offspring and was gathering her resources to effect a rescue. But this was an Indian tale, subject to the moralistic and epic infusions that characterize the subcontinent; much darkness must come before the first hints of light.

Indeed, as Tomamu progressed in her pregnancy, she once more took hold of Lal's deaf ear between her teeth. She did not whisper as much as gurgle, inserting her vociferations expertly in between Lal's unconscious recitations of Tennyson.

"Heard a carol, mournful, holy. . ." Lal intoned as he mindlessly slid along the sexual path.

"Yaar," she sang.

". . .chanted loudly, chanted lowly. . ."

"Our child is your true heir. You must disavow Jagdip." She sucked hard on his whole ear, causing it to pop and depressurize.

"Till her blood was frozen slowly. . ." Lal gasped, unsure of what had happened. ". . .the Lady of Shalott." But he concluded his carnal task happily, rolling back to sink into the post-coital dream.

The dream was restless. In it, he was riding his bicycle along a country road beyond the village. In dreamtime, the lazy afternoon dissolved into blackest night, illuminated at points by a blinding full moon. His bicycle struck a large rock, tossing him into a pool of watery mud and splashing his frightened face. His right ankle landed into a bear trap. The trap snapped shut silently, its rusting teeth tearing into his bony leg with a searing pain. Despite the pain of his bloodied and crushed leg, the dreaming Lal was pushed to consciousness of yet greater peril: the arrival of ominous visitors during this vulnerable moment.

They were four women of uncertain age and caste, all but their brown eyes hidden behind layers of tattered cloth, their attitudes staid and serious, but their movements slyly sexual. They gathered about his prone body but did not attempt to comfort him or to minister to his wounds. Instead, they simply stared at him. In the dream, Lal looked to his ankle, concerned not so much about infection, as the immediate threat of wild animals that, attracted by the scent of blood, might try to devour him. Yet no matter where he cast his gaze—to his ankle, to the moon, or to the trees— he was met by the unspeaking gaze of one of the women.

The fear began to rise up through his esophagus, threatening to choke his will and stifle his breath. Despite their oddly sexual allurements, these women were terrible creatures to be sure. And Lal could sense other dangers in the trees. Oddly, the moon bore down only upon his body and his bicycle; all else was cached in blackness. And where there is black, there are often unseen designs.

As the fear became unbearable, and Lal felt a scream rising in his throat, one of the weird women bent close to him and spoke in a clear and familiar voice. She said, "Who are you?"

Lal turned to the ground then, back to the muddy pool in which he had first fallen. There, framed by the eerie moonlight, he saw his fat sweaty face peering back at him. Then he awoke, finding himself once more upon the dry safety of his curtained mattress, with his mysterious lover lying still and soundless next to him.

At this part of the tale, Kalya's mind turned to minutiae. Of what relevance was a dream that ended so uncertainly? And, more importantly, in whose familiar voice did the weird woman speak to Lal?

"Whose voice do you think it was?" Ajee asked.

"I don't know, Ajee. Was it Lal's wife?" Ajee just shrugged and continued the tale.

More months passed; exactly how many remains uncertain. Still not large enough to be obviously pregnant, Tomamu announced to Lal that her pregnancy was near its end, and that a baby daughter was forthcoming. How she could know this was never asked; people knew better than to question demonic foreknowledge.

Despite Tomamu's exercises of suggestion upon his deaf ear, Lal had still not confronted Jagdip with his intentions for his familial legacy. The task would be doubly difficult since theirs was a tradition that excluded daughters from the line of inheritance. Yet there had been cases in recent history in which women had usurped family lands and power from their less competent brothers.

Tomamu was enraged by Lal's dithering, of course, and her blood rose to her head, causing it to swell and smoke. At these times, she would take Lal by the shoulders, throw him to the floor and engage in violent, impatient sex. Her heat would grasp Lal in his most cherished of parts, then seep from there upward to his navel and against his spine. Soon, his chest would be ablaze, his mouth dry and inflamed. Then, as sexual climax approached, his very brain would seem to expand and threaten to explode.

Through bloodshot eyes he would see his mysterious lover in a sea of red, appearing to fume as she bucked and swayed. Her rage was evident, and he felt his will being sapped by her motions, pulled through his penis into her womb. Could it be, he would ask himself, that Tomamu's unborn child fed upon his spirit?

During these months, the dreams continued. It was usually after lovemaking, when the spent body was compelled to sleep by chemical fatigue, that the four weird women returned to him. Sometimes he would be caught again in the bear trap, other times drowning in a pond, and sometimes being chased by dogs or by brigands. But always, as the fear rose to its most intense pitch, the same women would arrive and ask in that familiar voice, "Who are you?"

Kalya had never been one for stories that involved dreams. Her many aunties had often used allegories and parables to preach moralisms at her, and a dream was yet another lesson hidden amongst indirect images. She could certainly appreciate the dreams' effect on her poor forebear, however, as she too had endured the tedium of the recurring nightmare.

Like most children, Kalya's dreams touched the primal, tapped her limited but visceral experiences: the out-of-breath chase, the terror of impending abandonment, and, of course, the standard fall from a great height. Oddly, the latter was not a frightening vision, merely an exciting one to be anticipated as a child would thirst for a roller-coaster ride. In Kalya's case, the dreams of pursuit were the ones she most dreaded. In them, her forward vision would expand to more than 180 degrees as, fleeing across rolling hills and rocky valleys, she was chased by an unseen predator in glaring daylight.

Her impressions of Lal's dreams, as told by Ajee, were more sinister. Thoughts of such bizarre events during the dark night are always disturbing; to dream at night of a dream in night is a disconcerting pattern to be sure. She knew that this signalled a crucial change in Lal's behaviour. And, as Kalya predicted, the tale's telling progressed onward to a precipice.

On a warm afternoon on the eve of his new daughter's birth, Lal finally found the nerve to summon Jagdip to his study. Lal was a bit surprised to find his eldest son considerably taller than he had remembered him to be, and he thought he heard the stirrings of a melancholy but manly baritone when Jagdip spoke.

"Pa?"

"How is everything, Jagdip?" Lal asked, uncertain of how to broach the subject of the impending new addition to the family.

"We manage, Pa. Where is Ma?" Lal had not been prepared for such a response, nor for a direct question of this nature. In truth, he had no idea where his wife had fled. He had sent her to her father's house in Uttar Pradesh, but whether she had remained there was unknown.

"She has gone to visit her family, Jagdip," he finally said.

"No she hasn't. You sent her away, and she cannot come back. You did this, you sleep with another woman, and now you lie to me!"

Lal was rendered speechless by his son's forthrightness. Unlike his own father, Lal had never been a disciplinarian, and even now was unsure of how to deal with his son's insolence. Appropriate parental protocol would surely require that he brandish a thick leather belt and bellow primal male indignancies and threats of social, pecuniary and physical violence. But Lal's instinct was to furrow his brow silently and to examine carefully the lines of anger that had been driven so fiercely into the corners of Jagdip's mouth, creasing forever the handsome boy's pristine brown skin, and thus leaving a permanent anatomical record of these doings.

Lal mentally searched through stanzas of Tennyson for guidance. The poet's verse seemed so pointless now, useful only for describing long-dead white women and the mindless follies of suicidal soldiers. The feeling that washed over him was not the poetic thrush of lustful angst or sentimental wonder, but a deeply piercing guilt that bore into his stomach with nauseating slowness.

"Who are you," Jagdip demanded, "that would send his wife away? How can you keep our mother from us? I don't know who you are anymore, Pa." And once more: "Who are you?"

Aahhhh, Kalya realised. The dream becomes real!

Ajee's version of the tale said nothing more about Jagdip. It was assumed by most that he grew up well enough, became a landowner himself, though not a zamindar, since that station was outlawed upon

Independence, and had many children, as did his proper sisters and brothers. But his importance lingered that day in his father's mind, as the seed of responsibility once more took root in Narinder Lal's heart, and began to push away the spell that had taken such hold over it these past months.

Lal brooded that afternoon, failing to find solace in his books and in the prosperity that had newly enhanced his estate. He found himself crouched upon a chair on the walk-up, refusing to take visitors or speak to servants. His mistress was nowhere to be found, or else surely he would have sought selfish comfort in her arms and between her legs.

But Tomamu Nomei was busy with concerns of her own, for she would give birth that evening. Where she spent the afternoon is unknown, but many story-tellers have since speculated about her unnatural activities. Perhaps she had stolen into the woods to perform puja to a beastly nether-god. Or perhaps she had returned temporarily to her natural form, and had watched the humans from a safe perch in the near forest.

What is known is that she made her way back to the estate in early evening, beckoning the servants to prepare the instruments of childbirth. And as the final rays of sunlight were swallowed by the horizon, she brought forth a Chinese-eyed baby girl into the world.

In Ajee's version, Lal had not been present at the birth. Instead, he remained in contemplation in his chair, where he let the guilt of his actions wash over him in recurring waves. With each successive wave, he would question his worth as a man, his strength as a leader. Perhaps, at times, he dozed off briefly, and was catapulted back into the dream of the weird women. Or perhaps he sat there for hours in full consciousness, refusing to accept the solace of sleep, no matter how unrestful.

To be sure, at one point he tore into the house to find his wife's make-up mirror, a small hand-held variety. The servants reported seeing him transfixed upon his own image in the mirror as the day's light waned and finally disappeared. There is strength in numbers, and Lal had found a compatriot in his reflection. "Who am I?" he asked himself. "I am Narinder Lal, a father and a husband, and a zamindar of this village."

Kalya rolled her eyes at his point. Here was the parable's moral at last, in typical Indian fashion: the importance of duty. How typical and predictable, almost tiresome. It was, however, not an entirely unpalatable moral.

"And do you know what he did next, child?" Ajee asked.

"I dunno, Ajee. Did he kill the baby? Me, I would've killed Tomamu and the baby, and gone and found my wife!" Kalya knew the response that was required of her. Had this been North America, the thought of dispatching a newborn would be unacceptable, for, as she had heard so many times, a child has no responsibility for her parents' actions. But this was India, where evil deeds transcend generations, and where one is born burdened by the actions of past lives, destined to accrue and spend karma like the spiritual currency it is misunderstood to be. Tomamu's baby would indeed be guilty of her forebear's evils, and Lal would be a godly man for bashing its skull against a rock.

"Maybe that's what he should've done, eh?" Ajee said. "Instead, he dragged the wicked woman out into the field, under the full moon—"

"And the baby?"

"The baby Lal did leave with the servant in the house. He had only eyes for the devil-woman."

Tomamu was surprised, of course. While she was cradling her offspring against her breast, Lal had wrenched her arm and she was forced to abandon the child in the care of the mistrusted servant. Her diabolical designs were unstrung now, and she focused her energies upon two fronts: concern for her child, and control over the man. She hadn't the energy for seduction or for fury. Had she been allowed to gather her forces, surely she would have once again grasped Lal's deaf ear and poured into it powerful words of suggestion, forcing him back under her influence. Or perhaps she would have found the beastly strength that her animal heart pumped through her veins, to claw out her attacker's eye, and drag his bleeding form into the woods to be savaged by the wild things that lay in wait there.

But, inadvertently, Lal had chosen his moment well. He had dragged her through the maze of manicured bushes that circled the estate, into an ancient grove at the edge of the forest, one subtended by a massive grey fig tree that the clan had named Yggdrasil. Beneath the spidery branches of the ancient tree, he held his mistress by the nape of her neck, straining to ignore the sexual stimulation of this rough action. Avoiding

Tomamu's slitting eyes, Lal then forced her to look upon her reflection in a mirror, relying on the soft and magical moonlight to illuminate with truth a tissue of lies.

What peered back at Tomamu from within the mirror was not the face of a lovely foreign woman, nor the bloody terror of a demonic incarnation. What both Lal and Tomamu saw that night, where the reflection of the mystery woman should have rested, was the sleek and unfeeling face of a forest fox, a wild animal with bright and tympanic eyes.

Tomamu tore free of Lal's grip and raced past the tree trunk into the thickening forest, not bothering to hold the folds of her sari in a lady-like manner. Lal watched her run, seeing the sari's spot of whiteness shrink in the distance, until devoured completely by the enveloping night.

"And they never saw her again," Ajee said.

"And the baby?" Kalya asked.

At this, Ajee smiled her toothless smile. "The child was adopted by Lal and his wife," she said. "Raised like one of their own. They named her Shalott."

The Bihari night breeze was chilly now, and Kalya nestled protectively into Ajee's warm body. My village, she said to herself, casting her eyes in the direction of Whell, away from the trees, where the tree Yggdrasil still reached from the woods toward the estate. This is my village. It was here, or somewhere near here, that Tomamu had fled into the woods so many years ago, her animal spirit regressing to its unthinking default: fear and flight.

The sounds of an Asian night are always restless, confused by warm breezes that push through thick leaves and by the competing calls of various fauna as well as the occasional noise of human culture. On this night, Kalya made it a point to try to identify the individual sounds, separating the monkeys' howls from the dogs' whimpers and the night birds' squawks. From that panoply, she strained to make out the scurrying of the lone fox that no doubt patrolled its territory. All like a storybook.

"Ajee?"

"Yes, child."

"Was Shalott my great-grandmother?"

Ajee's eyebrows reached for her hairline. She pushed herself to her feet and beckoned for Kalya to follow her to the tent Subodh had prepared. "That's something you will have to decide, child."

The air was still as the pair disappeared into the tent, as if the world were silent when no one was there to listen to it. The storybook had opened when the night had fallen, and it had closed again with the closing of the tent. The waking dream would end just as the sleeping one was to begin. Kalya pushed herself desperately against her Ajee's warmth, content that the beasts of the Bihar forest could be held at bay by an old woman's snores.

2

ELEMENTAL

Here is one opinion. It is the arrogance of men that prevents them from perceiving the imperceptible, from allowing themselves to consider that which is not obvious. An example: honeybees can see in wavelengths that are invisible to human eyes, yet not until relatively recently could we accept that such imperceptible wavelengths exist—not until we were able to reproduce bees' eyes with our machines.

In Tibetan mythology, there exists a place called Shambhala, a divine city populated by ancient and current saints who will be reincarnated in a later age. The Hindus call it Aryavarsha, the land where the holy Vedas originated. To the Chinese, it is the Western Paradise. So many cultures, so many names, testament to what historian Karl Meyer calls "a widespread yearning for a city sublime." By Buddhist and Hindu reasoning, time is illusory, so the future Shambhala can exist in the here and now, simultaneity being a necessary condition of all existence. In such a philosophy, the world is less a movie and more a complex photograph. (Interestingly, a similar conclusion was reached by quantum physicists whose acts of mathematical observation in many ways brought into existence that which was observed, remarkably much in absence sequential time.) For their part, the Lamas have long described the physical dimensions of Shambhala, even its location relative to certain obvious Himalayan geological features. Yet no hiker has ever reported having stumbled upon the "city sublime." It is there to be seen, the mystics say, only by those prepared to see it, to those who will it into quantum existence by the power of their own undistracted observation alone.

In Caribbean folklore, a baby born with a skin of amniotic remnants on its face—a caul, as it is named—will be sensitive to the transactions of the netherworld, activities that occur all around us, but of which we regular dumb folk are blissfully unaware. Perception, it seems, is a function of destiny and will, not just of equipment. If these traditions are to be believed, will and perception shape the world and define its expanse.

The shaman, the wise elder, the prophet, and the mystic are all called visionaries or seers, testament to their critical ability to expand perception. The Norse god Odin sacrificed one of his eyes in order to obtain inner sight. The Vedic god Indra possesses a third eye, embedded in his forehead, allowing him to peer into men's hearts. The extension of perception, it goes, is a universal human ambition, reflected in mythology, religion, and dream. The interpretation of that which is perceived is a different matter, and is no doubt responsible for the world's diversity of spiritual beliefs. But according to any survey of global mythologies, one theme remains universal: there are things we cannot know or feel but that are nevertheless real.

That a nether-beast emerged from a Bihari forest generations ago to take human form is but a tale. That her ghostly blood courses thinly but unerringly through the veins of her progeny is perhaps also a fiction. Yet such legends are sometimes grounded in truth. The trick is to tell that kernel of fact from the many layers of embellishment that have accrued over generations.

If it can be assumed that such creatures do persist, in whatever form, existing alongside men yet remaining unknown to them, then perhaps differing natures may be elucidated. Tomamu Nomei, the seductress, was but a forest spirit who summoned sufficient will to form herself into a woman. Angels, some might argue, are but earthly beings living earthly lives. And gods. . . well, gods permeate the infinite and linger in the back of consciousness. One tradition holds that they are all manifestations of the one sleeping god who was necessarily dreamed up by fragile humans so that he might in turn dream the world and all the events within it. A sleeping god or a quantum mechanical god?

According to myth, a last creature of imperceptible nature is what fearful types sometimes call the vile "elemental." It was perhaps manifested, the story goes, from a brief vanity of the sleeping god, or from the darkest nightmares of our world's earliest creatures. In that time, a reptilian essence heralded the rise of living, passionate creatures. A taunting lizard voice still whispers in our ears from the wet evolutionary darkness of our hindbrains; the air we breathe still contains traces of a dinosaur's breath. Supposedly the oldest of the imperceptible things, the elemental remembers a time before men, before *Homo erectus* might have hunted and destroyed its robust manlike cousin *Zinjanthropus* out of fear, before Alexander the Great conquered the world, and before all pockets of the Earth were stuffed with chattering messy human beings weaving history and folklore like some great pied and mismatched quilt. Ancient castles in Scotland are said by tourists to reek of a foul animal stench, akin to rotting flesh, that has no obvious source. This is thought to be evidence of the passage of the elemental. But such insufficient summaries are for fireside ghost stories, complicated by delicious layers of tangential narrative. How much is truth?

For an imagined thing that predates humanity, yet lingers amongst people, it is safe to suppose that the elemental's thinking, its machinations and motivations, is sufficiently alien for us never to fully understand. While those tourists in Scotland may have smelled its rankness, and while others, experiencing a momentary spate of tranquil and lucid consciousness, may have caught a glimpse of it out of the corners of their eyes, the activities and desires of the elemental remain unknown, even in folklore.

A young girl slept curled up beside her snoring grandmother beneath the ancientness of the Indian night. Images of spirits and seduction, treachery and renewal, and predators and prey danced formlessly in her coalescing dream. A storm of dichotomies raged: old and new, living and dead, material and spiritual, male and female, human and beast, truth and lies, East and West. Hers is a memory of youth, a history. For she is grown now, raised abroad and returned to the ancestral soil. But this is not Kalya's story, at least not hers alone. Rather, in the brief respite she seeks in the familiarity of a Bihari village, a reckoning is sought with one whose own hauntings put to shame Tomamu Nomei's storybook banality. This is instead his story, in whose heart love and intellect conspire both to substantiate the perceptible and to manufacture the sublime.

3

Bucephalus

It is said that Alexander the Great loved his horse Bucephalus more than he did any woman or man. When Bucephalus was stolen by Afghani boys during the Great March to India, Alexander was so distraught that, instead of razing the country to the ground, he issued a reward for the safe return of his horse—-and actually paid up! Such trustworthiness from a tyrant was unheard of, especially when it involved the payment of a ransom. Whether fact or fancy, the event and its telling speak highly of the bond between the man and his beast.

When Bucephalus finally breathed his last beyond the Hindu Kush, Alexander built for him a magnificent mausoleum upon whose site stands a Muslim shrine today. The local shepherds still speak of "the horse temple," though they do not know why, its origins obscured by the passage of time. But more than two thousand years of intervening conquests, geophysical activity, the rise and fall of countless small empires, and the inevitable amnesia of generations has not completely suffocated the memory of this unique relationship. In the ensuing history of tyranny, it is said, only Caligula and Catherine the Great would rival Alexander in their opulent treatment of their steeds.

Yet the horses of Caligula and Catherine were mere animals, handsome stallions to be sure, but simple beasts whose fame was but the reflected glory of their owners' eccentricities. Bucephalus, on the other hand, was considered by some to be a demon-horse, a creature impervious to mortal wounding. Adorned with a pendant emblazoned with the image of the dreaded gorgon which matched the one that dripped from Alexander's neck, Bucephalus was among the many supposed supernatural weapons wielded by the young god-king. For such men, the love they claim to absorb and emanate is more complex than that felt by us mortals. In truth, we cannot know if Alexander truly loved his horse, or if instead the demon-beast held the young king by a debt of supernatural honour. We do know that Alexander would have given anything, perhaps even his immortal soul, to conquer all the lands before him, so strong was his need to fulfil what he felt was his Destiny.

It was said by some, usually the descendants of his victims, that Alexander was himself a devil. A Persian tale has it that Iskandar, as he was known east of Greece, had to hire a different barber for every haircut, since each would discover the king's devilish horns beneath his hair, and would thus require silencing. According to the tale, one such barber was shrewd enough not to reveal his surprise at finding the horns, and so was spared to continue to tend to Iskandar's flowing golden-red locks. The stress of keeping a secret of such enormity tortured the poor man so that one day he ran to the nearest well and screamed into it, "Great Iskandar has horns!" Of course, the words echoed against the wet walls of the deep well, and the proclamation was thus heard around the world. Alexander's demonic nature was revealed to all, and thence recorded in history.

In some small way, his namesake—Tristan Iskandar Diamandi—had followed his forebear's trek, displaying a minute degree of Great Alexander's desperate ambition, his oneness of will and unwavering confidence in Destiny. He was no devil, this new Iskandar told himself, having chosen the most unobjectionable of trades, and eschewing ownership and conquest of any sort at every opportunity. But there were parallels he could not ignore. Indeed, some friends theorized, Iskie searched out and meditated upon those parallels, secretly revelling in the origins of his middle name.

"Name me three such parallels," Professor Kumar had once insisted over several mugs of Kingfisher beer.

"All right," Iskie said. "I am Greek, and so was Alexander."

"Your family is from Sparta. You are from Canada. And Alexander was from Macedonia. I see no parallel there."

"Details." Iskie waved them away and drank deeply from his mug. The Indian sun was high that afternoon, beating down upon the Himalayan hill station much like the god for which it was once mistaken. Saner men, especially those as white as Iskie, would have sought cover. But the power of alcohol is such that subtle physical woes may be pushed aside for the benefit of compelling conversation. So it was with Iskie, who took no notice of the scorching of the flesh upon his shoulders and the back of his neck.

"Tell me others then," Professor Kumar said. *Who was this odd little man I've accepted into my life? Why do I indulge him so?*

"Like Alexander, I trekked from Greece to India, albeit via Canada and vicariously over two generations—"

"And albeit by design! Intentional coincidences don't count, my friend."

"Okay, okay." Iskie wiped the sweat from his forehead and waved at the insects buzzing around his ear. A mosquito had alighted upon his forearm. Waiting for the minuscule prick of proboscis against his hot flesh, he watched the mosquito with detached placidity. He never felt it, possibly because of the drunkenness that was seeping from his stomach to his brain, but he continued to watch as the mosquito grew fat with his own blood.

"Let me see . . . Alexander's father Philip had two wives . . ."

"He actually had several, Iskie."

"Yes, yes, but we only care about the two. Olympia and the other one. Olympia was Alexander's mother, and the other one had a younger son."

Kumar laughed patiently. "You're not very good with details, are you."

"Details are for accountants. The big picture, that's for great men like us. Thinkers! Scientists!"

"Go on," Kumar said. "About the mothers."

"Well, Olympia was so jealous that she had her rival's son roasted alive in front of his mother. My father, too, married twice. And because of his first wife, my mother and I never received any of my father's property when he died."

"So you're the second son, the one without a name. Your half-brother is the true Alexander, not you!"

Iskie did not respond, but his eyelids fluttered briefly. He focused his attention on the mosquito again. It was nearly sated and about to fly away.

"Kill it," Kumar said. Iskie didn't move. Kumar lifted a hand to do the job himself, but Iskie intercepted him awkwardly, drunkenly.

"We're scientists, Professor. We study nature. We don't destroy it. Isn't that what your Hindu religion teaches you?"

Trying to discern alcoholic nonsense from true character, Kumar squinted hard at Iskie. *Four years with him. Can I last four years?* For hours now he had been examining young Diamandi, sizing up his new graduate student. He was not physically outstanding, indeed, he was almost a dwarf of a man. It was interesting that Iskie himself had not pointed out that particular similarity between himself and the diminutive god-king.

But what struck Kumar first was the depth of his eyes. Even in this drunken stupor, he seemed to look beyond his listener, into some infinity behind his head, or perhaps to an imagined assassin lurking atop a distant knoll. His eyes were black pupils set against black irises, the infinite cradled within the neverending. They absorbed any watcher, surrounded him in a salty pool of warm amniotic darkness that tore down all personal defences. In such an environment, one became a porous sponge to absorb any of the nonsense young Iskie blabbered on about. Only it wasn't entirely nonsense. There was always a thread of thin believability that ran through his rambling alcoholic proclamations.

And how he liked to drink! Kumar had known him for only a few days, but had seen him imbibe spirits on all but one of those days. This was not a problem, since the drink did not seem to impair Iskie's ability to produce structured thoughts and useful scientific insights. But as an entomologist, a steady hand was often a useful thing. If it were not for Iskie's remarkably unwavering physical gentleness, Kumar would be concerned for his drunken ham-fisted destruction of living samples. *But to let mosquitos feed upon you?*

Iskie sat back for a spell, his eyes seeming to glaze over. This was not an indication of mindlessness, Kumar had learned, but rather the default condition of Iskie's mysterious irises. Like those of a nocturnal burrowing creature, they were brightly reflective and probing, never sleeping. "There's another parallel I can tell you about, Professor." He was not, it seems, prepared to pursue his earlier comment about Hinduism.

Kumar waited, but there was nothing more forthcoming. The black irises seemed to widen, to separate further as if examining something at a great distance. His lips reddened and thickened, and they seemed to Kumar to be in mockery of sensual Hindu sculptures. Iskie's whole body at times suggested an amalgamation of the worst of Hindu art: round, stout, unnaturally full and flush, and senselessly sexual. At such times, he appeared serene and plump.

There was a giant statue of the god Indra nearby. It predated Aryan times, and so reflected a sensibility almost completely separate from European thought. Indra's eyes were exaggeratedly oval and deep, reflecting the all-seeing wisdom that a king of heaven should possess. It occurred to Kumar that, when sufficiently soaked in beer, Iskie's eyes resembled those of Indra. But the boy's temperament, his curmudgeonliness and his insistence upon manufacturing mystery, were more akin to the more "modern" Hindu gods. Kumar likened his student to Shiva, the god of both yogic tranquillity and sexual insatiability. Iskie would have done well to have been born into a brown-skinned body.

As if reading his thoughts, Iskie said, "Do you know that Greek scholars thought that the Hindus worshipped Olympian gods?"

"No, I didn't know that. Is it true?"

"I don't know. It's what I've read. They felt that the ancient world was one great continuum with Greece at one end and India at the other. When Alexander and the later Bactrians arrived, they were shocked to find brown-skinned folk worshipping Heracles!"

"You mean Hercules? How could that be?"

Iskie giggled. "It's what they thought Krishna was. And some of the stories are similar, some of the myths. Alexander even chanced upon an

Indian settlement whose inhabitants claimed to be descended from the Greek god Dionysus himself! He believed it. . . he spared them."

Kumar made no reaction. He said, "Is that the parallel? Do you claim descent from a god, too?"

"No, nothing like that. Alexander did indeed believe he was descended directly from Heracles and Achilles on both parents' sides. I'm not so arrogant."

"So what are you trying to tell me?"

Iskandar became serious. He leaned forward and brushed a moth from his arm, careful not to hurt it. The solemnity that marked the facial pits between his cheeks and nose was compelling, sobering. "Alexander, in accordance with his time, did not distinguish between mythology and history. And neither do I."

The heat was almost unbearable now, penetrating Kumar's black linen pants and making his thighs sweat uncomfortably. The odours of drying earth, settling beer, and the ubiquitous cow dung were usually consoling, but not today. Kumar finished his mug of beer and poured the dregs onto his forearm, drowning two small flies that had settled by his moist pores. "And what's the other parallel?" he asked.

Iskie leaned back again, thoughtful in that detached distant way of his. "I, too, have my Bucephalus. But it's not a horse. Nor do I love him." He mumbled the last, unable to assert control over the finer muscles of his liquored tongue.

What would Alexander have thought, Kumar asked himself, if he had known that his trek of conquest would bear this unlikely fruit two millennia hence? Surely he would have balked at claiming a distant relationship to his brown-skinned subcontinental victims, as they were so obsessed with spiritual matters of little consequence. Moreover, the warrior-tyrant could never have predicted that his countryman and namesake, young Iskandar Diamandi, would be an unathletic drunkard pacifist unwilling even to swat a mosquito. Was that the Hellenic legacy of which Great Alexander had dreamed?

Diamandi's Indra-like eyes were pleading upward from the table top, in silent despair for the stereotype of Indian tranquillity that had thus far eluded him. "Who had been the true conqueror?" Kumar whispered to himself, sure that Iskie was too inebriated to hear him, and casually dismissing Iskie's last statement as drunken gibberish. "The general who loved his horse more than his men, or the stereotype of the country that has enslaved this young man's heart?" *Let him have his new mythology. I have to get back to work.*

Iskie watched Kumar go, uncertain if, in his drunken stupor, he had indeed said his goodbyes. Like an army of war horses pressed between the awesome cliffs of the Hindu Kush, his blood slowed between the stiffening walls of his heart. Here, at the feet of the world's mightiest mountains, ladders to heaven, the collision of East and West had first begun, drawing together the most disparate of religions and mythologies to struggle for millennia towards a common world view. Yet that confluence was marked most meaningfully and pointlessly by a barely remembered monument to a dead horse.

He had to laugh. It was, after all, an irony in the finest ancient Greek tradition.

When soaked in alcohol, his brain comfortably afloat in numbing spirits, Iskie sometimes came close to the tranquillity, the undisturbed, undistracted state of observation that would allow him to gaze upon the Watcher without fully doubting his own sanity. But he would usually fall into unconsciousness before that point was reached, waking later only more frustrated.

When Iskie rose to wash up and return to his research, the Watcher, if it were indeed real, went with him. A new patron took Kumar's place at the patio table, sank into placidity beneath the oppressive sun, and looked right through the imagined Watcher as it walked in Iskandar's footsteps. He didn't notice. They never noticed what wasn't there.

4

WASPS

The meeting of Kalya and Iskandar was an inevitable thing, really, given the underlying machinations of the universe, and of this peculiar India in particular. It makes an odd sort of sense that a woman who was perhaps descended from a ghost would come into the company of a man who refused to distinguish between the observable and the assumed, who presumed that mysticism would somehow abut the scientific method.

Kalya's cousin Subodh was a technician in Professor Kumar's lab. His tasks involved staining microscopic samples and preserving whole-body insects. Dr. Kumar was a laboratory scientist within a discipline that abhorred laboratories. But even the purist must admit that the day of gentlemanly naturalism, requiring only a butterfly net and a copy of Bloom's Taxonomy, was long past. The era of the microscope, and indeed of the DNA sampler, had arrived, and Kumar was intent on riding the peak of that wave.

Iskandar's role in the lab was difficult to ascertain. Young Diamandi hated both the indoors and most machines. The information within his transcript was uncertain as to how he had in fact passed undergraduate biochemistry given his obvious distaste for the subject. For Professor Kumar, this was but one more element contributing to the enigma that was Iskandar.

When he was a boy, Kumar had felt his calling in no uncertain terms. At thirteen years of age, he had dropped to his knees in mathematics class, profoundly moved by an equation the teacher had written on the chalkboard: $y = mx + b$, the equation of a straight line. That God had caused all the infinite points in a straight line to conform to the description offered by such an elegant, simple equation was indeed proof of His existence. When, later that same year, he had learned of Fibonacci's sequence—the infinite string of integers that begins: 1, 1, 2, 3, 5, 8, 13, and so on—that feeling had returned. For Fibonacci's numbers also described the dimensions of the Golden Rectangle, the shape that manifests itself in many biological systems, such as the ratio of human torso length to width and the ratios of surface areas spanned by the spiralling whorls of any seashell. That God had embedded mathematical precision into life itself was a signpost to the divine. This was where science and spirituality must intersect!

There was similar precision in the compartmentalization of insectoid bodies, in the spinning of arachnid webs, and in the seemingly chaotic but ordered relationship between predator and prey populations. As his expertise had developed, so had his realization that greater precision could be found at the molecular level, where both substance and energy interchanged in discrete quanta, and according to complicated but reasonable rules.

Order. Religion strove for order. Science was order.

That Iskandar did not seem to understand this truth was troubling to Kumar. It was insufficient merely to describe, one must also measure! One must quantify and elucidate relationships —estimated, if need be—between the quantities. To simply enjoy the butterfly's prettiness or marvel at the predatory sleekness of the dragonfly was pleasant but pointless. Yet he sensed in Iskandar a gravitation towards such aestheticism. That was the road of the poet, not of the serious scientist. He had invested many hours trying to invent a suitable doctoral thesis topic for the boy, but all paths, of course, led to the microscope.

"This species of mantis doesn't seem to produce haploid gametes. Why don't you investigate that?"

"No, Professor, I don't think so."

"All right. There's a species of red ant in this area that secretes a corrosive substance I assume to be similar to fumaric acid. Why don't you start there and see where it leads?"

"I'm sorry, Professor. I'd prefer not to do that."

Kumar huffed a bit, but showed remarkable patience and flexibility. "All right, Mr. Diamandi. What do you want to do?"

"I don't know. But I'm not interested in parts of animals. I want to know the whole animal, its role in the larger picture."

Kumar steamed silently for a moment. He was used to dealing with Westerners, even coveted their company. This was an integrated new world, after all, where lines between languages and cultures were becoming increasingly blurred. Still, he was not used to such frank and conflicted exchanges with a student. He would not have tolerated such contrariness from an Indian. Perhaps he gave this boy too much breadth. He chose his next words well. "We aren't behaviouralists here, Iskie. This is a lab. You knew this. Why did you apply for a studentship here if you don't want to learn laboratory techniques?" Despite his measured words, Kumar regretted the question as he asked it. Of course, it was a question that needed asking, that any sane administrator would have asked. But he knew what the answer would be: *Because Alexander came this way.*

Iskandar surprised him. "I do wish to learn laboratory techniques, Professor. But I don't want to make molecular minutiae the sole focus of the next four years of my life. And I am interested in the red ant and the local mantis and all of the entomological fauna of this region. That's what brought me to you. I recognize that you're a reasonable man—more than a scientist, someone capable of seeing the big picture."

"Does this crap work on your other professors?"

"Usually."

Kumar giggled complacently. "All right, maybe we can compromise. Read this and tell me if there's anything that strikes your fancy." He handed him the library call number for a textbook, one co-authored by

Kumar himself, on insects of North and Middle India.

Iskie accepted the slip of paper gratefully and went straight to the Institute's library to retrieve the book. Kumar was stuck in his ways, Iskie thought, but wasn't a bad sort. What Kumar failed to realize was that his lab produced drudgery work, bits and pieces of information that would never be synthesized into a whole philosophy. Kumar was not a shallow man, not at all. In fact, Iskie believed him to be one of the most thoughtful individuals he had ever met. But he was too close to his work, was unable to step back and see the universal. After all, Kumar had acquired great fame for having dug into the infinitesimally small aspects of life, honing myopia to an art form. It matched him well with his circle of similarly niched companions, particularly one Goran Damjanovic, the flowery administrator of a series of art galleries in the area. Between the two of them, Kumar and Goran could reduce a thing of beauty, whether scientific or fanciful, to a set of corpuscular observations whose discreteness belied the truth of the whole, much in the same way that individual hydrogen and oxygen atoms were so much less than their spawn, the magical fluid called water.

"Why spend so many years watching silly bugs?" Goran had said to Kumar once. Iskie had been listening in silence from the far end of the lab.

"Because insects are ancient creatures, Goran," Kumar had answered, offering a rather anaemic explanation, by Iskie's reckoning. "If we wish to understand the intricacies of our world, we are well advised to examine its foundations and tenets, from the quantum universe to the seas of bacteria to the populations of pollinating species and pathogen vectors which dictate how all life is spread on this planet."

"Goodness, Pradeep," Goran had huffed in his dismissive and patronizing way, even uttering some Slavic curses under his breath. "You cannot make something important just by using a lot of big words. Get a real job. Take up pottery or gardening."

Kumar had chuckled in response and had waggled a finger at his friend. It seemed to Iskie that theirs had been a conflict of show, not rooted in any real disagreement. And that offended him somehow.

Iskie sighed.

The librarian fetched the book promptly, but handed it to Iskie somewhat sheepishly, not meeting his gaze. India was a place of complex hierarchy, Iskandar convinced himself, so perhaps as a student of the great Pradeep Kumar, he was afforded some special dispensation or respect. It was a feeble explanation, he knew, but it worked for the moment. Iskandar went straight home to devour the book.

Home was a room in a local three-star hotel, immensely affordable given the weakness of the Indian rupee. He ordered up a plate of papadam, cracked open a bottle of the local cola, and set to reading. He would reward himself with a shot or two of brandy if the intellectual cogitations proved fruitful. He quickly discovered that while Professor Kumar was without doubt a stellar scientific mind and an excellent fellow to boot, he was a piss-poor writer. To Iskie's eye, the text, though technically correct and thorough, lacked a textured complexity that would allow the subject matter to sing.

And entomology should sing! It wasn't just the study of bugs, or, these days, the conflux of a variety of biophysical and naturalistic sciences; it was a testimony to the harmonious wonder of the most successful animals in Earth's history! What are angels but lithesome winged creatures that bring life, pain, salvation, and horror? How better to describe the honeybee, the hornet, the ladybug and the praying mantis? There was a special kind of beauty in the toil of the common garden ant as it struggled to accumulate and store food for the winter. There was grand poetry in the life cycle of the male honey bee, its sole purpose to impregnate and die while consuming as few resources as possible. Such Spartanism, such mindless dedication to the practical and the necessary was truth in its most brutal and unmitigated form. And what is art but our vain attempt to describe such truth?

The insects in this philosophy are art incarnate, their lives free of the misdirecting effects of illusion, conscience, sentiment, and civilization. The path of the mystic, Iskandar was convinced, was to return to that state of unabashed truth, to deny the distracting influences that daily living builds around us. The path of the scientist was to boil down that truth to its painful core, to stare it in the eye without flinching, no matter how disturbing it might be. He didn't know much about such things, about mysticism or what Edward Said or Somerset Maugham would have both called "Orientalism." But perhaps being in the land of yogis, just hours away from the Himalayas themselves, imbued in him a sense of this philosophy.

Spiritualism, mysticism, or whatever you wish to call it, Iskandar believed, must be a voice within the human animal crying out for a return to that state of insectoid unabashedness. Mythology is a manifestation of that cry, an outpouring from the semirational mind to recapture truths that cannot be observed but that are nonetheless felt.

What of tales of the sasquatch or the yeti, those semi-mythical apemen stalking the forests of the American Pacific and the heights of the Himalayan peaks? Possibly real creatures, but more likely a cry from our genetic heritage. When communities of *Homo erectus*, our distant ancestors, emerged onto the vast and fertile plains of Asia, they may have discovered another more robust hominoid, *Zinjanthropus*, whom they perceived as a wild man. Modern tales of similar wild men may just be a remembered cry from that time, an attempt to conceptualize uncertain facts into a world now dominated by provable, testable observation. We call that conceptualization, *mythology*.

Mythology, by Iskandar's reckoning, reflects biological truth. In all mythologies, there are tales of bisexual origins. Romulus and Remus, though brothers, founded Rome. To many monotheists, Adam and Eve started humanity. Zeus was father (with Hera sometimes mother) to the Olympian gods; Shiva and Parvati were parents albeit symbolically, to a pantheon of Hindu gods. Human society reflects this obsession, with dining establishments catering to couples, laws that favour pair-bonded families, and artistic representations of romantic love between woman and man ad nauseam. Even homosexual unions are still pair bonds.

Romantic love—its desperation, futility, ecstasy, and agony—is best observed amongst the insectoid angels, Iskandar believed. As a physicist understands the universe by examining the interplay between positively and negatively charged particles; as a Taoist recapitulates that universe by describing the yin and yang; and as human morality concerns itself, understands itself, within the context of good versus evil, so must a naturalist seek purity of dichotomous expression within the pair bonds of the animal world.

Mating ants grow temporary wings and soar to heights to complete coitus while plummeting to possible death. Male otters grip their lovers' snouts until they are bloodied just so that contact is maintained long enough for sexual completion. The plight of the migrating salmon is legendary, completing a Herculean swimming feat to reach the spawning grounds. And birds of all variety seek out compatible mates in an impossible cacophony of competing mating calls.

The technocrats, the lab hermits—the Kumars of this world—would have us believe that such things are the result of a biological imperative, a need to procreate. In truth, Iskie too believed it was so, that perhaps the core of that universal scientific truth was merely a couple of layers beneath the storied biological imperative. But then why the pervading dichotomy of male and female? Certainly, in some species there are one and sometimes three sexes, but perhaps they conform to a different universal truth. For the rest of us, even for subatomic particles, there exists that unavoidable compulsion to separate all things into dark and light, positive and negative, masculine and feminine. Simple sexual imperatives do not tell the whole tale, do not penetrate deeply enough into that thick sponge of cosmic truth.

Iskie sighed deeply, shaking the symphony of thoughts from his head.

He turned to a new chapter in the textbook, "Theorized Life Cycle of the Indian Fig Wasp," and was horrified to discover that the entire chapter had been ripped out. The odd behaviour of the librarian was perhaps thus explained, for he remained responsible for the condition of all the books in his care.

Iskie ran his forefinger along the book's crease, feeling the jagged edge of the ripped paper, hoping perhaps to extract emotional information from this unorthodox examination. Like many Indian books, the binding was poor but the paper quality was good. That spoke so well about a great many things whose pieces were well forged, but that hung together rather poorly. Much like a man, really, who spends so much time developing the separate aspects of his life—career, body, intellect, emotion—but who does not know how to bring them together for a common purpose.

The rest of the book was immaterial, Iskandar decided. The Indian fig wasp would serve as the focus for his studies. Destiny had so decreed it, and an Iskandar of any generation was loath to defy Destiny.

5

DESTINY

The librarian was a nervous middle-aged man of middling caste and uncertain sexual orientation. His greasy hair sat with difficulty atop an elongated head punctuated by shallow pools for eyes and labia-like lips. "Yes, sir, can I help you, sir?" he blurted with staccato timing, his posture unmistakably that of someone wishing to remain undisturbed, though who clearly understood his role in the organization.

"Yes. I signed out this book yesterday, and there seems to be a chapter missing."

"There is a fine for damaging a book, sir. I am so sorry, I must levy you with a twenty-five rupee fine, sir, unless you wish to purchase the book outright for five hundred rupees, sir."

"I didn't damage it. It was like this when I signed it out."

The librarian rose in mock indignation. "I am sorry, sir. Fine is levied immediately, sir."

Iskie sighed. "I just said I didn't damage it. I received it in this condition."

The librarian flailed his arms, his voice becoming more animated. "I am sorry, sir. Fine is levied." The man was actually perspiring, either from the heat, illness, having taken offence, or sheer nervousness. The sweat flowed so copiously now that Iskie feared he would shrivel like a prune and collapse lifeless onto the desk.

Iskandar was unnerved, but thought quickly. "Listen, dear sir, I'll make you a deal. I'll pay the fine. No one will ever know of how I damaged your book. I only ask, kind sir, as a favour to me, that you tell me who checked out this book before me." Quite conspicuously, he slid a one-hundred rupee note across the desk. He had noticed that the locals, when eager to play the role of pitiable sycophant, punctuated their speech with countless honorifics. Iskie remained incredulous that any sane man would be swayed by such obvious toadyism. But he had seen it enacted on many occasions, each time resulting in a kind of social lubrication. Roles, it seemed, were important and complex things here. Best to keep that in mind. His belly grumbled at having to address the gesticulating librarian as "sir," but Iskie wanted that information. This was, after all, part of the game, part of the adventure.

Refocused, but still encased in a suit of perspiration, the librarian immediately snatched the bill and scribbled something on a wad of paper, sliding it back to Iskie, though not meeting the young foreigner's gaze. Iskandar read the paper, harrumphed dutifully, muttering a thanks beneath his breath, and marched out the swinging door. The librarian watched him go, relieved to have the matter done with, and allowed himself to slip into a post-conflict state of denouement and relaxation. His full lips quivered slightly, and his concentration shifted to the limp one-hundred rupee note he caressed between thumb and forefinger. The actual sum was, of course, meaningless; it was the gesture that mattered. He felt his heart slowing, his mind returning to peace as his solitariness was returned to him, his rows of books creeping nearer to offer a weird paper embrace. In that quasi-meditative daze, he was certain he saw the swinging door snap close not once, but twice.

Iskie was not too surprised to find that the name on the paper belonged to someone in Professor Kumar's lab. It was an entomology text, after all, and Kumar ran the most prominent entomology operation at the

Institute, which, not coincidentally, bore his grandfather's name. But the fellow, if indeed he had the face pegged correctly, was only a technician with no need of casual textbook reading. Perhaps he, too, sought the greater role of their science in the grand panoply of human understanding. That was certainly part of the charm of this place, that even those whose life paths merely abutted the purely scholarly seemed to seek erudition for its own rewards, and not merely for its pecuniary potential. Such was the glory of a place yet denied the full forward thrust of the American cultural assault. The thought made Iskie smile, as would any small epiphany of self-validation.

"Subodh? Are you Subodh?"

"Yes, that is me. Tristan? That's your name, right?"

"Actually, I prefer Iskandar."

"Pleased to meet you." Subodh stripped off the latex glove of his right hand and offered it. Iskie shook it meaningfully. "How may I help you, Iskandar?"

The charm of the young technician slowed Iskie a bit. Indeed, all the young men who worked and studied at the Institute were similarly forthcoming, no doubt a fine testament to the social graces imbued via the Indian higher education system. Perhaps he should have invested his first days here in developing relationships, not just with Professor Kumar, but with everyone in the lab. After all, human interaction is based upon social nicety, not just mutual tolerance.

Iskie felt his thoughts slipping away, drawn to half-formed theories of social dynamism and the role of relationships in an evolutionary context. He shook his head to clear it, noting warmly that he would work through the theories later in the evening over a good shot of brandy.

"I'm sorry we haven't spoken before, Subodh," Iskie said. Subodh nodded briskly, and fingered the knobs of the microscope on his bench. "Um, you checked out a book from the library last month . . ."

"*Insects of North and Middle India*. Yes, what about it? Would you like my opinion of it?"

"Not really. . ."

"That's good, because I didn't actually read it." Subodh laughed charmingly, somewhat embarrassed. His eyes actually twinkled. He whispered, "It looked kind of boring, you see." Iskie shrugged in agreement.

"Actually, I got it for my cousin who was visiting from Canada. I was with her in Bihar last month, and she had requested that I bring a book written by our famous Professor . . ."

"Why?" Iskie made a face of disgust. "Why would a non-entomologist want to read such a thing?"

"You assume she's not in the business, eh? Ha ha, that's okay, she isn't. She wanted to know what kind of man had acquired such fame for erudition in India. I'm afraid it may have left her with a poor impression of intellectual life in this country."

Iskie shuffled his feet. He was about to blurt out his suspicion that Subodh's cousin had defaced the book, then thought better of it. "Is your cousin . . . still in India?"

"Yes, in Bihar. In our village. She'll be there until the end of the month. You are countrymen, I understand, both from Canada. Perhaps you'd like to meet her?"

Iskie's response was guttural, as if his heart had revolted against his brain, choosing a path based on feeling rather than reason. "Yes," he said. "I'd love to meet her." His intellect would rationalize later. It would argue that rural Bihar was the site of much of the entomological investigations described in Kumar's book. It would further point out that a trip to Bihar presented his best chance of escape from the laboratory and allow for the pursuit of purely behavioural studies, his true scholastic desire. His heart and mind would collaborate to paint a picture of scholarly adventurism wherein opportunities must be seized to maximize both productivity and fulfilment, and permit him to grow both in understanding and in wisdom. But the truth of the matter was that Iskie was directed by romantic principles of which even he seemed only cursorily aware. Those principles directed him now to follow a stranger to a remote village in a country that was still a mystery to him. He refused to hesitate, refused to question or forsake the path that shone so brilliantly before him.

Such decisions had always come easily to Iskie. A similar set of reflexive choices had brought him to India. He was guided by Fate, he was convinced. He longed for the existence of oracles such as had littered the road between Pella and Babylon in Alexander's day. The signposts of Destiny were always true, but they were sometimes subject to interpretation. It would have helped to have had the kind of confirmation an oracle could have provided. Such reasoning—that Fate is not to be denied, but embraced—would unfortunately carry little water with Professor Kumar.

Iskie took a more subtle approach. He would study the local fig wasps, he told Kumar. That would be the focus of his thesis. The details of the topic were yet to be fleshed out, but he was willing to include some degree of microscopic work, something to justify his association with the Kumar lab. He announced that his studies thus far, informed largely by Kumar's own book, had indicated a vital resource on the topic somewhere in Bihar—a nexus of living samples. So he'd have to be away from the Institute for a few weeks seeking that resource. And since Subodh was scheduled to return to his village in a day or so, Iskie would accompany him. The game was afoot and science would not be denied!

Kumar nodded and did not object, though he believed none of Iskie's animated story. He knew: it was a fool who stood between Great Alexander and his Destiny.

6

BIHAR

In high school, Iskandar had had a maths teacher whose father had worked on the Indian railroad. The teacher has spoken warmly of the rail system, of its charm and strong connection to the fabric of Indian society. If pressed, he would describe how, as a boy, he had watched his father painstakingly measure the gauge of the track, the distance from rail to rail. By the English standards of the time, the gauge should have been the breadth of a Roman chariot. But in some parts of the vast rail system, the Scottish and Irish engineers had won out. Their broad gauge, not that of the English, had been laid: a width equalling the supposed stride length of the mytho-historic Celtic king, Brian Baru.

For Iskie, of course, it seemed so fitting that a land of ancientness would have its first thrust into the world of technology be borne upon a measure of myth.

Iskie found that he liked travelling with Subodh. The journey by bus from the hill station to the nearest train station took a whole day, and the ensuing train trip would take another. Subodh had seized every opportunity to halt their bus journey, leaping from the vehicle and returning with various local foods. Things unnamed, unidentifiable, and sometimes unpronounceable were thrust into Iskie's open palm to be tossed down his throat. Keeping his mouth and stomach occupied allowed his attention to be drawn from the perilous bus trip down neolithic mountain highways, where remnants of rock slides and motor accidents abounded. Subodh took great delight at pointing out sites of deadly accidents, such thrills interrupted only by the passing of pretty girls through his visual field.

Throughout it all, Iskie took careful note of the preponderance of Hindu shrines along the roadways. Here, religion was not separate from life, he thought, but resonated with every action. He was actually relieved when their bus driver stopped briefly to perform puja by one of the shrines before taking a particularly dangerous stretch of road. At least one person on board should be on God's good side. He, too, directed a respectful nod to a statue of Ganesh when the bus pulled into the station, grateful for whatever divine protection had been granted.

He learned from Subodh that only tourists and fools bought first class train tickets. It was much too chilly there, Subodh said, and one always got a cold from the poorly cleaned air-conditioning system that spewed bacterial colonies directly into your face. If you could stand the stares, he said, third class was best because the windows were open, and you could buy food from the wallahs who ran alongside the accelerating or decelerating train.

But for Iskie and himself, he suggested second class. "It's not as crowded as third, and you won't get stared at as much, *gora.* But it's not freezing or sequestered like first class. Besides, we can best afford it." To be honest, Iskie was surprised not to find peasants hitching a ride on the tops of the trains, as he had seen in the movie *Gandhi.* Indeed, his guidebook had suggested that that might have been a common scenario. But this particular train ride was much like any comparable run in the West, except for the smells and sounds, and the scenery. Oh, the scenery.

Through flickering windows, he watched the Gangetic plains open up to him, widening at the horizon to subtend an immense vista of dusty terrain. There was starkness here, produced by a chronic shortage of fresh water. Yet life abounded! Cows were ubiquitous, either roaming aimlessly or hitched, as were bullocks and oxen, to carts or ploughs. Filthy dogs with hungry eyes and patchy fur scampered about randomly, often chased by small children wielding sticks. Thin leathery-skinned men, dressed in traditional dhotis or cotton dress pants and shirts, walked seemingly aimlessly along the roads parallel to the tracks, or sat in shops, sometimes pressing large glass bottles to their lips.

The women were more common and more diverse, he decided. Gripping the folds of their saris and toiling beneath the beating sun, they led queues of small children to muddy streams to wash, or tended to their personal hygiene publicly, though somehow remaining modestly concealed. Sometimes stained with dirt and hobbled by toil, or sometimes rising with queenly elegance and haughtiness, their beauty entranced him.

They were just part of the assault on, and seduction of his awareness.

The smell of antiquity wafted Iskie's nostrils. It was an odour he had encountered before, at the airport in Taiwan, and once while travelling through Java. Perhaps it was the smell of tropical decay. In such places, no doubt, humidity wreaked torture upon fabrics and compounds, rendering from them a common musky organic odour. He breathed deeply, conscious that each breath brought into his blood atoms that were once part of the bodies of Vatsayana, Akbar, Siddhartha the Buddha, and even Jesus Christ, Julius Caesar, and, of course, Great Alexander. In a very real sense, those men were now physically a part of him.

Whether he had taken those breaths in India or in Antarctica, that truth would still hold. Such is the power of chaotic air systems. Yet to be here, in one of the cradles of civilization, it meant so much more to consider such contingencies of history. He had no real personal ties to India, of course, except an imagined relationship with one of its ancient conquerors. But as a Greek, he felt that only in modern India could he experience what his ancient motherland would have felt like. The Olympian and Hindu religions had much in common. Their forms of art and dress, though disparate, were in his opinion more similar than dissimilar. And, of course, both civilizations were seats of comparable mathematics, astronomy, and philosophy. Pythagoras and the Buddha—Siddhartha Gautama—had been contemporaries, after all, both living in the so-called Axis Age of 500 BCE. From the two opposing poles of that continuum of ancient culture, those men and their peers radiated a new wisdom that signalled that the world had matured, was ready to coalesce into a single great humanistic philosophy based equally upon science and supposition.

Iskandar knew nothing of the Buddha, nor of his teachings, except what he had garnered from watching reruns of *Kung Fu.* But Pythagoras he knew. Pythagoras was a wild man who had lived in a cave on Samos and eschewed the hygienic and culinary norms of his time. He was a profound mathematician who had cared little for actual observation. "Why look at the stars?" he had asked of some astronomer friends, "when you can stay inside and think about them?" Pythagoras he understood. Pythagoras had beseeched the animal within.

"Subodh, why did you decide to become a lab technician?"

"What?" Subodh was busily examining a young beauty down the aisle, winking and smiling. He had little time for conversation when so engaged.

"Why," Iskie said, grasping Subodh's scalp with one hand and vigourously turning his face toward him. "Did you choose to be a lab tech?"

"Why not? It's a job. Pays well."

"There are lots of jobs that pay well."

"Yes, well, I could have been a lawyer like my father wanted. Or I could have been a doctor like almost every other young Indian man of means."

"But . . ." Iskie egged him on. It was clear that Subodh had no interest in this line of questioning.

"But," Subodh sighed, "those professions require that you invest every hour of every day of your life being them. I just wanted a job I could forget about when I wasn't in the office. I suppose I could have studied computers—"

"Or politics."

"Or politics." Subodh grimaced and returned his attention to the coy girl, who was trying hard not to look like she noticed him. Iskie would not let it go.

"Didn't the science beckon you, though?" Iskie asked. "I mean, you could have been a middle manager or a clerk or, as you say, some kind of computer guy. But you chose to study a science. Clearly, you had some sort of calling."

"No, Iskandar. Sorry. I don't know. Maybe. There was something interesting about chemistry in middle school, I suppose. Hey, look! She's got a friend!" Subodh directed Iskie's gaze to the coy girl,who was now joined by an equally attractive companion.

"Subodh, in our world right now there's a fight going on between religion and science. At least in my country there is. You're Indian, from a country famous for its spiritualism, and yet you chose the path of science. Don't you think it's important for you to consider why?" Iskie stared at him imploringly, refusing to notice the young school-uniformed women, who now were giggling sweetly.

Subodh sucked his teeth in frustration. "Iskie, do you know anything about Vladimir Lenin?"

"Not really."

"Good. Neither do I. But I'm sure that even Lenin occasionally took some time off from the revolution to have a beer and ogle the girls on the boulevard. You know what I'm saying? When we arrive, first thing we have to do is get you a drink." He rose with a smile and walked towards the girls, selecting an appropriate introductory phrase from a host of previous successes.

Iskie, meanwhile, tried to imagine what kind of chat-up lines Lenin might have used.

7

WHELL

One's exploring instincts are never fully in sync with the needs of the body. A lifetime of adventure television, of Indiana Jones and E M Forster, may compel one to seek adornment with a sola topee or fedora, the donning of a rucksack, and the purchase of a ticket to a faraway land. But the books, the films, and the dream never mention the microbes that infiltrate the intestinal lining, suffering the traveller to be himself travelled, the would-be conqueror to be conquered at the cellular level.

So it was with Iskie, desperately trying to maintain a sense of dignity and heroism between the waves of diarrhoeal pain. The parasites—a mere nuisance for contemporary Western travellers, and not the killers they could be—were not content to rest between the intestinal folds, but migrated via the circulatory highway to several other otherwise content organs: the lungs, the liver, and the brain. This was the result of trusting Subodh to select the foods purchased from various roadside wallahs. Never again.

The flood of fluids that regularly gushed from his lower orifices was now accompanied by the occasional fountain of vomit, despite Iskie's decided recent abstinence from food and drink. Soon would follow the migraine headache that would fissure his head along new crevices of pain, and the subsequent hours of self-pity and regret.

But, he knew, it would all be over by morning. Between waves of torment, his brain found sufficient calm to compute the time he had spent on the bed, perhaps five or six hours. When the sun rose anew, he too would rise from his sweaty bed, hesitatingly stretch his cramped abdominal muscles, and spend the next few days terrified of all Indian foods. The illness was in its final stages, after which there would be rest and reprieve. Professor Kumar's parting advice resonated inside his hollow skull, made so by the shrunken nature of his dehydrated brain: "Concerning Delhi Belly, my boy—in its worst form, first you'll be scared that you're going to die. Then you'll be scared that you won't die."

And, for the first time in a few hours, he chuckled softly and drifted into an exhausted sleep.

He awoke to the sound of the window blinds being pulled aside. He opened his eyes a crack and winced at the flood of sunlight through the window. It washed his body in warmth and exposed the silhouette of the woman who had entered his room. She stood at the foot of his bed, a fresh towel folded over one arm, and an unlit cigarette dangling in the hand of the other.

Iskie squinted at her, more concerned about the absence of pain in his gut than about his modesty. "I didn't think Indian girls smoked," he said at last, convinced that his illness had finally passed.

"I don't," she said. Iskie detected an American accent. "I just carry one around as a kind of oral fixation fetish." She threw him the towel, walked over to the night table, and fished a match from a drawer. She then lit the cigarette and drew several long drags from it.

"Ah," Iskie laughed. "Sarcasm!"

"Shh!" she spat at him. "Auntie doesn't let me smoke in the house, so be quiet. I'm Kalya, Subodh's cousin."

"Yeah, I figured that out. Um . . . how long have I been here?"

"Since last night. You were pretty delirious when Subodh dragged you in. You've been in and out of the bathroom all night. Don't worry too much about it. Same thing happens to me every time I come here. I think it's a kind of giardiasis. Consider it a rite of passage."

"Well, many things were indeed passed."

"That's an attractive thought." She sat the corner of the bed and eyed him cautiously. "You know, I kind of thought you were faking it."

"What?"

"When I came in here this morning, it looked like there were two of you on the bed," she said. "I figured maybe you and Subodh had a special relationship that we aren't supposed to know about."

"Well, I am Greek . . ."

"Good," she said, "you're not hung up on stuff like that. Maybe we'll get along, after all."

Iskie tried to sit up. He was weaker than he thought.

"It'll hurt for a few more hours," she said. "All that puking kills your abs. You just need your fluids."

He cautiously propped himself on an elbow, wincing again at the dull pain in his stomach. "Why were you concerned that we wouldn't get along?" he asked.

Kalya measured her words. "You know what men are like here." She peered at him insolently, dismissively, then sucked on the last centimetre of her cigarette. "It's like this place is the land that time forgot, as far as attitudes towards women go. Me smoking, or you being gay—it just would not be acceptable."

"I'm not gay."

"Congratulations. Does Subodh know?"

"Subodh isn't gay either!"

"Is that what he told you?" She snickered and tossed the burnt-out butt through the open window. "The shower is next door, and I think your things are still in your bag under the bed. We're going to have dinner soon, so I'll leave you alone to wash up." She went to the door, then paused and turned back. "Oh," she said, "I was serious about seeing two of you on the bed, by the way. I wasn't the only one. Tenali, the head servant, saw it, too. And Tenali's eyes are my eyes." She winked. "Hey, maybe Subodh was taking advantage?"

"Very funny," said Iskie, thinking it was anything but. Then he took a chance: "That wasn't Subodh with me. It was something else."

Kalya paused at the door and stared at him a moment. "Are you delirious as well as nauseous?" she asked.

"No to the first, but I'm a bit of the second."

"Okay, sit up." Kalya rifled through the night table drawers again, this time surfacing with a small leather bag. From it, she produced a hypodermic syringe that she filled from a small opaque bottle. "Roll up your sleeve."

"Hey, what is that?" Iskie protested, but he reflexively obeyed, exposing his bared deltoid to be jabbed. Kalya took a seat next to him on the bed.

"It's okay, I'm a nurse," she said, sticking the needle into him and depressing the plunger. "Well, sort of."

"That's reassuring. What did you give me?"

"Something for your nausea, a drug called diphenhydramine. It'll make you sleepy again, but at least you won't puke. So who was on the bed with you?"

Iskie shrugged and hung his head sheepishly. "I was kidding. No one. But ever since I was a kid, I knew that I was never alone."

"Guardian angel?" Kalya did not smirk. She seemed serious.

"I don't think so. I've always had the feeling that I was being followed by someone."

Kalya got up to leave. "You know," she said, "we brown folk have a word for that. We call it paranoia. See you downstairs."

"Downstairs" was actually down the hall. Iskie never did figure out why the residents of the Lal ancestral home referred to their one-floor house as if it were two storeys. But every family has its peculiarities, and in the grand scheme, this was a harmless one.

The hallway was long and ornate. He was taken by one particular hanging, a framed stylized printing of Tennyson's poem *The Lady of Shalott.* He walked down the hall very very slowly, surprised by his own weakness. For some men, perhaps, such debilitation would be a blow to their virility. Iskie had never been an exceptional physical specimen, so he had always refused to allow his manhood to be defined by his body's physical robustness or potency. But a man he was, and every masculine fibre in his body reminded him of this simple truth every time he chanced to glance at Kalya.

As was ordained, the compulsion he felt for her physically was undeniable. *Roxanne,* he whispered to himself, beseeching the name of Alexander's dark-skinned Asian bride. Roxanne had been the daughter of a chief, the finest upper-class woman her society could offer to the Greek conqueror. Kalya was a cigarette-smoking, sleepy-eyed, cynical girl from Canada who, it seemed to Iskie, probably had a penchant for foul language and who may or may not be a nurse. But she was still Roxanne to him.

He took every opportunity to study her over dinner. This was a difficult task since his attention was dominated by the polite questions of Subodh's mother (his father was away travelling, Iskie had been told) and by the fact that the presence of food, even this marvellous meal of biryani and various spiced vegetables, caused his internal organs to recoil in justified terror, the memory of giardiasis still quite fresh.

Subodh's mother, to whom Iskie had been instructed to address simply as "Auntie," was surprisingly Western in outlook. She thought nothing of entertaining her son's male friends while her husband was away. Like so many foreign-educated Indian women, her accent was slight and musical, her grammar more precise than most of the better-educated North Americans. And she knew enough not to impose her company upon the younger generation longer than was acceptable. She excused herself and retired to her bed, leaving Subodh, Kalya, and the ailing Iskie to sheepishly watch the servant clear the table. As she left, she glared at Kalya in an odd way, but said nothing.

After a while, Kalya blurted to Iskie, "Did you see that?"

"See what?"

"The way she looked at me. It was a warning not to spend any time alone with you. Appearances are everything here, you know." The words both hurt and exhilarated Iskie. However negative or playful, any discussion of the two of them being alone together was nevertheless promising.

"Iskie," Subodh said, rising from the table and beckoning the others to follow him onto the verandah, "tell Kalya about the girls we met on the train."

Iskie coughed, surprised. "You mean the girls you met. I didn't talk to them."

"I was our spokesman, old man, but we were nevertheless represented as a duo! Kalya, they live in Omas village, just over the hill. Maybe Iskie and I will go visit them later this week, *na*?" Kalya just smiled in mock wisdom. It was an old trick that Iskie had seen others try before: pretend you know something and others will eventually believe in your sagacity. He didn't buy it; Kalya was as clueless about her family as he was. She got up and rushed back into the house. Iskie fought the urge to follow her.

"So, Iskie," Subodh said. "How do you like Kalya?" He all but winked. "Quite a shapely lass."

"She's very charming. Not what I expected. Was she born here?"

"No. Her parents moved to Montreal before she was born. Our fathers are brothers, you know. Our family has owned this house, and much of the land around here, for centuries."

"Don't you feel—I don't know—guilty?"

"About what?" Subodh really did not seem to gather Iskie's thrust.

"Subodh, you have this big house, an education, servants. But the rest of the village is a bunch of neolithic huts. Hardly what I'd call an equitable distribution of wealth."

"I thought you said you didn't know anything about Lenin!" Subodh rejoined, laughing. Then he frowned and continued measuring his words carefully. "Things are the way they are, Iskie. Many Indians would answer you in religious terms, about how people are born into the stations they warrant. But I'm an educated man. I don't run to my supposed religion to justify things for me. All I can tell you is that we are what we are, and I don't waste my time burdening myself with guilt I cannot disavow."

"Very convenient," Iskie muttered under his breath.

"What did you say?"

"I said that's probably wise."

Subodh grunted at him. "You sound like Professor Kumar's friend Goran. Goran Damjanovic. Not met him yet? You will. He's also one for the passive-aggression."

Mercifully, Kalya returned clutching a clay bottle and three stout glasses.

"What's that?" Iskie asked.

Subodh lunged forward, grinning devilishly and exclaimed, "You'll love this!"

"Subodh tells me you like your spirits," Kalya said, pouring some of the bottle's contents into the glasses. "I mean alcoholic spirits, not the other kind."

"I knew I never should have told you anything."

"Told her anything about what?" Subodh asked.

"Never mind," Kalya said. "Iskie, this is the local moonshine. We call it arak. Given your weakened state, and the diphenhydramine in your veins, this'll knock you out in minutes. But you'll enjoy it while it lasts."

Subodh chuckled evilly. "You'll be surprised, Kalya dear. I've seen our Iskie here swallow gallons of hard liquor and yet return to the lab to finish the day's work! A true horse of a man where liquor is concerned."

The glasses were passed around and a suitably innocuous toast chosen. The vile fluid tasted like rubbing alcohol, and Iskie didn't dare ask why it was muddy. For all he knew, it was made from fermented sheep faeces. Sometimes ignorance was indeed bliss.

The substance didn't seep into his veins so much as it flooded them. It felt as though his brain were floating in a pool of the stuff, becoming pickled and malleable. Despite his fatigue and the injection of diphenhydramine, his hard-earned alcoholic resistance held him to consciousness, allowing him to revel in the arak's effects of altered perception. Or was it the environment?

He forced himself to take note of his surroundings. The moon was a sliver, but the sky was clear, almost crystalline. Unfamiliar constellations twinkled in the night sky, and the hum of identifiable nocturnal insects was comfortably near. He enjoyed the slight breeze that relieved the accumulated heat of the long hot day in bed, and the distant noise of chittering villagers and farm animals preparing to retire. The vale was an oddity, he realized. This was a province of sweltering heat, yet this particular locale seemed to enjoy its own separate, cooler climate, and maybe its own unique ecology. He let the science slip to his unconscious, preferring instead to cogitate upon matters of immediate sensory delight.

And he soaked in the vision of his Roxanne. She sat cross-legged upon a deck chair in the corner of the verandah, clutching her untouched glass of arak and staring at him with an amused look. Iskie allowed his eyes to roam across her body, tracing the magnificence of her full breasts, the welcoming quiver of her swollen reddish-brown lips. He didn't know how long he stared, but no one spoke. Her image was comforting, even meditative. And before he knew it, he began to slip into that familiar state where his field of vision collapsed to a wide tunnel, and where those otherwise unseen figures danced on the brink of his perception, teasing his optic nerve and playing with his sanity.

"Hey," Kalya said, "tell me again about your guardian angel."

Iskie glanced over at Subodh. Kalya's cousin was slumped in his chair and snoring, another victim of the arak's potency.

Iskie began to speak, but he found that his words were silent. He swallowed and tried again. "It's not a guardian angel. It's just a feeling that I'm not alone. Ever since I was a kid. You know how sometimes when you're alone in a silent room, you feel someone's eyes burning into your back? Well, I feel that way all the time."

"Maybe you've got a brain tumour. Or a sunburn on your back."

Iskie didn't laugh. "I thought of that. The brain tumour, I mean. Maybe someday I should get one of those scans. I certainly get enough headaches. Maybe it *is* a tumour."

"Maybe your headaches come from so many hangovers."

"That's ironic. You see, I drink *because* of my paranoia, not the other way around."

"Are you sure?"

"Yes, Kalya, I'm sure. It's maddening, you know, to always feel watched and followed. When I drink—and I mean drink—sometimes I think I can see who's there. It's not as maddening then."

Kalya didn't react. She never seemed to react. She just sat there, swirling the untouched arak in her glass, never taking her eyes from Iskandar's. "And? What do you see?"

"That's the problem. By the time I'm drunk enough to almost get it into focus, I pass out!" His black-on-black eyes twinkled, seemed to tear. Behind his demeanour of an excited explorer, Kalya could see, was great spiritual fatigue.

"Well," she said, "what do you think it is?"

Iskie smiled broadly. "You actually believe me! No one ever believes me!"

"Who says I believe you? It's just better than talking about the weather. So? What do you think it is?"

"The shade of history, a shepherd of Fate."

She blinked absently, dismissively. "I see. Poetic, but evasive. Well, we shall have to give it a name, no?"

"Oh, Kalya, it already has a name. I call it Bucephalus."

Kalya raised her eyebrows. "Alexander's horse?"

"Why," Iskie said, leaning forward, almost falling out of his chair, "does everyone here seem to know all about Alexander the Great? At first I thought it was an Indian thing, something to do with their educational system. But you didn't grow up here! Almost nobody back home would know the name of Alexander's horse. Do they give you a brochure at the border? Was there a big Bollywood movie recently that I missed?"

"Look, Iskandar, you seem like someone who should know this already, but I'll tell you anyway. Around here, nothing happens randomly. You meet certain people for certain reasons. Leave it at that. Right? So, why Alexander's horse?"

Iskie resisted the urge to insist on clarification. Save it for sobriety. "I'm Alexander, you see."

"I see," she said. "Then you should have named it Hephaestion. Wasn't that the name of Alexander's true companion?"

"Hey, it just follows me. It doesn't fuck me."

If Bucephalus the Watcher, the elemental, were indeed real, this is what it would have done then. It would have watched quietly as Kalya poured the contents of her unemptied glass back into the arak bottle and handed it to Tenali, the waiting servant. It would then have scampered silently after her as she guided the inebriated Iskandar back to his room, and left Subodh to be exposed to the mild elements. It would have settled into the corner of the room, observing carefully as Kalya pulled Iskie's slippers from his feet, leaving him unconscious on his bed, then tiptoed quietly back to her own room. Finally, it would have sat invisibly in that dark corner, as always, sleeplessly watching.

8

Fig Trees

Blastophaga psenes, the fig wasp, experiences a life cycle typically of only a few days. Its symbiotic relationship with the fig tree is one of the most celebrated in entomology, rivalling that of the pilot fish with the great white shark, or that of the crocodile bird with the Nile crocodile. So profound is this relationship that it has taken on divine status in parts of India, rising to the centre of a peculiar tradition among the peoples of the Western Ghats.

There are approximately 900 species of bisexual fig tree (genus *Ficus*) distributed throughout the tropical regions of the world. Associated with each fig species is a unique species of pollinating wasp that enter into the syconia—the fleshy, fruity, flower-bearing parts of the fig—to pollinate the female flowers inside. Without the arrival of the wasp, the fig tree would thus be unable to reproduce. Its dependence upon the insect is absolute.

In exchange, the syconia provide a completely safe environment for the female wasp to lay its eggs, one per syconium. After laying its eggs, the wasp dies and its body is absorbed into the developing fruit, feeding it. The male wasps, equipped with large mouths, are born first, chewing their way out of their receptacles, eating of the very plant their mother had died to feed. They immediately seek out the female larvae, which are not equipped with mouths large enough to extricate themselves, and chew out an exit route for them. The males fertilize the eggs of the females while the latter are still in their larval stage, then promptly die, their lives' purpose at an end.

The females emerge, their egg sacs filled, and immediately take to the air to seek out another fig tree of that particular species, expending their remaining days in this most vital of quests. So great is their drive to enter the syconia to lay their eggs that their antennae and wings are often damaged in their burrowing frenzy. It is a desperate life cycle that begins with escape, continues into flight, and ends in exhausted pain, only to begin all over again. It is one of the most striking examples of gender inequality in the animal kingdom.

A wasp that mistakenly enters the wrong species of syconium and oviposits will likely cause the demise of its brood. The fig likewise will fail to produce seed and propagate. Fig trees have thus evolved intricate entrances and chemical cues which select their specific pollinators. *Blastophaga psenes* is unsurprisingly one of the *agaonids,* the insect group showing the greatest host specificity.

In India, certain species of fig tree have greater social relevance than others, hence affecting the accessibility of the corresponding pollinator wasp species. Of particular interest is the banyan tree, *Ficus bengalensis*, whose role in Indian history and religion is certainly preponderant.

—*Insects of North and Middle India,*
by Pradeep Kumar and Jan Birbalsingh

"What is this preponderant role of which he speaks?" Iskie asked, delicately fingering the pages Kalya had torn from Kumar's book.

"I don't know. I stopped reading after the first few paragraphs." She shifted uneasily on the grass, glancing at the security of the Lal homestead a short distance from the hillock where they sat. "Is it safe here? Are there snakes or tarantulas?"

"You live here, remember? I'm a visitor. You tell me." Iskie lay back on the grass, shielding his eyes from the piercing sun while he squinted to read the text.

Kalya waved at the air, uncertain if the tiny things she thought she saw were in fact insects or floating bits of vegetation. Beneath her sundress, beads of sweat rolled down her skin, the sensation like that of ants scurrying across her flesh. The blades of grass would occasionally bend, whether from the press of spiders and millipedes or from eddies of air currents. It all made her quite uneasy, and she wished to be back indoors, or at least to be sitting on a blanket rather than upon living vegetation.

"Can you imagine the life of that female wasp, Kalya?" Iskie let the stapled sheaf of papers collapse upon his chest, and relaxed to watch his rounded belly rise with the tides of his speech. "To be born pregnant, to spend the entirety of your brief life looking for a place to lay your eggs, chased at every step by some predator. Then to die, never having known the conscious company of another of your kind. What kind of life is that?"

"I thought you envied insects?"

"Envy isn't the right word. I respect them. We mammals only came into our own since the dinosaurs died out 65 million years ago, you know. The fossil record tells us that insects have been thriving for at least 350 million years. Over three quarters of all the animals on Earth are insects. Clearly, they're doing something right."

Kalya lay down on the grass, quite against her nature, and propped herself up on one elbow. She turned to Iskie. "They outnumber us because they reproduce so efficiently," she said. "Their life is all about finding a way to reproduce. Maybe they don't know how to really live. Maybe that's why we're better."

Iskie bristled. "That's one way of looking at it," he said in a derisive tone.

"What's the other way?" she asked.

"That they have boiled the essence of living down to its bare bones. With an extra 300 million years of evolution, they've managed to get rid of all the extraneous stuff. For example, what is it that each of us wants and needs?"

"Money?"

"I'll assume you're joking. But money is a proxy measurement for what? For security, possessions, power. And why do we need security, possessions and power?"

Kalya sighed and rolled onto her back. "We need those things because we are essentially a greedy species."

"No!" Iskie sat straight up, his right hand extended in a cupping gesture. "We need those things because, whether we choose to believe it or not, they are useful for attracting a mate and for raising offspring."

"Ugh," Kalya said. "I don't think I like that."

"I didn't think you would," Iskie admitted. "Most people don't. The insect has done away with the layers of deception and rationalization that mask that basic imperative. We, on the other hand, still pretend that there's something more complicated, whether it's noble or insidious, about simply seeking the basics of life."

Kalya harrumphed.

"Well," Iskie continued, a bit subdued, "maybe those are the essentials of physical life. Spiritual life is expressed differently. But some philosophies would have all spiritualism dictated by physical need. The Tantrics, for example, sought divinity in sex. And we will agree, won't we, that sex is a physical need?"

Silence. A cloud momentarily occluded the sun, softening the harsh brightness. Kalya and Iskie both felt as if they had been brought down from a celestial flight, forced to perceive things once more with earthbound vision.

"Come to think of it," Kalya said at last, "the wasp life isn't so different from most people's. I mean, we do seek mates, it's true, and often we never really know them. Perhaps the fig wasp just expresses that more honestly by never actually meeting its mate. And to live in flight, forever seeking a place to die, and forever eluding hunters. . . well, isn't that everyone?"

"I don't know, Kalya. That's pretty dark."

"Well," Kalya said, "what do you seek, really, if not a place to die?"

"I figure death will find me eventually. No need to go looking for it."

Kalya laughed. "I was being morose. I'm sorry. Actually, I've always thought that that's what separates humans from animals. We seek more than just reproduction and the avoidance of death. We seek beauty, poetry, understanding. We lie on our backs looking at the sun and thinking about what goes through the minds of fig wasps. Fig wasps don't ponder us."

Iskie could feel the warmth of her body not centimetres from his own. Despite the oppressive heat of the day, he was drawn to the heat of her form, to the flowery scent of her skin, and to the outline of her figure against the grass. "The wasp is pursued and hunted," he said. "What hunts you?"

The corners of her mouth turned up in an enigmatic smile, but she remained silent. *A woman of secrets, my Roxanne,* thought Iskie.

After a long pause, Kalya finally reluctantly spoke. "I dunno. My creditors. Several ex-boyfriends. Perhaps one or two potential new boyfriends."

"I wish you'd stop being so damned mysterious and give me a straight answer!" Iskie wasn't really angry, but he liked his lines to be straight, his subtleties to be not so.

"Don't get all macho on me now, Iskie. So far I like you." Kalya rose to her feet and straightened out her dress, bending low enough for Iskie to glimpse an eyeful of glistening cleavage. He closed his eyes and breathed deeply, imagining the scent of that flesh, beseeching the beast within himself.

She stood before him, the sun at her back, with her hands at her hips. He couldn't see her expression, but imagined pursed lips and a creased forehead. "Come on," she said. "I want to take you somewhere." Never asking for clarification, he leapt to his feet and followed her into the village.

"Iskie," she said, "do you want to know something? I came to India because I defaulted on my student loans. I was feeling like such a loser, so I thought I'd come to a place where no one knows me and hide out for a while. It's nice not to have to answer the phone when the collection agencies call."

"Wow," Iskie said, " you *were* telling the truth. So what about the ex-boyfriends?"

"Do you want the whole story right away? Isn't it better to get it out of me a bit at a time?" Kalya asked. Iskie merely shrugged. They had re-entered the lower part of the village, a place of wooden huts with tin roofs and the occasional slab of concrete. A teenaged boy on a bicycle smiled at Iskie, ignoring Kalya entirely.

Several small children carrying seemingly heavy loads—a large cask of water, baskets of fruits and crafts—stopped to grin at Iskie. They yammered at him enthusiastically and to his total incomprehension. He smiled back appreciatively. One by one, they took Kalya by the hands and seemed to revel in her company, though they never dared to touch Iskie.

"Back home," Iskie said, "children would never be so friendly to perfect strangers, though I guess they're used to you by now."

"It's often what makes this place bearable for me," Kalya said. "Everyone's smile is genuine. How rare is that?" She chittered something to the children and they skipped away, but not before whispering to each other and giggling, casting a knowing glance back at the grinning Iskandar.

"Do you want children of your own?" Kalya asked.

"Of course," Iskie said. "It's my biological imperative. It's why we evolved. It's *how* we evolved."

"Never mind, science boy."

"Where are we going?" He stumbled along the mud path, eager to grab hold of Kalya to keep his balance, but knowing better than to do so.

"We're going to visit a woman who lives on the other side of the rice paddies. Her name is Eunice. She's from Guyana."

"Africa?" Iskie asked, knowing full well the correct answer.

"No, stupid, South America. She's West Indian, but she lives here as a kind of female *sadhu.*"

Iskie nodded. A *sadhu,* he recalled, was an ascetic, usually male and often a middle class, who had given up his worldly goods to spend the remainder of his life as a spiritually pure mendicant. No such path was typically available to women, though female sadhus did exist. Iskie wasn't surprised that a foreigner had chosen to emulate the lifestyle.

"She provides advice on. . . non-specific things," Kalya continued. "She was branded as a heretic back in the West. So she came here to live a simple life."

"Like you?"

"Whatever. Anyway, have you got a few rupees on you?"

Iskie fished around in his pocket. "I think so. This is going to cost me?"

"She's providing a service, bucko. You're a Western capitalist. You know how it works."

"Oh, man, she's a psychic, isn't she." Iskie felt his stomach go hollow. The day had been pretty good so far, complete with skywatching, reading about wasps, and enjoying the company of a terribly sexy woman. A low-budget fakir was not going to add to that score.

When they reached their destination, Iskie realized that Eunice's place wasn't so much a hut as it was a canopy spread over the roots of a great tree. The setting was lusciously pastoral, the hut nestled on the edge of the forest and against the corner of a rice paddy. The mosquito population was enormous, however, and Kalya was becoming visibly distressed. "We have to make this fast," she said. "You may like the little biting beasties, but I'm coming back one day with a flame-thrower!"

"On one condition," Iskie said, holding Kalya by the shoulder. "I'll go in and do whatever you say, but you must tell me about the ex-boyfriend thing."

"Sure," she said, brushing his hand off. "I was going to tell you, anyway." She swept aside a corner of the canopy and drew Iskie inside with her.

They sat in one corner of the hot little room, cross-legged, with Iskie's right knee in painstaking contact with Kalya's left. In the darkness, perhaps a metre in front of them, sat a very dark figure. Eunice did not rise at their arrival, did not even shift her weight. The immobility of her silhouette was ghostly, and Iskie felt a slight chill up his spine. Also, the musky odour of the place, complicated by the smells of an unwashed woman and the unmistakable wet scent of fungi growing under the canopy's darkness, assaulted Iskie's brain in a narcotic fashion. He found that he liked the effect.

Kalya nudged him. He shook some coins in his hands, sure that Eunice would recognize the familiar clang of money, and dropped them onto the ground in front of her.

"You know," Eunice said, "me been born wit' one caul." Her voice was not unpleasant, soothing Iskie with its femininity and grandmotherliness. The singsong Caribbean accent was welcome, too, a touch of the familiar in this most unfamiliar of places. "You know what be one caul?"

"No," Iskie said.

"Is one mask of mucous, boy. When one baby born wit' one, we say he got one caul. Explain it to de boy, Kalya."

"Sometimes babies are born with the amniotic sac unpunctured," Kalya explained. "When they emerge and the sac bursts, their bodies are covered in the membrane."

"You know what one caul can do fo' you, boy?" Eunice asked.

"No," Iskie said again.

"Tell de boy, Kalya." Kalya put her hand on Iskie's right knee. It was the most marvellous feeling, warm and dry, a much-needed comfort in this weird scenario.

Kalya said, "They say that people born with a caul are mediums or psychics. They can see ghosts."

"I see," Iskie said, unconvinced. "Do you see any ghosts here?"

"Rudeness is not appreciated, bug boy," Eunice said.

"I wasn't being rude! I really want to know!"

"You were being rude, fatty. Kalya dear, do you see de ghost?"

"No, Auntie. Is there one here?"

Eunice shifted her weight to lay against the tree trunk. Iskie watched her every move, as best he could in the darkness, with unwavering scientific curiosity. What did she eat? How did she tend to her hygiene? Did she ever leave the canopy?

She noticed his interest. "You tink me live like one animal, bug boy?"

"Yes. Yes, I do." His confidence was growing.

"Tank you, den. From you, dat a compliment, I know. You wish you could live like so, too, right? You wish you na need de demon liquor fo' let you tink like one animal, fo' let you see like one animal. You want so much to be de animal, poor bug boy."

Iskie said nothing.

"What about the ghost?" Kalya asked.

"De ghost not important," Eunice said. "Plenty ghost here."

"But," Iskie said, "I paid you to tell me about the ghost, I'm pretty sure. I suspect that's why Kalya brought me here. Please tell me about it."

"Bug boy," Eunice said, waving a finger at him accusingly. "Me na tell you what you want fo' know; dat's what de fakirs do. Me tell you what you need fo' know. Right? And dis is what you need fo' know. You listenin'?"

"Oh yeah," he said.

"Okay, you wan' one pen fo' to write it down, *na*? Sometime people bring one pen. Don't do no good. Dey always forget, even when dey write it down."

"I'll remember," Iskie said. "Please tell me. What do I need to know?"

There was an extended and uncomfortable stretch of silence, during which only their breaths could be heard. Eunice's breathing was particularly noticeable, its raspiness and inconstant rhythm unmistakable and distracting. Finally, she spoke. "What you see is na always what you get. And sometime you get ting dat you na see." There was no more.

"That's it?" Iskie asked.

"What you call it? Parsimonious, no? What? You wan' more specific?" Eunice was grinning in the shadows, that much was clear. Darkness and fungi breed an odd sense of humour.

"I would appreciate it," Iskie said.

"Okay. But me got fo' be mysterious, you understand? Dat's de way it work. Dere's a place where many men stay fo' rest one time long ago, many hundred year ago, under one tree. At da place, you go see de sun, and den you go be okay, ghost or no ghost."

"What nonsense is that?"

"Don' be rude, bug boy!"

"Sorry."

Kalya whispered in his ear, "Iskie, I think you're the sun. Think about it. You're round and sunny, warm and yellow." She giggled charmingly, straddling, as always, that line between innocent friendliness and provocative flirtation.

"No, Kalya dear," Eunice interjected. "Iskie be de moon."

The pair just stared at Eunice, but no elucidation was forthcoming. Quickly, they crawled out from under the canopy and hiked away from the cloud of mosquitoes, back towards the Lal home.

It seemed as though they had spent no more than a few minutes with Eunice, but the sun was now courting the horizon, and dusk threatened. The perception of the passage of time was a function of mental state, too, it seemed.

In these lands, the environment truly was dependent upon the time of day. Where earlier there had been the ubiquitous buzz of familiar insects, now there were the more ominous distant hoots and howls of forest birds and monkeys. The mud beneath their feet seemed to Kalya and Iskie to be darker and wetter than before, and they slid along uneasily.

Back in the heart of the village, most of the adults would be returning from the fields, and Subodh and his mother would be wondering where their guests had disappeared. So little science had been accomplished, so little work done on the Indian fig wasp. Yet the day had not been for naught. Some progress had indeed been made, though none of it rigorous.

"Not all knowledge is scientific, Iskie," Kalya said.

"I didn't say anything!"

"But you were thinking that Eunice is a crank, right?"

"Actually, I was thinking that I didn't get bitten by a single mosquito while I was under her canopy. Did you?"

"No," Kalya replied.

"Man, that's strange."

"That's not what's strange," Kalya said. "What's strange is that I never told Eunice that you're an entomologist. . . bug boy."

9

ROTTING FLESH

To dream at night of a dream in night is, without doubt, a portentous event. Its oddness is made more so when the dreamer becomes aware of the illusory nature of his environment—its maya, as the Hindus call it. Patrolling the frontiers of maya in dreamscape was what Iskie did best, flirting with the realization of the dream, threatening to puncture its comfortable membrane and to poke through into a sensationless reality.

Iskandar the Hellenic conqueror strolled with confident grace across the black and white dreamscape panorama, hands on hips and nose turned skyward. There were no scents in this dreamland, only sight and sound and the lightest of touches. He heard the plangent call of the loon, which was odd, for this was not Canada, but some geographical hybrid of India, Canada, and the moon. Even the gravity was something less than normal, allowing his hair to float in the air, each fibre alive, Medusa-like. He felt rough blades of grass against his sandalled toes and breathed scentless cool, clean air. These were the sensations of timelessness.

He walked towards the edge of the grassy plateau, towards that line where ground met sky. Beyond the edge, he knew, was a drop to certain doom, a plunge that would test the mettle of his hard-won virility. Only a god-king could face such terror without hesitation. Only the Iskandar of lore.

He peered over the edge to see the target that awaited him, yet only clouds were visible, concealing the mystery beneath. His dreaming mind imagined sharp rocks or upturned spikes, an acid bath or the opened mouth of a hungry monster. *What lies beneath?* a voice mocked him. *Destiny!* he shouted back, his dream voice echoing across the cosmos. He did not wait, did not contemplate. He did not step with one foot, nor dive like a swan. Instead, he drew his knees to his chest as if he were a foetus, and rolled headlong into the abyss.

Iskie awoke, not in shock but disorientation. His head poked through the membrane of maya, emerging into reality, wet with sweat. The arak poisoned his brain still, inducing in him alternating states of wakefulness and unconsciousness. As feeling seeped back into his limbs, he noticed that his right hand still clutched a bottle of the stuff, no doubt nicked from the pantry of the Lal home. And as his eyes struggled to regain their focus, he saw that he was in his room, lying in the dark on the same bed upon which Kalya had first found him stricken with giardiasis four days ago.

Breathe. Enjoy.

It was a moment suspended in time. Iskie's normally busy brain slowed to a comfortable crawl. He stared dully into the featureless gloom. His toes and fingers tingled, and his breathing was slow and unlaboured. The rise of his belly with each breath brought joy and contentment; the breaths came slower and slower still. He had stopped time, remarkably existing in that precious moment between waking and sleeping, holding that moment static against its will.

Through the corners of blurry and teary eyes, he noticed a dim figure in the corner, a shadow in darkness, black on black. The mysterious shade appeared to stand up from a crouching position. It moved out of phase, existing as planes of interplexing light, bending against the corners of the room. It then slipped through a crack in the door jamb, making no noise in its passage, but leaving behind the scent of rotting meat.

Iskie struggled to rise, dropping the bottle of arak as he did so, barely aware of its shattering on the floor. As he stood, the world swayed and constellations swam; this he knew, for he could see through the roof into the starry night sky. Somewhere on the other side of the world, a whirlpool formed in the ocean, swirling beneath Iskie's feet, making every step difficult. He stepped lightly across the room, and onto the door as he had seen the ghostly figure do. He moved down the hall, feeling himself to be floating rather than walking.

Breathe, enjoy.

There was a kind of rhythmic quiet in the Lal home, its cadence kept by the muffled punctuation of Iskie's bare feet against the wooden floor. His modesty returned to him when he became aware that he wore nothing but his briefs. But the smell of rotting meat disgusted and beckoned him, so that even semi-nakedness could not slow his dance-like passage.

With each step, his sobriety returned incrementally, though the alcohol in his veins would still have rendered immobile a less experienced drinker. His eyes gradually focused, but his thoughts remained a jumble, unable to rest upon any one theme.

The odour of rotting meat began to thin and soon vanished, but by now Iskie had decided upon a destination. He had wandered past Kalya's and Subodh's bedrooms, and had, in his unconscious, stupefied way, noted that both doors were fast shut, indicating that their occupants were asleep inside. Yet there was someone else awake. Someone in the pantry.

Iskie pushed open the swinging pantry doors and stumbled inside. A man sat at the table, his hand gripping a short glass full of clear liquid, his gaze seemingly focused upon a large bottle of gin atop the table. The man was in his mid-forties and quite handsome. But his forehead was creased with concern, his jowls heavy with sadness.

"Mr. Lal?" Iskie asked, cautiously.

The man looked up slowly and chuckled at Iskie's plump half-naked form. "What is this?" he asked. "Are there leprechauns in my house?" He had a pleasing accent, the product of an expensive education. But his words were slurred, their joyful tone failing to mask the heaviness of his heart. He was not, Iskie could see, an experienced drinker.

"I am Iskandar Diamandi, sir," Iskie said, summoning a sober and controlled voice, as he had done so many times before. "I'm a friend of your son, from Professor Kumar's lab."

"Yes, yes," Lal said. "I know all about you. My wife telephoned me, you see. Wouldn't do to have a man come home to find a stranger living in his house, would it." He laughed hollowly and sipped from his glass. His left hand was caressing a metallic object in his lap. "You must call me Uncle, Iskandar. That is how we do things here. And my wife is Auntie. Yes?"

"Yes. . . Uncle."

"But. . ." Lal refilled his glass and pushed the bottle towards Iskie. "But that is for tomorrow. Tonight we are drinking mates, and you may call me by my given name, Palvinder." He licked his lips and mouthed his own name curiously a couple of times. "We Lals have often had Punjabi names. I don't know why."

Iskie sat across from Lal, took the gin bottle, and held onto it without drinking. "We Diamandis have often had Persian names. I don't know why, either," he said.

"Here's to names that aren't our own!" Lal extended his glass in a toast then downed its contents in one go. Iskie dutifully refilled the glass. "Not a drinking man, are you, Iskandar."

Iskie smirked knowingly. "It's a bit late at night—or early in the morning—for me. But I've had a few run-ins with your local arak."

"Here's to arak!" Lal downed the glass again, and beckoned for another refill. His hands lifted from the thing in his lap. Iskie could see now that it was some kind of vase or container. "I used to keep a bottle of the stuff in here somewhere. . ."

"I understand you've been away on business," Iskie said, not eager to admit to having copped the bottle for his personal use. He was now becoming more aware of his lack of clothing. Lal was, after all, still dressed for his affairs. His brown pants were muddy at the cuffs, though, and his silken kurta was stained with sweat and smelled of booze. Even so, he was an officious figure, one that commanded respect and caused shopkeepers to strike rigid poses.

"Is that what they called it? 'Away on business'? I was in the city, making preparations for Subodh's wedding."

Iskie nearly dropped the bottle. "Subodh is getting married? When? To whom?"

"They'll be wed during the Chhath festival early next month. I thought you were his friend?" Lal asked seriously. Then he broke into a wide grin.

"Well, to be truthful, we only met recently." Iskie was abashed at that confession. He had never stopped until now to reflect upon the circumstances that had brought him so abruptly to this house in this village. His link here was truly tenuous, dependent upon a casual and embryonic relationship with Subodh, a co-worker he barely knew.

"You're an honest boy, Iskandar. I like you. Though I wish you wouldn't walk around my house naked. Might scare someone, you know."

Iskie pressed his knees together reflexively, conscious of his poor physique before Lal's impressive figure. "So," Iskie said, trying to sound nonchalant, "can you tell me about Subodh's. . . fiancee?" The word came exactingly. He found himself unable to imagine Subodh settling down with a traditional Indian woman. Kalya's words about Subodh's questionable sexual orientation hadn't been lost on Iskie. But he suspected that many of Kalya's words had to be questioned, or at least looked at from several perspectives.

"She's actually a distant cousin. I know how you Westerners are aghast at such things, but we do it quite regularly. Marry cousins, I mean. Most European royalty do it, too, you know."

You consider yourselves royalty? Iskie didn't dare ask. "Is it anyone I would have already met?" *Not my Roxanne!*

"Fortunately not, lest the poor girl be won over by your exotic ways. Subodh doesn't need that kind of competition, you know. She lives in Delhi, is studying to be an accountant."

"An accountant? Not really Subodh's thing, wouldn't you say?"

"Seems you know my son well, after all. No offence, Iskandar, but where can his laboratory pursuits take him in life, hmm?"

Iskie toyed with the idea of drinking the gin, but he worried about the potential breach of protocol of putting his lips to the communal bottle. "You'd be surprised, sir. May I ask in what line of work you are involved?"

"Why not!" Lal presented himself as the image of mirth, the good host. But the arak had wiped clear Iskie's inner eye, allowing him to see into Lal's heart, or at least giving him the impression of that power. Lal was troubled about something. "My ancestors spent their lives accumulating land in these parts, and some in the city, too. I'm essentially a landlord, Iskandar."

"A zamindar?"

"No, no. That function was outlawed decades ago, and for good reason! Zamindars exploited their peasants mercilessly. I rent my land to shops and businesses, not to peasants. It's a good living, one that Subodh will one day enjoy. But I fear the boy hasn't the financial wherewithal, the money smarts. His could be the last generation of Lal prosperity, you know." He smirked to himself.

Iskie watched Lal's hands: steady as a rock, especially when caressing that vase. His form was deceptive, but the man was essentially honest. He was looking for an opportunity to share something, and Iskie would try his best to give him that opportunity. "Where will the wedding be held?"

"Here, according to village tradition, underneath one of the big banyan trees in the forest." Lal almost beamed. His pride in family tradition was quite evident.

"Surely," Iskie said, sensing his opening, "it could not have taken four entire days away to organize a wedding that is to be held locally."

Lal put his glass on the table, and his face took on a serious, almost a frightening expression. He absently scratched the table's surface with his fingernails, and his left knee began to rock back and forth. "Actually, I also had to pick up a dead body."

Iskie's eyes widened for a heartbeat, then returned to their normal slitted state, their black eeriness drawing Lal's tale from him. Indeed, there was more truth to that than Iskie imagined. As had so many others, Lal was soothed by Iskie's oily optic pools, sucked into them. "And . . ?" Iskie said. "Are you going to leave me there?"

"No. Here it is. My last remaining uncle was in hospital for several weeks. Heart failure, you know. He was in a coma in Delhi, kept alive by life support. I instructed the doctors to disconnect the machines.

That's no way for a man to die, I say. Leave him his dignity!" Lal sipped again, his gaze distancing even further, slipping from the firm grip of Iskie's entrancing glint. "Anyway, I received word a few days ago that he had died the instant the machines were turned off. So they put his body in the freezer until I could arrange for its transport."

Iskie swallowed and tried to appear nonplussed. "So is it here? The body?"

"No. My original plan was to bring it back here so that we could do the cremation in the village. Much nicer than those crematoria in the city, or those floating meat fires in Varanasi, don't you think? I don't know how much you know about Hindus, Iskandar, but many look forward to being cremated on a raft on the Ganges. At least they did in my youth. It used to be quite a sick sight, really, since there was rarely enough wood to do the job properly."

Iskie's stomach turned a bit. The thought of generations of partly cremated corpses littering the holy river was not a pleasant one, at least not for his arak-riddled brain in these wee hours. And yet there was a certain beauty to that image, a fleet of parting loved ones set ablaze upon a river that was said to flow from God's long hair. It was so wonderfully ancient and primal, and yet terrifyingly pagan.

"Anyway, I left for Delhi to collect the body," Lal continued. "As I was being led to the freezer room where the body was kept, I couldn't help but notice the detached manner of the staff. Do you know what I mean?"

"I think so," Iskie said. "It's like abortion doctors back home. Because some of them find what they do distasteful, they start to refer to the foetus in very clinical terms, as a way of protecting their emotions. Is that what you're talking about?"

"I hadn't thought of it that way, my friend. My feeling was *How bureaucratic*. Bureaucracy is India's lasting legacy to the British empire; it's a virus that we developed, and it has infected the whole world, it seems. But that's not what I mean. The fellow who showed me the body was so clinical, so insensitive and willfully unaware that my uncle had once been a father, a brother, a husband."

"Well, in his defence, the clerk must have to process hundreds of bodies a month. . ."

"Yes, yes, I understand that. I don't fault him for his attitude. It's just that it got me to thinking. . . What if Uncle Hari had awoken from his coma, would anyone have noticed?"

Iskie was silent. It was indeed a provocative and horrifying thought. Surely, there were enough terrible urban myths circulating that the possibility of such a thing happening was not altogether foreign to the human mind. "Uncle. . . Palvinder, I don't know much about such machines, but I think an alarm sounds when the coma patient wakes up."

"But what if he woke up *after* they disconnected the machines? What if they put him in the freezer just as he was waking up, and the bloodsuckers were too callous to notice?"

Iskie leaned forward, an arm outstretched in a gesture of convincing sincerity. "I'm a scientist, Uncle. Believe me. If he was too weak to wake up while the machines were helping him, there's no way he'd have had enough strength to wake up without the machines."

"That's what I keep telling myself, Iskandar. And yet when I saw his body, there were fresh scratches on his face, as if he had awoken in agony, without the strength to push open the freezer door, but enough to mutilate himself in his crazed anguish."

No longer caring about protocol, Iskie pressed the gin bottle to his lips and drank very deeply.

"Here's to my Uncle Hari!" Lal toasted, and he and Iskie imbibed further.

"So what did you do?" Iskie asked.

"I couldn't bring the body home like that," Lal explained. "I had it burnt in a crematorium in Delhi, and brought back the ashes." He tapped the vase on his lap. "We'll spread the ashes over the roots of one of the banyan trees, maybe even the same one we'll use for the wedding. But you mustn't breathe a word of this to anyone in the family, do you understand?"

Iskie nodded briskly and drank again. The gin entered into an unholy union with the residue of arak in his stomach, causing him much discomfort. But he was well able to ignore it, his conscious thoughts centred on other things. "It's not possible," he whispered into the bottle, not loud enough to be heard by Lal. "You're mistaken. Seeing something that isn't there. He couldn't have been alive." The mental image of a man tearing into his own face in his death throes was one he could not shrug off. What terrible hauntings his ghost would surely inflict on the living.

The memory of the smell of rotten flesh was still strong. Stumbling all the way, he followed it back to the safe haven that was his bed. He could no longer see through the ceiling to the stars, no longer peer into the hearts of men. He clutched his knees to his chest and rolled headlong onto the bed, plummeting back into his favourite amniotic dream.

10

UNCERTAINTY

When Alexander first arrived in the subcontinent, he was shocked to discover an isolated community that claimed descent from the Greeks. The inhabitants of a little town called Nysa, nestled somewhere between modern Pakistan and Afghanistan, rushed unarmed into the Greek phalanx. "We are children of Dionysus," they proclaimed, insisting that the Greek god of wine had fathered them during his mythic journey to the East.

Alexander, of course, took this as a sign that his own military quest was divinely sanctioned. He was, after all, retracing the steps of Dionysus the Olympian, reconnecting the disparate pods of Hellenic tribes that the god of ecstasy and intoxication had supposedly scattered. The community showed Alexander their grape vines, their Mediterranean wines, their bay leaves, their laurels and ivy. And they pointed out their physical features, which, if one squinted enough, were undeniably European. It was then that Alexander did the unthinkable: he spared their lives. Perhaps it was the reminder of a home left thousands of miles in the past; perhaps it was his perceived duty to sanctify and preserve all things vaguely Olympian; or perhaps it was simply the human need to curtail his path of conquest and destruction, if only for a little while.

For whatever the reason, the god king's refusal to let this one vulnerable pocket remain to his rear signalled, to the minds of some, the beginning of his downfall. The first bronze scale had fallen from his armour; his tyranny could be assuaged. His path into India was now touched with uncertainty.

Iskandar's eyes opened to a flood of sunlight that washed in from the open windows. The voice that had pulled him from dreamspace spoke again, this time more slowly. "Awake, Iskie, awake!" It was Subodh energetically commanding Iskie's body as if it were a marionette to be bent to the puppet master's will.

Subodh crawled onto the bed and straddled Iskie's chest. "This will wake you, old man." He trickled a stream of warm brown liquid onto Iskie's pale lips.

"Man!" Iskie protested, struggling to free himself. "What is this?" He licked his lips reflexively.

"Chai!" Subodh rolled over to lie next to Iskie. He handed him the cup and gazed wide-eyed at him, teeth exposed in a boyish grin, waiting for further peals of protest and curmudgeonliness.

Iskie wrapped his palms tightly about the cup, coveting its warmth. He sipped the tea slowly, thankful for its revivifying sweet milkiness after a night of alcohol abuse. Usually it was Tenali, the humourless head servant who could disappear like a shadow into the wallpaper, who brought him his morning tea, and that was enough of an imposition. But to wake with Subodh upon his chest. . .

"To what do I owe this honour?" Iskie asked, slowly and sarcastically.

"This will be a grand day, Iskie." Subodh clapped his hands and rubbed them together with unrestrained glee.

"Oh?"

"Remember those two girls we met on the train?" Iskie didn't respond, but slurped the chai greedily. "Well, I've arranged for us to meet them this morning!" Iskie sputtered his chai up his nose and into his sinuses, to his great discomfort.

"But—"

"Never mind your research, old man. You can take one day off, no? Besides, maybe the girls will enjoy hearing you prattle on about your bugs. You can tell them all about mating patterns and things like that."

"But. . ."

"And Kalya has things to do without you, you know." Iskie was silent. Subodh was clearly holding back an explosive grin. "So get dressed, eh?" Subodh leapt off of the bed and sped through the door. His head popped back into sight moments later. "And don't forget to pack a rubber or two!"

Iskie clutched his forehead in anticipation of the headache that was sure to follow when he was fully awake, fissuring his brain and sapping his will. Undoubtedly, this day would be a trial.

Kalya and the elder Lals were nowhere to be seen. Odd, for this was their breakfast hour. Instead, Tenali was waiting for Iskie in the car park.

Tenali had never seemed to like Iskie much. Ever since that first evening when the young Canadian had risen from his giardiasis induced reverie, only to sink yet again after his first exposure to arak, Tenali had worn a barely concealed scowl around him. It seemed that to serve the spoiled Lals was discomfort enough, but to wait upon a chubby pink-skinned foreign alcoholic was simply too much.

"Good morning, sir," Tenali said, his scowl less severe than usual. He knew only a few words of English, but he could enunciate greetings impeccably as if he had been reared in the House of Windsor. He handed Iskie a paper bag.

"What's this?" Iskie asked. Tenali just glared at him. Iskie recalled Kalya's earlier words: *Tenali's eyes are my eyes*. He glared back.

A voice called out, "Lunch!" Iskie turned to see Subodh seated, his face beaming, on the back seat of the polished black Ambassador sedan. "Get in, old man."

Iskie got into the car beside Subodh, a bit overwhelmed by the vehicle's luxuriance. Ever since he had first seen these elegant automobiles along Delhi's embassy row, he had envied their passengers. In truth, he cared little for automobiles, never having understood what so many young men found so fascinating about them. But the Ambassador auto was special. It hearkened to another era, one in which proper gentlemen wore bowler hats, and their prim anorexic escorts were bedecked in faux pearls and parasols.

This was the face of India that both beckoned and disgusted him. Its legacy of British colonialism was one that allowed an undeniably attractive aesthetic at times: garden parties that could have sprung from the books of Jane Austen, and opulent households whose army of servants was unknown in the West. But these things, of course, also underscored the yawning chasm between rich and poor. The thrill of riding in an Ambassador was thus tinged with guilt.

Tenali settled into the chauffeur's seat and started the engine, and they were underway. Iskie found himself feeling rather kidnapped. For all of his adult life, he had directed his own path, choosing to live as he pleased and to move as he pleased. Even his fanciful relegations to the whims of Destiny were possible only because of the control he wielded over his own comings and goings. To be in a car with a driver who openly disliked him, speeding to an unknown destination to socialize with girls he had little desire to meet, was a somewhat unnerving development. But he did not feel in a position to protest.

They sped along unpaved roads awhile, then climbed steadily up a curving path that took them along the outskirts of the village's pine forest, another signature of the vale's unique ecology. Iskie craned to see out of the Ambassador's unusually high window, feeling like a small child being taken on a Sunday drive. The forest floor was littered with pine needles, centimetres deep. In the recesses of his scientific brain, Iskie pondered the ramifications of this phenomenon. Pine needles decayed into an acidic sludge, making the soil unproductive. Signs of erosion were everywhere, too, in the exposed tree roots and sheer fringes that bordered the forest. These observations led Iskie to conclude that, despite the illusion of pastoral timelessness that characterized the region, environmental change was most definitely afoot.

Perhaps, he thought, this was a dying village. One did not need the scent of rotting flesh or the meaningless words of a village psychic to arrive at that conclusion. To a trained scientific mind, such dire portents were indeed ubiquitous.

The Ambassador trundled along, jerking slightly as they passed onto a paved highway. "What's that?" Iskie called suddenly, indicating a white and red structure by the shoulder of the road.

"A postal station," Subodh answered.

"Stop!" Tenali pulled over and Iskie leapt from the car, fishing frantically for something in his back pocket. Subodh watched him in mild amusement, but waited patiently and silently for his new friend to return.

"May I ask," he said, as Iskie took his seat once more inside the Ambassador, "did you post something?"

"Yes," Iskie said, regaining his breath as the Ambassador continued on its journey. "It's a letter to Professor Kumar."

"Interesting. I didn't know you two were such good friends."

"No, you idiot, it's not like that. He's waiting for an update. I told him I have my thesis proposal written, and he'll receive a copy in a few days."

"I see. Did you tell him anything about me?"

"What's to tell? You're on vacation, right?"

"Right," Subodh said. "And have you?"

"Have I what?"

"Have you written your proposal?"

"Virtually." Iskie avoided Subodh's inquiring gaze and instead turned away to digest the scenery of rural India. Tenali would honk his horn liberally to alert the many ox carts and overladen bicycles of his approach. The occasional vegetable stand, manned by entire families of vendors, would flash by his periphery. And once on this trip he even saw a wizened old man controlling a shaggy bear on a leash that danced by the roadside.

What ancient wonders and beasts inhabit these woods, he thought to himself. *What untold mysteries wait just footsteps off this path*? But that, of course, was the avenue of the naive Orientalist, to seek intrigue where only poverty and disease await. And yet the compulsion was strong. The need to perceive an aspect of the subcontinent's mystique was surprisingly potent, and he wondered how much of it was informed by his own culture's susceptibility to New Age doctrines, and how much of it was his own personal need to co-opt his scientific training, to seek that which could not be explained by observation and experiment alone.

No, his proposal was not yet written. But he was inspired on all fronts, and he was certain he'd have it done in a few days. As a pathological procrastinator, he often found it useful to declare that something was already done, thus giving him a ready deadline and the motivation to complete it. By the time Kumar's response arrived via the slow Indian postal system, Iskie's proposal would be half written, he was certain.

The Ambassador rolled to a stop alongside a grove of trees bearing unidentifiable red and orange fruits. "We're here," Subodh announced.

"We're where?"

"See those two figures under the tree? That's Seema and Sonali. Delicious, *na*?" He all but licked his lips and patted his tummy. Iskie squinted through the Ambassador's window to make out two thin delicate figures reclining beneath the branches of a spidery tree. "Which one do you want, old man?"

Iskie sighed, uncertain of how to respond. "You choose," he said at last. Subodh climbed from the car and waved dismissively to Tenali. Reluctantly, Iskie followed, wishing he had stayed in bed with a bottle of arak.

The fading dream that morning, fuelled by the magical qualities of the local moonshine, featured Iskandar the conqueror of the lunar dreamspace plummeting past worlds of shifting environments. He yet clung to sporadic memories of Technicolor forests and yellow deserts summoned from the infinite corridors of his subconscious.

At no point in the dream did Iskandar encounter other sentient beings, only unspeaking animals. Once, an orange and red fish had floated millimetres from his face, and had stared into his oily optic pools with iris-less fish eyes and teased a wet cold kiss from its articulating fish lips, until finally backing up into a receding oblivion. And a forest fox had brushed against his shins, sending statically charged particles racing along his flesh. When he'd bent down to caress it, the fox had snapped at his hand, its fangs dripping saliva, then had raced off into the protection of the trees.

Standing in the womblike protection of a real forest grove was decidedly different from the dream. First, the colours were not as vivid, the foliage being uniformly green, with only the flash of the occasional fruit, blossom or insect to disrupt the homogeneity. Second, there were sensory elements here that were absent in the dreamscape: the ubiquitous buzz of flies and mosquitoes about his ear, the drops of perspiration that rolled down the sides of his face and legs, feeling like ants scurrying across his flesh, and the subtle and pleasant odour of percolating floral pheromones. And third, of course, was the presence of human beings who insisted on speaking and being spoken to.

Iskie and Subodh exchanged words of introduction and pleasantries with the girls. Somewhere in that standard transaction, Subodh and one of the girls separated themselves from Iskie who found himself suddenly, uncharacteristically, struggling to carry a conversation by himself.

The young Indian girl stood coyly and silently, seemingly in expectation. *Which one is she? Seema or Sonali?* Iskie took a guess. "What do you study. . .Seema?"

"Business administration and commerce," she said.

Success!

"I see," Iskie said, quite uncertain of how to continue. He scratched the side of his head and craned his neck around to survey the grove. "Nice day, isn't it?"

"Yes, quite," Seema replied. "Subodh told me you're a doctoral candidate in entomology. Is that correct?"

"Yes. Yes, it is."

"Please, tell me about your studies." Iskie studied her hard. There was *no way* she cared anything about entomology. No young business student does. And yet, unlike Western women, Seema projected so well the facade of fascination. For the first time he took stock of her comeliness. Waifish she was, but not unattractively so. Quite the other extreme to Kalya's curvaceous womanliness, Seema instead suggested a delicate Audrey Hepburn look, batting long lashes atop kohl-blackened eyes that seemed much too large for her small oval face.

He motioned for her to sit next to him as he dropped to the grassy floor. Seema fastidiously straightened her silky lenga and deposited herself to his left, conspicuously within touching distance. A quick glance over his shoulder revealed Subodh and Sonali similarly arranged some

"Well," he said, uncertain of how to begin, "I'm studying the life cycle of the local fig wasp."

"I don't know anything about that," she said. "Does it sting?"

"I. . . don't know," he admitted, at a loss for how to continue.

"Then tell me about its life cycle. What's so special about it?"

"It lives only to reproduce," he said, invigorated. "Each species of fig wasp can only lay its eggs in a certain species of fig tree, and the fig tree can only be pollinated by its specific species of wasp. Each spends its lifetime in search of the other."

"How romantic," she said. Her face beamed charmingly as she crossed her legs and grasped her knee with both hands. "Which species shall you study?"

"Um, I haven't thought about it yet."

"Well, what species are available locally? You are staying in this area, *neh*?"

Iskie's jowls quivered slightly. "Yes, yes, I am. Well, the most prominent species of fig tree in this area is the banyan tree. You know it, right?"

"Yes," Seema said. "But clearly you do not. We are sitting under one right now." Iskie's embarrassed gaze drifted upward to the branches of the great spidery tree. He had mistaken it for a baobab, but clearly baobabs did not grow here. The tree was animalistic, held in static constriction like a photograph of a pouncing predator. He searched for syconia along its branches, for the nests of his precious wasps, but could see none. That was odd, since the local banyans reproduce year round, and their syconia should be brightly coloured to serve as beacons for the wasps.

It took some minutes to realize his mistake. He had been fooled by the lushness of the tree's leaf cover, convinced that it was thriving and in its prime. But the source of the greenery was the vines of adjacent strangler trees, whose witchy embrace cloaked the banyan in a living blanket of parasitic vegetation. "This tree is dead," he said.

"Is it?"

"Yes, I'm pretty sure," he confirmed. "Odd, isn't it? That something dead and inanimate can so convincingly emulate the living." *Things are not always as they seem.*

"You speak as though you've seen a ghost," Seema said. She pursed her full lips and frowned a little. "Have you?"

"And if I have, what would you say?"

"I'd ask if it was a brown-skinned or white-skinned ghost." There was a brief pause, then Iskie found himself chortling. Seema, too, offered a dainty grin. Maybe today wouldn't be so much of a trial, after all. He asked her about her family, her plans for the future, even what colour toenail polish she preferred. He was surprised to hear that she was pursuing a minor in theology. It had never occurred to him that Indian universities would offer courses in theology; the word always held for him such strong connotations of Christianity.

The names of gentlemanly theologians of old flashed through his forebrain: Saint Francis, Martin Luther, Thomas à Beckett. It was such a Western goal, he felt, to use formal religious training to rationalize the political status quo or the boundless pursuit of wealth. And yet he was pulled back to the tactile present by the undeniably Oriental face before him, so clearly bedecked in the garments of privilege and elitism. Here, too, religion could be used for purposes of socialization. What was India's religious caste system if not an instrument of social control?

"It's an odd combination, I think," he said. "Business and religion. What's the connection?" He slid towards the tree trunk, eventually pressing his shins against the dead bark. Seema followed suit, reclining next to him, peering up into the tangled brambles of decaying branches that were held aloft by the strangler vines.

"Do you know who the Jains are?" she asked him.

"Yes," he said. "They're a kind of religion aren't they? Sort of an offshoot of Hinduism?"

"That's fairly accurate. In Jain belief, all things contain a holy life force, *jivha*. To preserve *jivha* is the most saintly pursuit. Their holiest saints are therefore people who have starved themselves to death rather than ingest and destroy living things."

"Seems fairly self-defeating. I wonder what Darwin would have said."

"Wasn't Darwin obsessed with physical evolution? I doubt that he would have ever considered the spiritual demands upon a species. Mahavira, the great figure of Jainism, is often portrayed entangled in vines, afraid to move lest he disrupt *jivha.* Much like this banyan tree, I suppose. You can sometimes see Jains walking down the street with brushes or brooms, whisking microbes and insects from their paths so that they don't get hurt."

The memory of watching a mosquito grow large on his alcohol-ridden blood touched Iskie then. He would not have swatted that mosquito, not even if it had meant his own health. Yet he happily consumed meat and vegetable products, blissfully unmindful of how they had arrived upon his plate.

"Because they can't be involved in the slaughter of animals and plants," Seema continued, "the Jains became competent business people instead, leaving the horticulture and husbandry to the Hindus and Muslims. Many grew to have great wealth. That's one connection between religion and business."

"And is that why you study it?"

"To be honest? Partly. Also, it helps to understand your customers, as all good businessmen should."

"And what are your personal beliefs?"

She leaned toward him then, wearing a devilish smile that stretched across her pixie face. "I believe in the sanctity of love," she said. "I believe in embracing all that God has given us, the pleasures of the mind and the body, without pause for guilt or regret. I believe in abandonment, in succumbing to temptation." It sounded practised, almost like a phrase plucked from a Harlequin romance. Seema's eyes slitted as she became enchanted by the oily black pools of Iskie's enigmatic orbs. She reached out a slender finger to touch his lips, to trace their smooth outline and gently to pry them apart.

Iskie was paralysed, unavoidably drawn by her flowery scent and comfortable repose. He was fixated on her full lips, so moist and tender. He felt an urge to lunge at her, to bury his face in her slender neck. Rarely had he felt such a potent sexual compulsion. Yet he recoiled.

"Is something wrong?" Seema asked.

"No. . . No, nothing."

"Do you not like girls?"

"What?"

"You're from America where there are fewer inhibitions, *neh*? It's okay. I have a cousin who is a homosexual."

"No! No, I'm not gay. I'm not a homosexual." Where were Subodh and Sonali? He couldn't see them anywhere.

"Then I did something wrong? Was I too aggressive? Please, tell me what to do." By Iskie's reckoning, she was a character from a science-fiction story, a sexy space alien who was all too willing to please the clue-less human male hero. "Or," she added, "Is there someone else?"

"Yes. . . No."

"Yes and no? Then she doesn't know that she's someone else?" Iskie did not respond. He had not felt so abashed, so foolish, since adolescence. He was a grown man now with many sexual encounters to his record; these scenarios of uncomfortableness and uncertainty were supposed to be far behind him. "Iskandar, if there's no commitment and no assumption of fidelity, then what is the problem?"

He sat up straight and looked her unwaveringly in the eyes, his own wide open, exposing the infinite black abyss into which so many had fallen. He grasped her head firmly and pressed his lips against hers, his body rejoicing at last.

His action was animalistic, completely contrary to the desires of his rational mind. Was that so wrong? In some neglected back area of his brain, there came the thought that it was what Eunice the Guyanese psychic would have wanted him to do, to beseech the beast within, to act on instinct as he had always claimed to do.

Seema's tongue was hot and swollen, tasting of sour berries and sweet chai. He caressed her incredibly soft cheek, then moved his hand down to massage the side of her neck, feeling a quickening pulse and the first touches of perspiration. With both hands he cupped her small breasts, then struggled to find the fringes of her blouse, to lift it over her head. Overpowered anew by the scents previously trapped beneath her clothing, he breathed deeply and allowed himself to be engulfed by her presence. Limbs entwined, they rolled against the trunk of the dead banyan, two figures performing an instinctual act of life before a shrine to death.

Iskie marvelled at her boyish form, surprised by the sexual potency of a woman so unlike his preferred physical type. He struggled to free himself from the imprisonment of his clothing, helped frantically by Seema, whose staccato breaths belied her impatience and straining need.

One last fleeting responsible thought took hold of Iskie. He paused in his disrobement to reach for the paper bag Tenali had handed him that morning. He emptied its contents onto the grass behind Seema's head, and was relieved to see a couple of sandwiches, a mango, a bottle of water, and two condoms. Subodh had taken care of him. He pressed her to the forest floor and bent to his task, compelling her to look up at him, to see his sweaty reddened face framed against the dead banyan brambles held above him by the strangler vines.

In India, Iskie had discovered, in *this* India, this unusual place where everyone knew Alexander's history, where magical arak gave him magical powers of perception, and where sweet young girls threw themselves sexually and improbably upon chubby pink foreign boys, one felt things more potently. The odours of Seema's slick and undulating body bathed him in a pheromonal shower, extinguishing the last embers of reason from his mind, and drew him into mindless ecstasy.

Seema, too, was overcome. Unable to vocalize, she could only grunt and stutter. Iskie and Seema, their limbs locked in coitus, were animals trapped in the cage formed of their mindless ardour. Seema reached out to the dead tree trunk with her right hand and absently scratched it with her fingernails, leaving four shallow grooves in the wood.

"Who are you?" she hissed into Iskie's ear, as her pleasure escalated. "Who are you that can take me to such heights?" More words from a Harlequin romance, no doubt. But they were words Iskie had heard once in a dream, the context long forgotten.

"I'm the moon," he stuttered back, giggling. He was uncertain whether Eunice would have approved.

"I'm being fucked by the moon."

"Not for much longer!" he roared. "The moon is coming!"

11

PURSUED

Never before had she noticed them, except perhaps as yet another buzzing nuisance. But the new insight she had been given into their behaviour, their specialized niches and their desperate hunt for a particular tree, lent Kalya Lal a new appreciation for the golden-brown fig wasps that she now saw everywhere.

They would buzz and flutter, racing through the heavy, hot air with primal desperation, their biological clocks ticking in sync with the thump-thump of Shiva's creation drum. It was a dance whose steps had not changed in millions of years. It made Kalya feel both small and a part of a larger mechanism. Her time on this Earth was brief, though not as brief as that of the desperate fig wasp. Yet the signs of eternity were all about, and she recognized them now with Iskie's borrowed sensitivity to nature: the ancientness of the trees, the endless life cycles of all the organic and, indeed, inorganic systems about her; they hearkened to eras that predated humanity's arrival.

The wasps were intriguing. If angels were to take physical form, to insert themselves into the natural background and flutter unnoticed to partake of the tangible universe, might they not alight as insects? And if alien civilizations were to send probes to function autonomously and single-mindedly within the Earthly domain, why not disguise them as flying bugs? They might just as well be celestial beings, after all. This Diamandi guy, it seems, had chosen his specialty well.

Quite against her natural tendency, Kalya had taken her lunch outside, braving the mosquitoes and stray dogs that would unerringly pester her when the odours of her bowl of dal and rice and her blood-scented exhalations percolated through the air like the invisible fumes of a feral feast. She brought with her a sheaf of papers, some blank for composing letters and some already creased and darkened by the words of another. The temptation was strong to return to the shade and comfort of the house, to hide from both the sun and the animals, but she opted to stay.

It was a common belief that picnics and camping trips were tranquil and calming. But she had always found them trying experiences. She didn't mind perspiring when engaged in a physical activity, but to do so while sitting still was intolerable. And you could not swat every fly, brush away every ant, shoo away every curious dog. There was more peace indoors, she had concluded early on.

Her mind clutched a memory from childhood, that of camping on the outskirts of the village with her grandmother, her brothers, and Subodh. The boys had scampered about in the mud and leaves, engaging in those apelike physical diversions that so captivate the male of the species. But she and Ajee had crouched in an intimate embrace, sharing tales of familial history. The tale of Tomamu Nomei, told so well with Ajee's melodic and creaking subcontinential accent, had both warmed and chilled her. It was a welcome link to her past, after all, but also a disturbing tale of otherworldly and bestial insight. In obeisance to the timbre of the tale, she had made it a point that night to commune spiritually with the animals, to swing in her mind alongside the howling monkeys and hooting owls. Then she had happily hid from it all against Ajee's sleeping form.

She had awakened the next morning with enormous mosquito bites and a scorpion hiding in her shoe. Ajee had crushed the interloper before it could do any damage, but the memory was nevertheless etched permanently into her youthful heart. Her disdain for nature had begun that morning.

To many who came here to Whell, the crispness of the vale's air, so different from the muggy heat of the rest of the state, was a welcome joy enlivened by the diverse fauna and flora and the rolling landscape. Comments on the sweetness of the breeze, the particular softness of the sun, and the vividness of the green meadows and wild grasses were common, as were visitors' deep sighs upon straddling the threshold between the Lal estate's manicured tameness and the ancientness of the village below.

Kalya, too, could appreciate such things. Indeed, she was often lost in the beauty of the village's seamless melding with the contours of the land. Bright Bihari faces sang to her a melodious tune of sylvan acceptance, and quickening colours danced beneath a reflecting sky, spelling vitality and warmth. The smells of cones, grasses, and wildflowers would often mix with the more pungent odours of village husbandry and cookery, forming an odoriferous mist that settled comfortably upon the entirety of the vale. Yet for Kalya, the delight was bounded by the fringes of the forest, beyond which lay shadows.

If the story of Tomamu Nomei had not convinced her of the evils of the forest, and if the scorpion had not anchored that fear in reality, then surely the dream she had had that night with Ajee had clinched the matter. In it, Kalya had been the forest fox, chased almost to exhaustion by unseen predators, until trapped in a snare to be consumed at leisure beneath a dreamy full moon.

Of course, the dream had been informed by Ajee's tale. But it became her sheer cliff, the metaphoric trigger that always drove her to adrenaline panic. Others feared darkness, enclosed spaces, or plummeting over a cliff to jagged rocks below. For her, terror lay in being the target of the chase, her perspective stretched wide to subtend a field of almost 180 degrees, her panting breath and thundering heartbeat almost deafening. According to a psychology course she had taken in nursing college, Freud believed the dream state to be a reflection of anxieties within the personal subconscious. Jung, she had been told, believed that the dream state was the product of a racial subconscious, whatever that was.

On her sheaf of papers rested a fig wasp. She was able to recognize it for all the lessons and lectures Iskie had been giving her. A female, of course, it was allowing itself a brief rest before continuing its desperate search for an appropriate fig tree in which to oviposit and die. There was an image Iskie seemed fond of impressing upon her, one in which the flying insects were divine tears, each containing a drop of truth or a question that each mortal must ask of his heart. "What is the message here?" she asked the wasp, who of course paid her words no mind. "Am I resting too long before finding a place to lay my eggs and die?" It was an adolescent question, she knew, that hearkened to those endless teenage crises that screamed, Why me?! to the uncaring world. Yet for Kalya specifically, there was a bit more substance to the angst, as there would be for any unmarried woman torn between the individualistic values of the West and the paramount familial imperatives of the East.

Her days here in India were numbered, she admitted to herself. Auntie and Uncle were already grumbling about posting matrimonial ads for her in the Delhi newspapers. As if local Indian men would want one such as her: foul-mouthed, smoking, unable to cook and much much too old. She was sidling up to thirty, after all, a grandmotherly age by some standards. She would have to leave before they acted on their threats, before her potential dishonour blackened this home.

That was the problem with this place. It defined you by your connections and your milestones, not by the content of your character. What is your profession? Who are your parents? How many children do you have? How many servants? Never: What is your stand on. . .this? or Whom do you admire?

She caressed one of the letters in her pile. It was dog-eared and worn by the many times it had been read. Each time she picked it up, she wanted to burn it. Yet, like an insidious addictive drug, she craved its torment. Anything that can inspire strong emotion, it seemed, was something hard to let go of, even when that emotion is unwanted.

If Iskie were right and all human impulses were manifestations of the biological imperative, that supreme evolutionary law that compels us to survive and procreate, then what was the rationale behind her need for self-torment? Where was the competitive advantage in keeping and reading this troubling letter? Looking again at the wasp, she knew the answer. This piece of paper reminded her that, if need be, there was a fig tree waiting for her back in Montreal.

"Dearest K.," it began. They all began that way. She had found it enchanting at first, sort of romantic in a childish Edwardian literary way, as if the first letter of one's name could somehow indicate a special kind of intimacy. That was certainly in Neil's character.

It was therefore doubly disturbing to have discovered that Neil's ex-girlfriends (and, perversely, his mistress of preference) had all been named Katherine, Kathleen, or some derivative thereof. That, too, was certainly in Neil's character, to have chosen his lovers based upon the convenience of their names. Perhaps it would have been more romantic had he displayed a preference for names that sounded pleasant when spoken aloud after the words "Neil and" or "Neil loves."

All was possible. This was a man, after all, who, almost every morning, would fax press releases to major media outlets detailing the minutiae of his life. "Neil Falter to wear plaid," and "Orange juice proves to be a morning bowel irritant, Neil Falter decided today" were among his more creative submissions. This was not a joke to Neil. He truly did believe that the minutiae of his life would prove fascinating to the outside world. Kalya was therefore not surprised and, in fact, quite amused when Neil had put ads in local drama circulars to announce his open casting call for the role of "Neil's best friend."

Only six individuals responded to the ad, but they were a varied and geeky lot, complete with the obligatory Doctor Who scarves and the occasional nervous leer in Kalya's direction. Why each had chosen to audition was a mystery she'd never cared to explore, preferring instead to watch them from the safe shadows in the rear of the rented auditorium. From there, she had looked on in horror as Neil had had his applicants run through the extremes of amicable conduct, from sucking sycophantism to rancorous rage.

In the end, Neil had declared them all inadequate, all unworthy of being his sidekick. That was his way, she was convinced. He cared more for the process than for the outcome. And how that reflected on his relationship with her was, of course, her primary concern. Was the process of wooing and courting more important than the goal of coupledom? That was what she should have asked Neil, if only she had known the right words, the right concept, back then.

Iskie would have known. He would have applied his own version of Darwinism in which all behaviours were informed by the biological imperative. Courtship is for securing the most appropriate mate, Iskie would no doubt say. The goal is to procreate and to establish an evironment of maximum opportunity for one's offspring.

And what of the process? Is there no value in that? Neil would ask Iskie.

The "enjoyability" of the process is valuable only inasmuch as it serves as a reward to encourage fertile individuals to engage in courtship activities that may lead to gene flow, Iskie answers in her mind. After all, smooching teenagers aren't aware that they're pair-bonding for the purposes of procreation. They're only aware that it feels good.

No doubt Iskie would express such sentiments much more eloquently than was done in her mind's absurd theatre. But the virtual Iskie boasted certain traits that the real one could not hope to adopt: predictability, compliance, and eternal congeniality. Still, she preferred the real thing.

"Dearest K," she continued reading. "I've not heard from you in some time. Your absence has permitted me a needed, though unpleasant, respite during which I've been able to consider the priorities in my life. I know now that you are one such priority, as is the life we can, and should, make together."

When she had first read those words so many weeks ago, her heart had leapt for joy. The little boy had at last grown up, had at last found that lightly trodden path out of male adolescence. The letter's potency had flowed from both its excellent phrasing and its brevity, both characteristic of Neil's communicative style. Whether by design or by circumstance, he always kept her waiting for more.

The next letter had been as equally appeasing. The first had come etched onto blackened birch paper, folded into the shape of a flower. This second came emblazoned upon gold-coloured parchment, wrapped tightly about a finger-sized wooden baton. They were undoubtedly symbols of female and male genitalia. Neil tended to be blatant in his supposed subtlety. It was his preferred kind of sarcasm.

"Dearest K," the letter began, as expected. "Being without you now is cold sobriety, made more so unpleasant for its reminder of our heady drunken time together. You were a drug from whose addiction I strived to release myself, only to realize the gnawing torture of withdrawal. I need you still."

Like the symbol into which it had been folded, the first letter had betrayed a feminine sensibility, citing the touchstones of female stereotype. The second was less complex, more pathetic in its blatant manipulativeness, more stereotypically masculine in its misguidedness. Yet there was charm in such floundering, too. Neil was master of the psychological game, showing both carrot and stick in rapid succession. And that had always made him that much more attractive—and infuriating.

Kalya did not consider herself to be overly analytical. That, too, would be a stereotypical female trait that Neil would no doubt explore and exploit. In fact, she had first consumed the letters with an explosive release of joy and relief, pleased that she would likely be returning to familiar love, to a fig tree of proven hospitableness.

But an element compelling caution had shone through, triggered by Neil's insistence upon addressing her as "K," reminding her of his laziness where romance was truly concerned. At no point in either letter, or in any of the subsequent notes he sent, did Neil make any specific references to Kalya or to their time together.

She had had to ask herself: *Were these form letters?*

It would certainly be Neil's way, to turn even their breakup and potential reconciliation into his own brand of performance art.

Her response to the first letter had been a sick overpouring of sentimentality. Her loneliness and fear had leaked through her normal veneer of impermeable strength. She now regretted having sent that letter.

Her response to the second letter had been more cautious, more of a traveller's postcard detailing her experiences in India, but betraying no emotion. Neil had continued his flip-flop, having sent in response a gushing note of indirect apoplexy:

Dearest K,

The nights grow colder in Montreal, though the sun still shines bright. The wideness of my empty bed betrays the emptiness of my world. I am lost and detached from the trunk of human toil, unable (or unwilling) to seek adhesion with greater society, for I am without the glue that binds me. . . without you.

It was not his best work by far. Actually, she found it laughable for its ironic encapsulation of juvenile suckiness wrapped in the big words of a highly literate and erudite road scholar. But Neil's psychological game plan was more evident because of it: he would reveal the struggle between the abandoned little boy in his heart and the grown man who must yet participate and thrive in society.

It was a ploy to engage her maternal instincts. She was damned if she would let it work.

When she had failed to respond, more notes had followed, all of comparable length and content, all boasting a careful balance between juvenile need and mature masculine strength. And none ever addressed her by name or made specific reference to her or anything she had done.

The rested fig wasp took to the air again, no doubt in search of a syconium of the right species. The letter upon which it had rested showed no sign of the wasp's brief stop. In fact, it looked more pressed and pristine than ever before. If these were indeed form letters, how many did Neil Falter have? And how many times had he used them? It was an odd choice of weapon—the personal letter—to both lure its prey, injure its target in the name of romantic retribution, and perhaps snare that target for long-term captivity.

Flowers and a box of chocolates would have sufficed.

12

SELEUCUS

One of Alexander's most senior generals was named Seleucus. In his honour, historians often make reference to the "Seleucian" period of Indian history, those years in which Alexandrian Greek thought moulded and shaped much of Indian craft, religion, science, and values.

Seleucian culture was a soup of Vedic and Hellenistic ingredients. There are some who say, for example, that the ancient Indian medical science of Ayurveda was shaped by classical Greek medicine. Both disciplines are informed by a reliance upon the elements—earth, wind, water, and fire—both to diagnose and treat illnesses. Conversely, it is possible that Alexandrian observation of Indian methods allowed the incorporation of Ayurvedic methods into Greek consciousness. Who can say which was the progenitor and which the progeny?

Or maybe their parallels at the two extreme ends of that continuity of ancient culture is indicative of the constancy of the human imagination, rather than an accidental meeting in history; perhaps there exists a shared psychological thread that weaves throughout our racial unconscious. Both Vedic and Greek philosophies would argue that we are products of the universe of earth, wind, water, and fire. Surely we all would be drawn to the underlying truths of those elements, notwithstanding the layers of manufactured culture that strive to separate otherwise very similar civilizations.

History has chosen to stress the differences between peoples, while mostly ignoring these marvellous overlaps at the frontier of cultural exploration. It should therefore not be surprising that in this India, this weird place of Caribbean psychics, psychedelic moonshine, angelic wasps, and animated corpses, every schoolboy is taught the minutiae of Alexandrian pursuits, the trivialities of cultural collision.

One often hears the story of Seleucus's fascination with the "wool that grows on trees," the tree being a recurrent symbol in Alexandrian myths: a thrusting wooden penis with which to both violate and seed the world. Seleucus lacked the referential infrastructure to appreciate a thing like cotton, that magical vegetative wool that sprouts across vast tended fields. His imagination was constrained by both the looming shadow of the phallic tree and by the supremacy of husbandry in his mammalocentric world. His people were similarly mystified by "honey without bees," that thing we call sugar, a sweetness extracted from plants instead of from animals. It seems that the meeting of Greek and Indian was as much a negotiation between the worlds of animal and plant as it was an encounter of alien fraternal races.

In its purest historical sense, the Seleucian period represents the first of two pre-eminently important cultural collisions; the second would not come for another two thousand years, when Christopher Columbus would drive three ships across the Atlantic. The Seleucian collision brought the world a continuity of ancient thought, and a much-needed injection of wonder at the true size and complexity of the human world. It was the joining of two ends of a very long thread, a return home for the human race, which had been splayed across the Old World with only a partial appreciation for the true depth and glory of its legacy, only vaguely remembered through myth, superstition and religion.

Alexander and Seleucus had followed the trail of Alexander's supposed ancestor, the god Dionysus, and had found a subcontinent of Greek-like thought, lifestyle, theology, and richness. They were, in some ways, among the first diasporic adventurers to seek out a spiritual homeland, among the first to witness the beauty of deceptively incompatible human philosophies that refuse to commingle.

Iskie held Seema's hand lightly in his own. It felt delicate and ethereal, a sensation of inconclusive pleasurableness. They trod lightly upon the forest floor, kicking the damp leaves and clumps of unidentifiable vegetation. He was not lost in the moment per se, but keenly aware of every nuance of his own body language, and every sound and stricture of Seema's jagged but girlish movements.

"Any fig wasps yet?"

"Nope," he replied. In truth, he had not been looking. His brain was betraying him, denying him the intensity of focus that was his gift. Instead, his vision was a kaleidoscopic mess of pastels and blood red, distracted by the thumping of his own heart and the uncertainty of his recent actions.

"Well," she said. "What's it look like?"

"Brown jacket, about yea long." He held his hands apart a couple of centimetres, forgetting for the moment that her hand was attached to one of his. "And it's more or less silent."

"I see," she said.

"Also, it prefers the upper canopy. We're unlikely to find one at our level, unless it's feeding, resting, or dying."

She made a noise of understanding and they continued on. Iskie's primary sensation was one not typically mentioned in romance novels or in other manuals of human intercourse: the stickiness of his loins, the viscous film of semi-glorious dirtiness that echoed across his skin. A vanity of civilization was the immediate post-coital shower, a luxury denied him here in the woods.

It was not necessarily an unpleasant feeling, just an unusual one. In a strictly theoretical sense, the post-coital scenario is a necessary connection to the grand trunk of animalia, shared by all humans and beasts, a uniquely natural phenomenon. Yet an uncomfortable sensation rippled over his flesh, stretching his tight meninges, the membrane about his brain, causing him both mild pain and irritation. His jaw would clench and unclench with a throbbing, orgasmic regularity, his intellect scratch against the walls of emotional distraction to achieve some kind of form and function, to put a word to his state, define it, and thus master it. Shame, it seemed, can manifest itself in odd physiological ways.

"Where have Subodh and Sonali gone?" Seema asked him. Perhaps she was concerned for her friend. More likely she was trying to fill the awkward silence.

"I'm not sure," Iskie said. "He probably gave her a ride back home. Don't worry, we'll get you home, too."

She stopped and looked at him. "Are you trying to get rid of me?"

"No, no. I just didn't want you to be concerned. Come on, let's look for wasps." He willed his jaw muscles to relax.

Seema clutched his hand more tightly. She gradually moved closer to his side, feeling the deliberateness of his tread, his resolute drive and direction. She could not know this was an illusion, that Iskie had no idea where he was going. He walked to spite his feet.

"Iskandar," she spoke softly, almost cooing in harmony with the avifaunal chorus, "would you like to make love again?"

She was close enough to feel Iskie's body stiffen, his breath shorten but for a heartbeat. "No, thank you," he said, and was abashed by the suddenness and coldness of his response.

"Did you not enjoy it?"

"Of course!" Iskie stopped for a moment to take both her hands, and to lock her pixie face into the theatre of his black irises. "Are you joking? Of course I enjoyed it!" He let slip a smile and an awkward giggle, engaged again by her unmistakable charm and liveliness.

She seemed to accept his answer and they walked on, choosing to turn south at the stump of a dead cork oak. "These trees weren't indigenous to the area," Iskie said. "I wouldn't be surprised if they were planted by the Bactrians, the Greek colonials from Afghanistan." He pursed his lips and looked down. He had changed the subject too abruptly, he realized. "I don't want to have sex again because my body is still. . . tired. It's nothing personal. It's not you."

Seema was plainly intrigued by his choice of words, but she put aside the topic for the moment. "Tell me again why you study insects," she asked instead, "and I don't want to hear about ecosystems or agriculture or industry."

Iskie kicked the ground harder as he shuffled, deriving some pleasure from watching the decaying vegetation dissolve in the scalding air. There wasn't as much animal life as he had hoped, only the occasional darting shrew, the ever-present mocking of unseen birds, and the comforting cacophony of insect hisses. But the signs of animal life were everywhere. Dessicated turds littered the bases of trees, often sprouting weird fungal growths, and scratch and gnaw marks were visible on the barks of some of the whiter trunks.

"It's simple," Iskie said, almost in a sigh. "The insect is the path to the divine, the bridge between the programmed life of the beast and the social and sporadic lives of people." His diction betrayed the practised nature of his words. His meninges tightened.

"And why is that important?"

A wave of rage rippled through him, like a spirit passing soundlessly through his body, raising his hairs and scratching his brain stem. He blamed it on the wet heat of the afternoon and on the unending buzz of his beloved though overabundant flies and mosquitoes. But it was disturbing to be unable to direct his intellect at will, to be so relentlessly subject to the forces of metabolism and emotion. A menagerie of manufactured romance compounded by the pixie's teacherly tone stoked the discomfort, and he struggled to rein in his reflexive vitriolic response.

He calmed himself and stepped more firmly into his soliloquy, as always choosing his words with care. "Don't you ever wonder what truly separates man from beast. . . if anything?" She looked at him with wide eyes, an expression he took as acquiescence. "It's an important question," he continued, "for establishing our role in the process of universe. I say process because the universe is more than a thing—that would imply inertia, stasis, and simplicity. The universe is an undulating set of almost infinite forces and realities. We can never know all there is to know about it because its nature is such that there is always something more to know."

He paused to scan their surroundings. This area of forest was starting to look a bit familiar. "In such a realm of chaos, of ever-spiralling currents of complexity, we *need* to assess a function for ourselves. Our ego demands it."

"All right," Seema said. "So what is our function?"

"I don't know!" he snapped. "No one can know. That's part of the chaotic complexity of the system, to deny us absolute self-knowledge. But if we are merely another kind of animal, then our function is simple and, dare I say it, not exemplary. But by all scientific reckoning, we are nothing but animals. Every analysis, every observation shows it to be that way."

"And is that such a bad thing?" she asked, again playing the schoolteacher, leading him with the lilt of her voice.

He bristled. "No, not at all. The beast is noble and vital. The beast is quasi-eternal, constrained in natural history only by the bookends of tragedy." He paused, surprised by the poetic content of his own words, the genuine despair in his voice. He took a moment to redefine the naturalist detachment he cultivated so, to strip the tremor from his voice. "The dinosaurs were killed off by a catastrophic meteor strike 65 million years ago," he said. "Because of their sudden disappearance, the age of mammals was permitted to begin. Do you see? The beast exists in a continuum of illusory timelessness, and that continuum is bracketed by violent global death. Every 50 to 100 million years or so there's a mass extinction. Did you know that?"

"No, I didn't. But I think you're getting off the topic."

Iskie surveyed the ground. They were in an area of densely layered pine needles, splayed across the ground like artificial turf, though matted and decaying. He imagined he could smell the acidic sludge seeping into the soil, poisoning the ground. The pungent odours of a vibrant ecosystem were missing here, replaced with the dry scent of scorched air. "You're right. I'm getting off topic. What do you believe? Are we people or animals?"

"We are people, of course," Seema said with the kind of confidence Iskie had seen before in those he would characterize as shallow, though that was clearly an unfair assessment. A new sensation washed over him, one that did not wrack his meninges or stoke his incipient headache, but rather calmed his breathing with a kind of poetic despair. He envied her confidence, her security in her acquired spiritual superstructure.

"How do you know we're people?" he asked. It was his turn to adopt the inquisitive teacherly tone, though he did so without disdain or sarcasm, inspired as he was by a genuine curiousity.

"Easy. Animals are dumb. We harness them for work. They still obey and love us, even though we kill them for food and products. We are better than they are. I'm sorry if that offends some of your American sensibilities, but it's true. The Hindus revere the sacred cow. But, if you ask me, they—we—still work them and abuse them. At the end of the day, animals are a kind of capital. And we are the ones who manage that capital."

"I see," Iskie said, deep in honest contemplation. "But I can't say that I share your certainty. After all, chimpanzees and humans can give each other blood transfusions. Did you know that? Genetically, we're almost identical. I don't think anyone who's ever owned a pet can deny that most animals are as emotionally complex as we are. The differences, dare I say it, are pretty much cultural!"

"You can't possibly mean that."

"Well, maybe I exaggerate. But let's think about it. For a long time philosophers thought that humans were the only tool users. But then we found that chimps use tools, too. Then they said that humans were the only ones who develop complex societies. But a lot of insect species have highly complex societies, including class structure and slavery. Nowadays it's popular to suggest that animals cannot laugh or feel emotion. But I don't think that's really well grounded. There are many reported instances of supposed altruistic behaviour among animals."

"So," Seema said, seeming to grow weary of the topic. "Do you not believe that there's a difference?"

"I don't know! But I think that there must be!" He swallowed hard. "And I suspect that the difference exists in sexuality." Seema's eyes brightened with a renewed interest. Iskie checked himself, aware that he was perhaps venturing down an uncomfortable path. He spoke carefully, striving to keep his balance atop that tightwire between the sky of limitless scientific dispassion and the morass of emotion beneath his feet. "I believe that the range of human sexual pathology separates us from the natural world."

Seema giggled to herself. "Dogs don't get horny?" She blushed at her own words. Iskie felt his headache returning.

"That's not what I mean," Iskie said. "By an accident of evolution, humans were granted constant sexual desire. This is particularly true for women, who, unlike other mammalian females, are not bound by cycles of estrus; our women don't go into heat." He paused to consider a point. "Well, not in the veterinary sense, in any case." Seema was looking at her feet, kicking absently while shuffling along. "Sexuality is the fundament of all human societies," he continued. "Pair bonding is encouraged by many social institutions. Cars, for example, are built to seat people side by side. And couples are encouraged to procreate. That's why we have such a thing as institutionalized legal marriage, to validate offspring and allow social control of the resources needed to procreate."

Seema's eyes were glazing over. But Iskie didn't care. He often refined his thoughts by speaking them aloud, more so now that his discomfiture suddenly demanded the vocalization of his position in a kind of formal reassertion of principle and purpose. "Even though we have social and innate pressures to pair-bond and to maintain fidelity, we have a powerful biological urge to have sex outside of our pair bonds!"

"So?"

"So? So the conflict between our biological imperatives and our social imperatives causes many of us to develop so-called perversions. I think that a pervert is simply someone who defies social custom in order to satisfy his sexual need. Why do we have kinky sex? Why do we have anything but boring missionary vaginal sex?"

Seema blushed visibly, perhaps recalling their own typical sexual union only hours earlier. Despite this mild titillation, her attention was wavering. But Iskie continued. "Why does every human society have its selection of sexual sadists and sexual powermongers? I believe that the conflict between society's demands and biology's needs is what truly separates man from beast. Nowhere else in the animal kingdom, except perhaps for caged animals, does this conflict exist. We are defined by our sexual pathology."

Seema still looked at her feet, trudging along atop the decaying pine needles. She no longer exuded a practiced sexual glow.

They emerged onto a familiar clearing that appeared swampy in places and was bordered by the seemingly expanding blanket of pine sludge. They were on the outskirts of Whell, Iskie realized, and he began to search for a familiar tattered tent. It was a spontaneous decision, one not born of the deliberate purposefulness by which Iskie strove to define himself. Best to sometimes appeal to the reptilian hindbrain, to sometimes listen to that whispering lizard voice that spat suggestions from a hidden dark, wet history.

"There it is."

"There is what?"

Iskie paused. Seema stood at his side, her soft breathing conspicuous against the silent forest backdrop. He regarded her with detached contemplativeness, considering his options. He was at a threshold, he realized. To step beyond was to bring Seema into his new world, which included Eunice and Kalya. The right decision was not readily apparent. Where were the romantic principles that usually directed him? His stated path of rationalized adventurism was suddenly dark and featureless. His hand, oft guided by Fate, was stilled, as he abandoned his usual practice of reflexive decision making. Regardless, what choice did he really have? The pleasant yet unsettling warmth of Seema's flesh against his side was his answer and his guide. He must lay quiet his mind and be led instead by instinct.

"I want you to meet someone," Iskie said. "She's a sort of psychic, or so she thinks. She's from a country called Guyana. You've heard of it?"

"Of course. I'm an educated woman, you know."

They sauntered to the tent, feeling the chill of a wet breeze ripple across the skin of their backs. The scent of mould was strong, and it made Iskie's nostrils twitch.

"Do we have to go inside?" Seema asked, scrunching her nose in distaste.

"No. I want to, though. You can wait outside if you'd like."

The gloom of the place was deathly, with fungal growths protruding from tree trunks like alien orifices and eyeballs, poking and peering and sucking. "No thanks," Seema said. "I'm coming with you."

Iskie squatted by the opening to the tent and delicately peeled back the canvas. Inside he could just make out a sprawled shadowy figure breathing with belaboured undulating infrequency. "Excuse me," he whispered. "Eunice?"

The psychic stirred. "Eh?" she issued weakly, seeming to rouse from an unsettling sleep. "Bug boy?"

"Yes, it's me, Iskandar. Kalya's friend. Can I come and see you? I've also brought a companion."

"Jesus Christ, bug boy. You got nuttin' better fo' do dan fo' wake one old lady?"

"Sorry. I'm really sorry." Iskie closed the flap and began to turn away.

"Bug boy!" Eunice called back to him. "Me na expect you back so soon. You may as well come in, na. Bring de gyal wit you."

De gyal? Ah. Seema. He took Seema by the hand and the two of them gingerly entered Eunice's otherwordly domain. Once again, Iskie was made uneasy by the darkness and dankness of the place. As before, he could not make out Eunice's face in the thick blackness.

"You still wan' fo' know 'bout ghosts?" Eunice asked sleepily.

"Ghosts?" Seema asked, more than a bit on edge. "What ghosts?"

"You askin' de wrong woman and de wrong questions, bug boy."

"In my village," Seema said, "there is talk of a ghost, a *bhut*. This one sucks the milk from the cows and goats, and once it pushed a baby calf back into the mother's womb!"

Eunice chuckled. "Yes, de elemental. Sometime she be de shadow of divinity, na, what a god does dream when a god does sleep. She very mysterious. And sometime she be a devil."

"She?" Iskie asked.

"Whatevah. Me say she, some say he. Who care? Never mind de elemental, she not important."

Iskie fished some coins from his pocket and slid them over to Eunice. "What about my ghost? Is it an elemental?"

"Forget yuh ghost, bug boy. Me go talk 'bout you." She paused strangely, then directed her voice at Seema. "You is a pretty one, you is. Big fish eyes, na. Golden light and shiny. Like de sun. But not as bright."

"What about me?" Iskie said. "What did you want to say about me?"

"Bug boy, yuh story begin in India."

"What do you mean?"

"It begin here, in India." A pause, but no clarification was forthcoming "You is de hero. Each of we is de hero in we own story. And de hero must undergo travail and strife, and must change. And maybe yuh story end in India, too. Me na know."

Iskie suddenly felt that had been a long day. It had begun with a weirdly vivid dream and Subodh crouching on his chest. It had progressed to a sexual union with a beautiful young stranger that, instead of sating both his anatomy and ego, had instead unsettled him in an adolescent way. And now Iskie found himself once more huddled in fungal misery with a weird fakir from the other side of the world.

"Give me something I can use," Iskie said. "If you can't help me with my ghost, help me with my work or with my love life or something!"

Seema glared at him. But Iskie remained unaware.

"Okay," Eunice complied. "Dis be what me got fo' you. You want de big pitcha, de big story, de deeper meanin' of life, and shit like dat."

"Yeah, shit like that."

"Don't get uppity, bug boy."

"Sorry."

"All right den. You say you want de big pitcha, right?

"The big picture? Actually, I never said that. You did." He had followed a command from his brain stem, had heeded a cry from his reptilian core, beseeched that ancient beast within. The forgotten odours of fungal decay assaulted his nostrils anew, bringing to the fore some of those same beastly raw emotions from the primordial mother soup. He felt a steady growl bubble subvocally in his throat, timbering in resonance with a rhythmic scrotal itch and the irritating prickliness of his meninges.

"You nah say dat? Okay, bug boy. You wan know 'bout ghost or you wan' know 'bout yuh-self. Which one? Before you answer, all me know 'bout ghost be, how you say, teery." Iskie took her last word to mean *theory*. "But what me know 'bout you be very very specific, very important."

Iskie sighed. "Fine," he said. "Tell me about myself."

"Like me been sayin'," Eunice continued. "You wan' know 'bout de big pitcha, right?"

"Right."

"You talk big like one perfessah. You like dem bugs, you say, 'cause dem older dan de dinosaurs. Dem be de bridge 'tween we people and God. Right?"

Seema gasped. "How did you know that?" she asked Eunice. "Were you listening to us talk outside?"

Eunice laughed gruffly. "Nah. Kalya been tell me."

Seema frowned. "Who is Kalya?"

"Nevah you mind, little fishy sunbeam. You rest quiet. Let de bug boy answer me."

Iskie remained expressionless, his eyes focused on the shadow that was Eunice's face. "Right," he said. "You're correct. I study what I study because I'm looking for, well, meaning. I think. I don't know."

"And dat's why yuh tink you follow de footsteps of de old Greek king, nah?" Eunice paused, then whispered, "Kalya been tell me dat, too."

"No," Iskie replied. "My interest in Alexander is separate. There are some. . . similarities between our lives."

"Whatevah, bug boy. De old Greek king bring yuh science to dis spiritual land, and you tink you do de same. But we na need yuh science here, you know. We got we own. In point of fact, you na bring nuttin' 'cause yuh story start here in India, like me been say already."

Iskie cleared his throat and tried to shake a fungal dizziness from his head.

Eunice went on. "So de old Greek king been seek he divinity in India, too, yuh know. Everyone here know dat. He been seek he wine god and he soldier god all de way out here."

"Did Kalya tell you that, too?" Seema interrupted, her tone spotted with pips of disdain.

"You be quiet, sunbeam," Eunice countered. "So, bug boy, what me got fo' tell you be dis. We all been here one short time. Yuh bugs been here much longer. And de spirits and de gods and de stars been here longer still. So what? What me mean to say? Me mean to say dat one quest for love be just as important as one quest for God. You undahstand? Love, bugs, de end of de world, exploding stars, nuclear war—it all important and not so important."

"I don't understand what you're trying to tell me," Iskie said, straining to maintain both dignity and eloquence.

Eunice belched a frustrated guttural sound. "Look, yuh don' need pretend to search fo' God, when all you wan' be one kiss. It okay. It *human*."

Seema grinned devilishly. Iskie sprung to his feet and ran out of the tent, gasping the hot Whell air like a newborn's first breath. His head was clouded, his blood percolating with imagined poisons. Eunice called to his back in a creaking shrill voice. "Bug boy, you can come see me one more time. No more."

Iskie's body stiffened at Eunice's words and ominous tone. But he would not look back, drawn as he was to the scents of living freshness that beckoned from the village. Seema noticed his stiffness, the rigidity in his fingers as she slipped her left hand into his right. They walked on, mostly in silence. Seema tried to puncture the wordlessness, sometimes with formless commentary about Indian religions, but usually with comments Iskie found irrelevant or unnoticeable. "What a fake" came out of her mouth more than once, one time followed immediately by, "But maybe she knows about the ghost in my village!" She also pressed her body against his side, rubbing her bare leg against his own.

They made their way through the village of huts, dodging the occasional trail of goats and the ubiquitous gaggles of glowing children, each eyeing Iskie with mischief and suspicion. As they climbed the manicured hill up to the Lal estate, Seema pulled away from Iskie, sensing the impending inappropriateness of their coupledom within the boundaries of Victorian Lal prudishness. Still, their recent partnership was evident to whoever happened to look into her eyes, to see the sparkles of girlish glee that glistened in Iskie's direction like white and yellow sunbeams. It was certainly evident to Kalya, who, sitting with her lunch and letters upon the lawn, watched them stroll towards the house, Iskie's gait as rigid as that of the soldier-king he so wanted to channel.

13

YGGDRASIL

It was an odd experience for Iskie, who felt torn between competing world views and emotional impulses. The domain of science was one of purported rationalism, defined solely by measured evidence and the parsimoniousness of proposed models. The realm of psychics and their ilk was poisoned by pointless speculation, unsupported by the preponderance of evidence, and excluded by the emotionless slashing of Occam's razor. The fakir would ever be at odds with the naturalist, seeking to impose a predetermined conceptual superstructure upon the evidence that asks simply to be observed, not deified. Thus, one of the glaring flaws of the more popular religions gnawed at Iskie, namely, that Christianity, Islam, and Judaism were all desert religions whose fundamentals were established upon Vulcan's searing Middle Eastern forge, hence insisting upon their austerity, their hallucinogenic contradictions, and their water worship, despite the inapplicability of such things to the myriad environments to which such faiths had spread. Madness, it all was madness.

The Hindus, Buddhists, and animists were no better, he reminded himself. Regardless of the poetry or enlightenment from which they claimed to have sprouted, they were slowed by their conquest-fraught histories and by inexcusable taints from previous lingering faiths and political designs. The final products were nothing more than religions written by committee—acceptable to all, but poetic to only a few of the deeply devout. Or so much he had learned from Seema, who was admittedly concerned with matters of an organizational, commercial, or quasi-political bent. Of course, that was one poison that both spiritualists and scientists lapped up with glee, the beastly institutional slowness that made careers and focused power, but did little to forward the disciplines' ultimate goals. In that sole sense, he found parity with Eunice, recognized in her a fellow-traveller who had bucked the constricting norm. In that one manner, perhaps, the paths of the mystic and that of the true scientist could run parallel, if never actually cross.

As they approached the Lal house, he distanced himself physically from Seema, a course of action that she herself had initiated. Iskie struggled to find context, to bring out the full force of his presumed intellect. Seema's proximity bristled against him, shortening his breath and tightening his jaw. It was her world view, he realized, her insistence upon reducing all matters to the coarsely commercial or to the pathetically transient human that defined her limitations, excused her from the class of seekers in which he himself had declared membership. He winced then, not in pain or horror, but in shame for the flight of masculine rationalization he had so suddenly and easily manufactured.

Kalya appeared unconcerned, a sunny smile playing joyfully on her full lips. "Hello," she said. "I'm Kalya."

Seema's friendly expression soured but for a heartbeat, as Kalya's name resonated in her recent memory, joined now with her previous familiarity with the Lal family and history. Her visage softened reflexively, smoothing to radiate youthful brown congeniality and show off the contours of her perfect skin. "A pleasure to meet you. I'm Seema, from Omas village."

"Ah, you're Subodh's friend."

"Actually, my cousin Sonali is with Subodh. I think Iskie is more my friend now." She beamed at him, seeking momentary connection in his irises' icy pools of black circumspection. She found instead theatric beatitude. "But I do know some of your other cousins from the area."

Kalya's face betrayed no emotion. She answered in perfect congenial rhythm, displaying the timeless grace of the Lal familial legacy. "I see," she said. "Please stay for dinner."

"Very kind of you," Seema said, her tongue playing absently behind her bottom teeth. "But I must be going."

Iskie finally spoke. His voice scraped across the late-afternoon heaviness, restrained but lifting into a train of shrillness. "I was hoping Tenali might drive her back. It's a bit of a hike."

"Of course. Tenali!" Kalya summoned the dour manservant with a very unladylike shout. Tenali, it turned out, had been lurking in a garden at the corner of the vast lawn and came running with car keys in hand. If Tenali were here, then perhaps Subodh had also returned.

Iskie felt his pupils shrinking, felt his consciousness fall backward, away from the scene before him. There was a wall he could build, he was convinced, that defined his scientific dispassion. It separated him from his experiments and from the biota he studied. This was the power of true science, the brand handed down by the Greeks, to separate the moral neutrality of the observed from the maelstrom of the observer's variable emotional states and biases. The magic of quantum mechanics was another matter, to be sure, but for Iskie's purposes, genuine dispassion was not only possible, it was the hallmark of his vaunted intellect. It was his mantra.

Withdrawing into himself, Iskie found repose and balance, the variable tightness of his meninges and his headache notwithstanding. All the while, Seema's doe-like demeanour beamed upon him. A slice of the sun she was indeed, if one were to consider solely the energy of youth and the heat of excited flesh. So hot, so bright.

Seema searched his face in quick darting glances and sought purchase among the facial nooks and niches known only to a lover, however brief their intimacy had been. Behind her, Kalya issued commands to Tenali, her words muffled by the layers of soundless distraction that intervened between the actual ongoing events and Iskie's dispassionate reverie.

The repose of his mind hearkened to unconscious memories of arak-driven dementia, slowing time and dulling his senses. Iskie returned Seema's curious look, while from the corner of his eye he noticed how the whispers of Kalya's loosely tied ponytail danced against her cheeks, etching jagged shadows upon the milky curvature of her skin. But she would not look to him, engaged as she was with the conveyance of information to the silhouette man, Tenali.

But Seema's glare was unwavering, and hardening by the moment and her unusually bright eyes seemed to cloud over beneath the blackness of Iskie's unresponsive countenance. Her delightful face, heretofore sensually unrestful, found sullen immovability in an expression of fear and disappointment, and perhaps disdain. Her lips parted as if to speak. Or did Iskie imagine that? Regardless, no word issued from her lips.

And so Seema marched off proudly with the chauffeur, never looking back, not even when she stretched to wipe the grass from the seat of her skirt, a gesture of blistering and hostile finality.

Iskie lingered a moment in this strange emotional middle ground between fatigue, displacement, and social awkwardness. As always, he found solidity beneath his feet by seeking a grander context; the animal had been beseeched, but it had also been reined in, perhaps prematurely. Eunice would be disappointed, and perhaps he should be ashamed. The invisible lizard whispered sweet benedictions from the wet darkness, reassuring and easing him, and allowing him to turn his full attention to the woman who remained. His Roxanne.

"So," Kalya finally said, peering up at him from her grassy nest among the letters, "I guess you've had an interesting day." Her mood was impossible for him to gauge. He had known women to hide their true feelings behind gracious facades, but in Kalya's case his tools of perception were weak and uncertain. He considered mytho-historic references for context: Roxanne, Helen of Troy, Jeanne d'Arc—which was she at this moment?

"I guess," Iskie said, not knowing how to continue, feeling unclean beneath the purity of her gaze. So he changed the subject, suddenly noticing the folded papers on the grass. "Who are these letters from?"

"Well," she said, seeming to choose her words carefully, "I was going to show some of them to you. But now I'm not so sure. Nothing personal, right? I just don't think this is something I can share right now."

The arrow had been launched with military precision. It was camouflaged as a non-hostile personal dictate, a plea for privacy and deference. Its intent, as Iskie saw it, was to wound, to deny him further purchase on that slippery slope of ascending intimacy—if indeed intimacy was what they shared. He took brief cover once more behind his invisible wall of convenient dispassion.

"Okay," Iskie said, suddenly more uncomfortable. He was acutely aware of the tone of his voice, the information conveyed with every shift of his weight, every bat of his lashes and stutter in his voice. "Where's Subodh?"

"Not back yet. Still traipsing about with the other one—Sonali?—I guess."

A less concealed missile, that was, aimed not at his head or heart, but at his feet, perhaps; intended to warn, not wound.

"Did you know he's getting married?" Iskie asked.

"Of course I know. He's my cousin." She smiled wickedly. "Though sometimes he forgets."

"What does that mean?"

"Nothing. You know, he's marrying another of our cousins. Her name is Anjali. You'd like her. She looks a lot like me!" This was no sling or arrow, but something that might resemble an olive branch, a potential return to flirtation. To be clear, it was not an invitation to climb anew that peak of intimacy, but simply a reminder that the mountain was still there.

"You know," he said, "I've never actually had a chance to explore the estate fully. I mean except for those times you and I went wasp hunting." She stared at him, offering no encouragement or dismissal, only vague acknowledgment. "So I was hoping you could show me around a little."

"Is that a request?"

"If you wouldn't mind, would you please show me some more of the estate?" He added a theatrical flourish of his hand, hoping to incite something resembling a smile. He did not.

"Okay," she said. "But not too long. I have things to do." She sprung to her feet and walked toward the rear of the house, away from the village. Iskie quickly followed, feeling as though his limbs were flailing about in these weird circumstances. She lead him to a complicated path through ever-thickening vegetation that was carefully manicured in the English style.

Hedges grew steadily on either side of the path, turning sharply at right angles and accentuated by large bulbous flowers of indescribable gregariousness. Purple stamens jutted from delicately folded petals of white, pink, and tan. The word "orchid" came to Iskie's mind. But he knew it was simply an intellectual vanity, not actual information.

He was jolted on occasion by darting fauna. They appeared to be spirited grouse or peahen, bobbing across the path with springy brutishness. It was a maze, he realized, though a small one. He was treading a romantic Victorian labyrinth with his Roxanne, his senses dulled by the competing whispers of invisible lizards.

"Where are we going?" he asked.

She answered flatly, never looking him in the eye. "The flower nursery. It's Tenali's obsession." More subtle missiles

"Figures. That man's a weirdo."

"Because he likes flowers? It shows an appreciation for beauty."

Iskie scoffed. "Everyone appreciates beauty."

"Yes, everyone appreciates stereotypical beauty. You know, the beauty of youth and bright colours. How many appreciate unusual beauty—the beauty of character and right behaviour?"

Iskie chose not to acknowledge the obvious arrow. Instead, as was his wont, he retreated to the comfortable ground of intellectual cogitation. "I'm not sure I know what right behaviour is," he said.

"Don't say it," Kalya interrupted. "Don't say that right behaviour is just a cultural reflection of your oh-so-important biological imperative." She almost spat the syllables, but was stalled, perhaps by the unintended venom of her delivery. She fished in her clothing for a cigarette, but did not find one.

"Okay," he said, not knowing what else to say.

"Right behaviour is civil behaviour," Kalya continued, calming somewhat. "Carrying yourself with respect for others and without barbarism." Again Iskie chose not to comment. Of course, within his fortress of dispassionate intellect he explored several interesting responses, including his preferred argument that civility was nothing more than adaptive behaviour whose purpose was to allow sustained social discourse, which in turn facilitated free procreation and the safe maturation of offspring. But just this once, he had the good sense to stay quiet.

"You know what I hate?" Kalya asked.

"What?"

"People who run their lives according to technicalities. Like trial lawyers. The whole criminal system. Crooks get off because of technicalities."

"Well," Iskie said, "the letter of the law must be adhered to with minimal interpretation, to ensure fairness across the board. That's why technicalities must be honoured."

"I'm not stupid, Iskie." Her eyes slitted. "I know. I accept the necessity for such things. But I hate them. Hiding behind technicalities is *uncivil*, you see? It's a way to be dishonest while being as honest as possible. You see?"

"Yes, I understand."

"Do you?" She started down the path again, weaving along the impossible twists of the chest-high hedgework with expert navigation. She stopped again. "Iskie, do animals have to contend with infidelity?"

"Interesting question," he said, relieved to be allowed to putter in his favourite intellectual playpen. "One part of the biological imperative is to obtain the best possible genes for one's offspring while simultaneously securing the best resources from one's mate. You see? Often, that combination requires infidelity."

"And among animals. . ."

"Non-human animals?"

"Among non-human animals," she glared at him. "Is such infidelity a divisive issue, as it is among humans?"

The temptation was strong to run behind his invisible wall of dispassion, to slow time and consider the nuances of this conversation with a deliberateness that was denied him. Instead, he loosed the reins on the beast, the whispering lizards screeching now in horror. "It's arguable that it's actually not divisive among humans. A large proportion of all human births are the result of extramarital affairs that are never discovered; genetic tests have shown this to be true. Plus, many societies, while not openly advocating such dalliances, have certainly condoned them through a lack of official reprimand. In fact, it can be argued that infidelity is one of the powerful and necessary forces in both human biological and social evolution, allowing for greater gene flow and competitive resource allocation. . ." He suddenly recognized the formalism in his voice, its dry textbook content and tonality.

She looked at him expressionlessly, as if waiting. "But is it right?"

"Kalya, right and wrong are such subjective human concepts. We're talking about biology here. Biology is morally neutral!"

"And therein lies the difference, Iskie. You say that you're interested in the thing that separates man from beast. Well, there it is. Simple morality. Maybe we can't agree on what morality is, but we have it and animals don't."

It had been a long day. Sometimes, as Subodh had once remarked, even Lenin took time out from the revolution to ogle the girls on the boulevard. "Kalya," Iskie said, painstakingly. "I'm sorry for being such a . . .an oddity at times. I take being a scientist very seriously. Sometimes in seeking dispassion and clarity, I give short shrift to things that are 'unscientific,' things that are value laden. I shouldn't do that. I'm sorry."

"I don't want your apology, you idiot. You are what you are. I'm trying to get you to understand something. Your science isn't without values. Knowledge is itself a value, don't you see? We say that knowledge is better than ignorance or mystery; that makes it a value. And what I want you to get is that if you're going to function in this world alongside value-laden humans, you're going to have to acknowledge your own values, your own biases. Because you've got them, buddy. Complete detachment is a myth."

Iskie raised an eyebrow. "Did you ever study quantum mechanics?"

"No," Kalya said. "And don't explain it to me now. That would defeat the purpose, right? Of getting you to back off from your scientific religion."

Her choice of words startled Iskie. *Scientific religion?* He shook it off, refusing to be relegated to the nonsense school of pataphysics. "I'll just say that quantum mechanics shows us that detachment is impossible. That the observer always affects the experiment. In some ways, simply by observing a thing, the observer establishes the existence of that thing. To take what you said, the scientist always brings his values to the world he's studying. It's always been something for subatomic physicists, though, never for biologists or anyone working without an electron microscope or multidimensional calculus—"

"Iskie," Kalya said. "Here's the value I want you to get. Okay? Trust is earned, and does not survive the invoking of technicalities. And when you lose trust, it's damned near impossible to get it back." She wiped her forehead, then paused to retie her hair. "Get it?" He didn't answer, but stood silent, cowed and bewildered and a little scared. "Now I want to show you something." She marched ahead with deliberate slowness, threading out of the steepening labyrinth with confidence, the hardened muscles of her thighs labouring unseen beneath the feminine shimmer of her linen skirt.

As the hedges receded and the bramble cleared, Iskie saw that they were within the forest that snaked along the village perimeter, the same forest from which he and Seema had emerged earlier, though from the opposite direction. Kalya led him to a grove of banyan trees within the forest, each seeming larger and more impressive than the last. They stopped beneath a particularly expansive tree, its branches radiating an astounding ten metres from the trunk.

"This is the oldest tree that I know of," Kalya said. "I was saving it for you. I think it has the kind of syconia you were talking about."

"It is surely impressive," Iskie said, looking straight up into the impenetrable tangle of branches. He felt as if he were peering up through history. "The mother of all fig trees!"

"One of my ancestors named it Yggdrasil. Do you know what that means?"

"Mmm," Iskie murmured. "In Norse mythology, it's the ash tree that overshadows the whole universe."

"Iskie," Kalya said, looking at him with surprising warmth, "there are some letters I want you to read. I want to show you my experiences with trust."

14

The Sleeping God

The entirety of human history is but an instant when compared to the ancientness of the Earth, a single frame in a lengthy motion picture. Geological periods lasting hundreds of millions of years occupy the playing time in that movie, providing a lush and ever-changing tapestry upon which life has chosen to paint its random and delightful parasitical designs. Such periods, lasting longer than the sum totality of sentient life, have arisen and faded on many occasions, leaving behind only ossified evidence and tortured landscapes. Alien terrains once characterized our Earth, their evolving nooks and ragged valleys giving rise to peculiar biota of completely foreign and vanished orders sprung from unfamiliar philosophies.

In a time we dreamily call the mid-Permian, some 250 million years ago, a forgotten ocean named Tethys stretched along the latitudinal area that now separates Tibet and Nepal. And a supercontinent sprawled across the globe. Its name was one of primal elegance and titanic indignance—Pangaea—matching well the Hellenic charm of its adjoining sea. In these days, the god Shiva's fire howled in the belly of the world, jetting through holes in the crust to quake the ground and melt the rock. The quantum mechanical god Vishnu, it goes, slept beneath it all, dreaming the universe. From his navel sprouted a lotus, upon which the incarnation of divine grace, the greater god Brahma, also slept, dreaming the events that transpired in Vishnu's universe. Brahma opened his inner eye, and a world came into being. He closed that eye, and the world vanished. Together they slumbered, Vishnu and Brahma, dreamer and dream, lover and loved, thought and sense.

Pierced by Shiva's fire and shaken by the beat of his drum, the Pangaea monstrosity split into an orphanage of directionless masses that swam apart like a brood of fish bursting from a single egg sac. Two daughter supercontinents, one that would become known as Europe and Asia and the other a twisted geologic stepchild, began a low-speed collision of centimetres per year, a cataclysm that would last a heartbeat in geologic time, but 200 million years by way of human reckoning.

The collision was a beautiful cacophony of slow fusion, a meeting of rock with mud, of water with air, and of biota with biota. The geologic stepchild pushed aside Tethys with godlike muscularity, constraining her voluminous tears to stream in rivers that would soon be recognized for their holiness. Shiva would rejoice, would spring to his feet in dance. Delicious wet soil was churned up, dragging with it nitrates and phosphates lapped up by the confused and displaced biota, fueling a green infection of the suture that now characterized the mating of continent with stepchild, pushing aside the mighty mother Tethys with contraceptive disdain.

Overthrust portions of the stepchild stacked upon one another, fed by Shiva's fire and encouraged to reach for the sun. The tears of Tethys could no longer bathe this behemoth, for its altitude would know no equal on the Earth. The Greeks would know Tethys as the wife of Oceanus, the Titan and world-girdling sea, and as the mother of countless rivers. The Hindus would not know her, but would bathe in her most revered creations, the rivers that would seem to flow from Shiva's long hair as he supposedly reclined and danced at the head of the stepchild's overthrust, on Kailasa, the Hindu Olympus nestled at the mouth of the great Himalayan range.

But Shiva only knew one dance, that of a circular two-step that he dressed up as an elegant cosmic ballet. The stumbling dance required that his torch and drum play both creation and destruction. As a result, the end of the Permian would see the biggest global extinction of life ever to be experienced by the embryonic Earth. Half of her children would perish, fifty percent of taxonomical families and ninety percent of species. Entire living philosophies inconceivable to hard-wired human brains would vanish forever with a disdainful shrug of Shiva's left shoulder. Brahma's restless sleep would cause him to moan then, bits of his immense body pinched and bruised by the events transpiring on his beloved Earth, in his restless dream.

Save for a few treasured niches, oxygen was evacuated from the waters, and rainforests were cooled. The Earth was a planetary garden no more, beaten as she was by the higher purpose—or vanity—of gods. But the remainder of the supercontinent Pangaea would find its voice, rotating in the warmth of the ancient seas, coaxing the flourishing of hot life anew, until the Earth was a jungle teeming with lush vegetation, fearless insects, and the terrifying thunder lizards we would call dinosaurs.

The stepchild's overthrust, what men would know as the Himalayas, would have been finally visible as the world's highest points when Shiva grew clumsy yet again, faltering in his two-step and raising the flame instead of the drum. It was 65 million years ago that an errant pebble from that galactic ancientness found its way into the eye of the childish Earth. It would make contact in the Gulf of Mexico, raising tides and dust, blocking out the sun and splintering the crust. The sleeping god would feel the pain in his side, feel the spill of souls dribble from his snoring mouth. The thunder lizards would perish, of course, as would countless species of animals and plants. But some, among them the lithe and mysterious insects, would persevere, whatever secrets accrued through millions of years of racial memory safely stored in the vaults of their genes.

Shiva sat for a while, regaining the yogic serenity that the sadhus insist he invented, perhaps afraid to dance again lest his clumsiness cause yet another catastrophe. The lingering drops of Tethys's mother milk dripped from his ascetic hair, pooling at the feet of the new mountains at the stepchild's suture, coalescing into a mighty river that raged down the plains of the new subcontinent, nudging the odd plants and spores that were differentially scattered, outbred or preserved from the days of that slow beautiful collision, and perhaps awakening other ancient elemental things that did not leave geologic evidence of their passing, but that are nonetheless dreamt by Brahma with fatherly judiciousness.

Precious deltas and vistas were fed by the torrent, sprouting oases of sustained life. Similar niches emerged thousands of kilometres to the west, in the fabled fertile crescent. New animals born of a new philosophy soon grew to prominence, reaching for the mantle of rule left vacant by the destroyed thunder lizards. The lizards, of course, remained as but a genetic whisper, emerging in emotion and reflex, issuing unheard suggestions from the wet darkness of the human hindbrain. As with all who strive for such dominance, the humans were streaked with understandable arrogance and a presumed special relationship with the forces that gave them rise. They pooled at these new lush vistas, benefiting from ready access to resources, freeing their oversized brains to consider issues of wider or lesser importance: knowledge, gods, morality, and conquest. Human civilization, born of arrogance in the wake of planetary catastrophe, saw first light in these two vistas, these Western and Eastern cradles.

Brahma dreamt of one such arrogant man in the Western vista. Alexander saw the path of gods who tread regularly between civilization's two cradles. He would follow that path, destroy all that lay in his way, and connect with the ancientness that flowed in his veins. In the divine dream, a million babies were born, cried, grew up, married, procreated, and died. Some committed foul deeds, a few rose to celestial moral heights, and most conducted lives not unlike those lived by the billions of non-human beings cast beneath hundreds of millions of years of geologic renewal. Wars were fought, books and songs written, ideas thought, crimes committed, prayers offered, and voyages undertaken. In one restless dream, the Greek king camped with his men beneath an enormous girdling tree, eating rotten shellfish and drinking coconut milk. Mortal eyes would have missed the amorphous forms that surrounded the soldiers, the elemental storm that paradoxically raged invisibly and soundlessly about them. If only they would look up, look through the layers of illusion that bound them to a linear existence, that yoked them to lives not so unlike those of the millions of species of beasts that had come before. But they rarely did.

The motion picture is a vanity, a visual crutch that depends upon that manufactured dimension, time. That the cosmic dream resembled a motion picture was a curiosity that was not to be analysed by the unconscious mind of a non-existent god. After all, time could be removed and the natural state of simultaneity restored. When it was, events transpired at once, the dream becoming impossibly but unmistakably chaotic. One such simultaneous event was the transfiguration of a forest fox into a beautiful woman, or so the story goes. Another was the instantaneous arrival of another arrogant but chubby Western man into the Eastern cradle, his prior existence unnoticed or unimportant, given the universe's true simultaneous nature. His story, you see, begins in India.

That this man and the daughter of the forest fox stood together beneath the same tree as that against which an arrogant king had once rested, embraced by the same storm of invisible and silent forces, would have been amusing and ironic to the sleeping god, if only he were real, and not the manufactured deity of an overly-religious people. Perhaps in his amusement he would have restored the temporal nature of the dream-movie, allowed himself to watch events transpire in agonizing sequentiality. He would have seen this arrogant man and the daughter of the forest fox return to the tree day after day, ostensibly observing those boring fig wasps with such ridiculously narrow "scientific" intent. He would have seen a fractured trust become sutured together, leaving a noticeable scar akin to the Himalayan scab that marked the wound between continent and stepchild.

His god's eyes, the fables tell, were inner eyes that would see all dimensions and all spectra. Surely, he would need to squint and concentrate to perceive the little story told between these people, obfuscated as it was by the storm of events unperceived by humans. Maybe he would have taken the time—for after all, time was an illusion, they say—to watch the pink man read delicate letters of intimate pain presented to him as offerings of trust. Brahma the dreamer, Brahma the voyeur, Brahma the watcher of romances—blasphemous characterizations, to be sure. With his godly perception, he would have seen the man stiffen with the remaining embers of a shame he did not even know that he felt. One hopes the beneficent one would have offered help with this, licking away that blackness from Iskandar's spirit, though such was impossible for a sleeping deity who, after all, was mere fiction.

It is possible he would have cared more for the flying treasures, the repositories of invaluable ancient biological knowledge locked in the flesh of Earth's oldest animals. A god's attentions cannot be monopolized by only one of his creations, as the invisible ones, whose presence no human society has ever doubted or proved, also require to be dreamt with vigour, lest Brahma's attention waver, his inner eye blink, and such creatures' existence quietly end. But it is pleasant to consider that a mythical being of infinite resources might find satisfaction in the hesitant, awkward, but warm and wet kiss between the pink man and the daughter of the forest fox. It was a lengthy kiss, leading to others and more, days in the making. It was a small thing, an inconsequential thing, given the infinite number of events occurring simultaneously elsewhere in the universe. But it was *no less* important. If the sleeping god were to look away, the lovers would falter in their existence. Their first kiss was thus worthy of his watchfulness, as were the instances of escalating physical intimacy that followed in subsequent days.

One would think that the fictitious sleeping god had seen many such identical scenes of love, had lazily noted the affectionate nudging of thousands of species, even those whose emotional core was dissimilar to the modern primate's. Yet his own emotional timbre was perfectly reflected in that of the humans, a species whose members uniquely and occasionally sought the celestial in spirit, in thought, and in action. If only the sleeping god were real, and not himself dreamt by imaginative humans, he would have the sense to worry, no doubt squirming uncomfortably on Vishnu's navel-lotus. He would see that the scab that grew atop the wound of broken trust had not fully healed, proving a poor bedrock indeed. Shiva's fire still burned, volcanoes were still active, and change was yet afoot.

15

KUMAR

"You know, you should not wear a brown belt with blue pants. It's quite gruesome on the eye," Goran Damjanovic said.

Pradeep Kumar grunted in response, stooping low to unlace his boots.

"And look, your socks are actually different colours. One is black, the other is very dark blue. Close, but not the same."

"Goran, I could really care less."

"Actually," Goran said, "you *could not* care less. To say you could is to imply that you do care some. You see? Unless that is what you do wish to say."

"I think you practice being annoying, Goran."

"No, I do not, Pradeep. It is a gift. It requires no practice."

The two turned away from each other and, as one, gazed lazily through the train window and out towards the dusty plain. The locomotive was noisy and bumpy, tolerable only for its magnificent and unobstructed view of the Indian countryside, made so much more tangible by the lack of windowpanes. Upon the wind was a delicious scent, hinting at cool refreshment and wet repose. The monsoons were coming. Not now, perhaps not for a couple of weeks yet, but they were coming.

"The great wheel turns, Pradeep."

"What?"

"Look, look at the sunset. Just a few hours ago we watched it rise. Now we can see it set beneath all this depressing flatness. Do you not feel like we are in the hub of a great wheel? If we look up at the spokes, I think we get dizzy!" Goran chuckled weakly. Kumar frowned at him. Croatian humour often did not translate well to English, especially when that English was then processed by an Indian brain.

"You know we're not at the hub, Goran. The sun is the hub. We are the spokes. The Earth goes around the sun."

Goran frowned in annoyance. "You are too literal, *Professor*."

"You're the one who insists upon socks that match."

"Precision is not the same thing as literalness."

"That's a precise argument."

"Exactly." Goran scratched his armpit absently. A yawn was bubbling somewhere, but was yet to be realized. "Look, we can already see the moon. The great wheel, it turns."

This time Kumar nodded. "Makes me feel old. The wheel has always turned. It always will turn. We only get to see it turn a few times."

"And you think there are fewer turns ahead than there are behind. Is that it?"

"Something like that."

"I am blessed, I think. The great Pradeep Kumar is truly a sentimental softy, and it seems that only I am privy to his softness. Truly blessed I am."

"You flatter yourself." Kumar stiffened. A howl erupted from the distance. A wolf, perhaps. No one showed signs of noticing. The rest of the carriage seemed unaware of the world outside the train. Most had drifted off to sleep, slaves as they were to diurnal rhythms writ deeply into their chromosomes. "Don't worry, there are no animals here so dangerous that they can reach us in a moving train." Kumar thought it best not to mention that Indian trains were known to stop in their tracks for extended periods.

Goran's face fell. "You suggest I am afraid of distant animal sounds?"

"No, no. Not at all. Just making conversation."

"I see. Let us converse then about this place we are going. It is called Whell, correct?"

"Yes," Kumar said. "A village in Bihar. The region is described pretty well in one of my books."

"Whell described well. I see."

"There'll be some sort of festival going on while we're there. They call it Chhath. You'll like it. Also, it's a good place for finding certain insect species. Complex interactions with the locals, that sort of thing."

"But we are going to a wedding, not collecting samples." It was not a question, but a statement, with the slightest hint of a command.

"Goran, one can always collect samples. One of my new students will also be there."

"Yes, I know," Goran said. He pointed to the sheaf of paper to Kumar's side. "Tristan Diamond. What sort of name is that? Sounds like an actor in adult movies, or an unsuccessful British pop musician. Very unpleasant."

"It's Diamandi, not Diamond. And he goes by the name Iskandar." Goran harrumphed and reached for the sheaf. Its title was, "Blastophaga Psenes And Its Agaonid Interaction with Ficus: A Doctoral Thesis Proposal."

"How dreadfully boring," he said. "Why don't you read detective novels or comedies? You are travelling to a wedding, a joyful occasion, and yet you choose to read this catatonic bilge?"

Kumar snatched the sheaf from Goran's hands and filed it back among his papers. "If you were not so amusing in your predictability," Goran said, "I might need to choose someone else to spend my time with."

Kumar knew he was being baited. But he could not resist. "And how am I so predictable, Goran?"

"I believe the psychologists call it passive aggression."

"How so?"

Goran smiled deeply, showing a glint of yellow teeth and stretching wide the pores on his cheeks. It made Kumar shiftless. "You choose to wear mismatched socks because you know to do so would elicit a response from me. You comment on my cowardliness regarding the wolf noises, then deny having done so. Now you play the wounded academic defending the work of his idiotic student. All clever scenes designed to engage me, perhaps just to hear my perfect grammar and attractive accent."

Kumar said nothing. He returned his attention to the darkening panorama.

"Come, Pradeep. Passive-aggression is a sure sign of intellect. You should be pleased. You have shown me you are a smart man." He paused. "And I have shown that I am smarter!"

Kumar watched the moon brighten in the sky. It wasn't quite full, but would be so in a few days. In this twenty-first century, few people took the time to notice, let alone to chart, the phases of the moon. This was a dreadful shame since so much could be learned from the lunar passage. Many animals, insects among them, behaved differently depending upon the amount of lunar light present in the sky. So much of human civilization reflected the lunar cycle. In a sense, civilization depended upon the lunar cycle, from the harvests to female fertility, that magical gift of evolution that freed us from estrus and from our slavery to the bestial seasons.

He opened Iskandar's treatise and reread one of the more troubling passages. It concerned the disruption of ancient syconia-seeking behaviour by the partial die-off of an ecosystem. A clever thought, it was, but a bit severe, unrefined and immature. Then there were his occasional diversions into spirituality. To be fair, they were not obvious diversions, but rather were just hinted at through the unusual use of certain adjectives and through a style that drew one's attention to the more angelic qualities of wasps. There were even allusions to the humanities, even literature and "the feminine hurling itself at the masculine in an eternal circle of pursuit and flight." His language was more poetic than clinical; not a good thing for serious entomological work. Surely, Iskie had known his teacher would object to much of this. Even if Subodh's wedding hadn't elicited an unexpected invitation, Iskie should have known that his clumsy entomology and inappropriate philosophizing would have summoned a worried Professor Pradeep Kumar to Whell. So many churlish intellects clamouring for recognition. God help us!

16

ROXANNE

Yes, yes. To dream at night of a dream in night. . . troubling, and certainly portentous.

The colours were purple-grey, with the occasional orange streak that marred the sky and dreamscape. So often in dreamland there is no ambient sound. But this time there was constant noise, something akin to an asthmatic exhalation. It had no source, but rather seeped from the ether, accompanied by a sickly sweet odour. One would have expected the smell of rotting flesh, considering the half-eaten deer corpse that lay off to the side. Instead, it was as if a cloud of warm honey had settled onto the grove, coating every surface with a sticky smelly reflectiveness.

The thing about dreams is that there is no rationale, no reason for circumstances, just the circumstances themselves. The fear bubbled in her blood. The urge to run increased to a desperate pitch. But she was restrained, not by any device or tether, but by the additional fear of open spaces. It was a war between instincts: to flee from the terror that was ceaselessly in pursuit, or to remain in paralysis away from the open field that was the only path to freedom. Such was the nature of dreams, to constrain options irrationally. *But there are always other options!*

From where she crouched, cowering in a mossy grove, the forest creche was a mere twenty metres away. Therein was home, safety, blackness. But the openness was foreboding. So charmingly illuminated by moonlight, it would be as a blank canvas hilight to her obvious and vulnerable form. She could bolt. She was small and fast, propelled by inhuman fear that was like rocket fuel in the veins. As the hurried breathing of the predator became louder behind her, all her nerves fired, all her muscles tensed and readied to spring.

Still she hesitated, stricken with a paralysing fear that made her eyes hurt. Her fevered blood inflated the arteries in her head to migraine extremes. Then she felt the tingle of hot breath on the back of her neck. It sent a horrific flush down her skin, and tripped the spring that launched her forward into the moonlit openness. She raced with abandon, too tightly wound to scream, too high on adrenalin to choose a trail, to presage potential obstacles or to consider other options.

For reasons known only to the gods of slumber, she was dressed in a constricting formal gown and tight shoes. She found the wherewithal to kick off the shoes, but now scampered barefoot upon sharp rocks that lacerated the sweet bottoms of her feet. The dress was snagged on a twig, then two, then twelve. She strained to tear free, to run naked towards the beckoning warm blackness. But the branches held her firm.

The predator was seconds behind her, galloping at full tilt, fangs bared. She cowered under the assaulting moonlight, unable to wrest herself free or to reason an escape. Still, she would not turn to face the monster, could not behold it with her dream eyes. For if she did not look upon it, it could not become real.

His lips always tasted of wild berries even though he never ate such things. One would think a man so in love with alcohol should be stricken with bitter saliva and noxious kisses. But Iskie was a feast of oral delights whose every touch was a focused exercise of passionate precision. His head lay upon her left arm, and she stroked the line of his jaw with her right hand. He was not a handsome man, not like Subodh and Uncle Palvinder. His was a hot cellular beauty that bubbled through his pores and sublimated from his corneas. He was clumsy, pale, and oddly shaped, but acted with such skill where her flesh was concerned. His words were argumentative and often clinical, but were thoughtful and usually honest.

And his eyes—discs of reflective darkness, black within black: they were anatomical collapsars whose quantum pull was irresistible and strangely calming. To awake under their gaze was to be soothed and embraced by the infinite. Vampirical was the lure of those eyes.

She extended her lips to taste again of that sweetness, to feel the day wrap about them. His eyes were open, but he remained unmoving as if in dreamless slumber. He, too, was considering the happenstance of the beauty before him, attempting to will the clock to remain still, to dwell longer in this space between moments.

"We have to get up," she said.

"No we don't," he said.

"If Auntie finds you in my room there'll be serious shit to pay."

"We have time still."

"No we don't, Iskie. She'll be up soon. And when she's awake, she knows everything that happens in her house."

"You know," he said dreamily, "orthodox Hindu thought has it that time doesn't really exist."

"Yes, yes. Maya is the illusion of a sequential universe. I know all that. I'm supposed to be the Hindu here, you know. Can we get up now?"

"If time doesn't exist," he continued, pausing briefly to nibble on the tip of her nose, "then there's no rush, is there?"

"I think I liked you better when you were bed-ridden with giardiasis. Get up!" Then, suddenly, she molested his mouth with her own, ingesting his essence with a furious desperation that surprised the both of them. Their lips remained sealed for several heartbeats until Iskie, slowly and unwillingly, pushed himself away. "Go!" she commanded.

Iskie pulled his trousers on and shuffled wearily to the door, feeling again like a teenager in his mother's home in Toronto. He turned back to pick up his half-empty bottle of arak and swept his Roxanne with a lingering glance. *Is this the dream, or is this the waking?* Finally, he waddled down the hall to his own room. If he were to bump into Mrs Lal on the way, he would feign drunken waywardness. Auntie would not be pleased by his state. But it was better than her knowing the truth.

Kalya rolled in the wrap of sweated sheets, yawning and stretching so much so that the hairs on her arms stood proudly, while her very skin seemed to wail in elegiac anguish. Yet this was joy, made more potent for its fragility. She would wait an hour or more, give Iskie time to be found waking in his own room, then time more for most of the others to have finished breakfast. Then she would emerge into the day's radiance to wallow again in ostentatious lethargy.

There was a stillness in the air, an immobility of ethers. If the passage of time could be measured by the cyclical shifting of the natural world, then the present was truly trapped between moments, with tinderbox-dry leaves perched at the ends of branches, afraid to fall lest they restart the clock.

At the dawn of the quantum era, when men first learned to peer deep into the minutiae of the atomic universe, physicists were shocked to find their own faces staring back at them. Niels Bohr would proclaim that "There is no deep reality!" When asked for clarification, he would offer, "Reality is created by observation." Again and again, experiments at the quantum level would cause the scenario to be replayed, pushing physics towards metaphysics, and increasingly constraining God to exist in the infinitesimal spaces between discrete quanta of energy. The true nature of the universe, that there is no innate truth except that which we choose to observe and to create through observation, was finally accepted. Einstein was horrified. Lamas were bored.

The Hindu and Buddhist heaven is a quantum paradise, a city of celestial perfection that exists outside of time, between instants. Through the power of observation alone, believers claim, the discrete quanta that compose time itself could be appreciated and pried apart, allowing one to reach between them and extract a handful of truth, glimpse a movie-still of paradise.

Iskie looked upon his world without the benefit of a Lama's observant discipline, but rather with the time-dilation effects of premature drunkenness. To his arak-addled brain, the beads of time were almost visible. They hovered soundlessly, thickly coating all of reality with their minuteness. He breathed them in, tasted them on his alcohol-coated tongue, and exhaled them without effect. But he could not as yet squeeze in between them.

Kalya found him as planned, in the maze just a few metres from the start of Yggdrasil's grove. She could smell the arak on his breath, but said nothing. This was not the time for such moralism. This was the time for wasp hunting. And there was no finer wasp hunter than a drunken Iskandar Diamandi.

She brushed her lips against his, tasting the pungent arak residue. "Come," she said. "We must chase angels." She pulled him to his feet and led him into the grove, clutching his hand.

Yggdrasil's trunk was like a pillar holding up the sky, the aged contortions of its bark like so many taught muscles straining in a clever parody of Atlas. Like that banished Titan, Yggdrasil was bent in pain, a scoliotic blemish against a clear blue timeless maw, with mighty arms that flailed outward in heroic anguish, spidery fingers outstretched with arthritic fragility.

Iskie peered up into the web of ancientness, seeking out the nodules that would contain his precious wasps. Kalya had cracked his quantum reverie. But this new vision gave him a different taste of it. For this was no mere tree, but a monstrous pouncing beast imprisoned in immobile time, trapped between the moments. "Did you bring the book?" he asked.

"Yes. Want me to look up something?"

"The chapter I was reading last night. The one about local customs. Can you find the passage?"

Kalya pulled the tome from her tote bag: *Insects of North and Middle India* by Pradeep Kumar and Jan Birbalsingh. She read aloud: "'*Ficus indica*, commonly known as the Banyan tree, took its colloquial name from the Hindu caste *Baniya*, the merchants who some say worshiped the species. It is also known locally as *Vat* or *Bad*, and is featured prominently in local lore, particularly in Hindu and Buddhist mytho-history. Its importance to the local culture may have led to an artificial prodigiousness, causing a proliferation of syconial sites beneficial to its complementary agaonid wasp species.'"

"Stop there," Iskie said. "He doesn't develop that thought, you know.

He just leaves it there. He goes on to describe the unique cytochemistry compared with that of similar species. But he never returns to the ecosystem."

"Well," Kalya said. "He can't do everything. The book is only so big."

Iskie grunted. "Let's consider what he didn't. The humans worship the banyan. . ."

"Well, I don't know about that. Let's just say that they respected and appreciated it."

"Okay," Iskie agreed. "The *baniya* caste took care of the banyan tree. Right?"

"Yes," Kalya said. "In my great-great-grandmother's time, there were big bazaars held under the banyans, under Yggdrasil in particular. The *baniya* merchants would set up big tables under here, and everyone in the region would come to trade. At least, that's how Ajee used to describe it."

"It doesn't happen anymore?"

"Not here it doesn't," she said. "Maybe in other parts of the state. But this village only has one source of wealth—the Lal estate." She said it with only a hint of emotion. Iskie was hard pressed to say what that emotion was.

"Okay," he said. "In the book, Kumar implies that because humans coddled the banyan, it thrived. It was more successful than other fig trees in the region. And it follows that the associated wasp must have also thrived, since there would be so many more syconia. Right?"

"Why not?"

"Well," Iskie said, "because it didn't thrive. That's why not. At least, the wasps didn't. From what I've seen of the forest so far, there don't seem to be any more banyans than any other kind of fig tree. And I've counted only a handful of syconia in each case."

Kalya shrugged.

"So," Iskie continued, "the question is, what is killing the banyans, or what is keeping the wasps from proliferating in the banyans that remain?" He paused. "Sadly, I don't know enough about botany to be able to tell if the banyans here are actually thriving or dying. As far as I know, this might be the healthiest banyan grove in the world!"

"And yet you *do* know that it isn't. Somehow, you do know, is that it?"

"I don't know how to phrase it." Iskie scratched his head, contemplated taking a swig of arak. "I get a sense that this ecosystem is collapsing. I don't mean the whole forest, just the area of Whell and Omas villages, including this grove. The whole vale, really."

"Spent much time in Omas village, have we?" Kalya asked.

"Look, this is serious. I'm no ecologist. I wish I were. But if I'm right, then all the people who live in these villages are in for hard times ahead."

Kalya looked at him like he were an idiot. "Iskie, they're already having hard times. Or hadn't you noticed?"

"I know, I know. But look. Certain species of insects and amphibians are known to be biological keys. The slightest changes in the ecological balance can cause such species to change dramatically."

"Like frogs," Kalya said, subtly reminding Iskie that she was a kind of scientist, too.

"Yes, like frogs. Changes in the health and number of frogs can be an early indication of ecological shifts. But other species, like maybe these wasps, might be indicators of changes or collapses that are already well underway."

Kalya sighed. Only Iskie could manufacture gloom on a radiant Sunday morning. "All right. What else have you got?"

"I saw a strangler tree killing a banyan tree," he said.

"What? Did it hide behind a bush and pounce? Were you afraid for your life?"

"Very funny, Kalya. It's a slow parasitical process. But, it was eerie, like a snapshot of a. . . an arboreal molestation." Iskie seemed pleased with his choice of words.

"And where did you see this?" She asked.

"Outside Omas village."

Kalya said nothing.

"Look, if I saw one strangler, then there must be others here." Iskie sighed. "I'm no botanist, but my gut tells me that that's a sign of decay."

"Or it might be a sign of health, Iskie. Even the lush, green jungle has parasites, doesn't it? Aren't lots of predators usually a sign that there's lots of prey? I'm not the expert here, but it sounds reasonable to me.

Maybe you're just too used to seeing ghosts."

"That's not all!"

"Okay. Go on," she said.

"There are pine needles everywhere!"

"So what? There have been pine needles since I was a little girl. It's one of the things that make this area so special. What do pine needles havc to do with anything?"

"Why are you taking this so personally?" Iskie demanded. "I'm trying to help your village. Look, pine needles decay into an acidic sludge. The soil here is being slowly poisoned. The peasants planted the pine trees to get sap to make turpentine, right? Pine wood makes poor firewood; it's shitty fuel. That means you have to plant more of them than other species in order to get the same amount of energy. And pine roots aren't deep enough to stop or slow erosion. So topsoil is being washed away. The human hand has brought slow death to this region. This, my dear, is an ecosystem in collapse."

It seemed to Kalya that the blackness of Iskie's eyes had grown to a become a shadow across his forehead. But she was intent on reclaiming the sunlight before he squandered it all. "So are these syconia occupied? Are we going to catch any wasps today?" Her voice was cheery.

Iskie stroked Yggdrasil's trunk absently. "I think they must be. The monsoons are coming, correct? That's why it's so dry. If I'm right, this tree has syconia that are occupied year-round, but which might peak before the monsoons."

"Why do you think that?"

"Well, I have no proof of this. It's just speculation. The rains would kill wasps in flight, and really slow down the implantation phase. So it makes sense to have evolved a system whereby most of the wasps are still maturing safely in the syconia while the rains are at their peak."

"Or," Kalya said, "maybe the monsoons destroy syconia. Maybe it makes more sense to have them as empty as possible when it starts to rain."

Iskie's face looked flat. "I didn't think of that," he said. "Why didn't I think of that?"

She snatched the arak bottle from his unclenched fist. "Because you're drunk all the time, idiot." Iskie didn't argue the point. Kalya stored the arak in her bag, next to Kumar's book and Iskie's wasp-catching paraphernalia. She wondered if this was to be the standard kit for the new generation of Orientalist naturalists—clumsy tools, fermented poison and a poor reference.

Iskie sulked for a moment, then shook it off. He rolled down his shirt sleeves as a sharp breeze chilled the sweat on his skin. The uneven weather was one of the perplexing, and sometimes frustrating, characteristics of the region. It was yet another factor that seemed to lift the vale out of contemporary Bihar, both ecologically and culturally, as if the region, with its chimeric forest and sister villages, was a kind of Brigadoon, a transient, ethereal settlement detached from the regular passage of time.

"So that Falter fellow of yours," Iskie said. "Do you still love him?"

Kalya did not waver, but answered confidently. "You can never stop loving once you've started. If you think you can, then it was never love in the first place, was it?"

"So that's a yes."

"And are you still screwing that little girl from Omas village?"

"No!" he spat, suddenly annoyed. "And that's not the same thing!"

"No, it's not," Kalya said. "I merely point out the inappropriateness or, shall we say, insensitivity of your question."

Iskie slumped to the base of Yggrdrasil's trunk, feeling complete sobriety return to him, growing increasingly aware of the sequentiality of his universe, and of the juvenile quality of their conversation, considering their bodies and vocations. "I don't think it's inappropriate for me to ask about your feelings for another man."

"Maybe not," Kalya said, still standing above him. "But your choice of how and when was not exactly the best." Iskie grunted. "But I'm serious. It is over with the girl, right?"

"Her name is Seema," Iskie said. "And yes, it's over. It never really began. You were always my first choice—"

"Yes, yes. I'm your Roxanne. You've said it many times. I like it. But I don't really understand what it means."

Iskie reached up and pulled her to him. She melted against his form, settling effortlessly into his embrace, their bodies forming an ugly knot in Yggdrasil's wizened hide. "There was an Italian painter," Iskie said, "named Il Sodoma, who was so taken by the romance between Alexander and Roxanne that he painted a magnificent tribute to their love, complete with smiling cupids at their wedding." This made Kalya smile. "She was Persian—Sogdian, to be exact—and the daughter of the tribal chief Oxyartes. Some heartless historians say that Alexander married Roxanne for political reasons alone, to show his men that it was their duty to spread Greek genes and culture throughout Asia, to lead by example. They say his true love was for his best friend Hephaestion. But I believe Alexander was truly overcome with the knowing of her, of Roxanne."

"Hmm," Kalya said. "Sounds like the making of a jealous little love triangle."

Iskie kissed Kalya lightly on the forehead. He squeezed her hard, wanting to be as close to her as was physically possible. She did not complain, though she did wince. "I sometimes imagine a stiff, focused Alexander," he said. "He was so completely filled with kingly duty and military goals. The only beauty he encountered, he either used for political leverage or destroyed it as a matter of strategy. Then this Alexander treks across half the world, growing old and bent with wounds and fatigue, and beaten down by disease and alcohol abuse. All he has to push him on, despite his men's pleas to return home, is a singular belief in his destiny—-to retrace the steps of Dionysus and conquer the world. He must have been so alone, so desperate for warmth and assurance. And then he was faced with an otherworldly beauty unimaginable to Western eyes. So lonely and ripe for love, his heart must have melted then."

"What happened to her, to Roxanne?" Kalya asked.

"She was eventually murdered by Alexander's jealous friend Cassander."

Kalya shuddered. "It's always about death with you, isn't it?"

"And it's always about jealousy with you."

"Oh," Kalya said, "I think it's always about jealousy with you, too. You just haven't figured that out yet." Iskie squinted at her, struggled to position her between his eyes and the glaring sun.

"The only thing that I'm jealous of," he said, "is every square inch of clothing on your body." As she bent to kiss him, he was once more cast into the quantum foam, straining to pry apart the delicate particles of infinitesimal time. As Iskie held his Roxanne to his body, he imagined himself pulling his knees up into a foetal embrace to plummet breathlessly into that void of timeless instantaneousness. He yearned to capture a heartbeat and constrain a kiss to last a lifetime, while Kalya was cast again into the waking dream, willingly consumed by an incandescent moon.

17

SCATTERINGS

Which one was the sleeping god, after all? The preserving one who reposes in shallow-breathed slumber, or the quiet lotus-sitter whose inner eye stares intently at all events within the dream? Vishnu or Brahma? Preserver or creator, watcher or watched, dreamer or dream, lover or loved.

From the dream percolated embers of light that were flailed by the breeze. Though whipped about by the unpredictable currents that hinted at the coming monsoons, they would appear to navigate with non-chaotic intent, retracing the same untraceable trajectories that were wrought from the first godly exhalations, just a few breaths prior, a hundred million years ago. Dipping and diving, evading the swallows, the bulbuls, and the naturalists' nets, they stopped only to eat and to rest and to revel in their passage through the unseeable materials, many eventually alighting upon gourdlike syconia, only to oviposit, then to sink down to be amassed with the rest of the dream, to be spat up again with the next exhalation.

About Yggdrasil's trunk they swirled. Through its branches they swarmed. Within its crevices they hunkered. To see their light was to perceive the elemental storm. The two lovers of Whell, entangled in the magic of happenstance, chased them like stars and danced to their celestial melodies. Day after day these two would come with their entomological tools, scampering about the grove, just as the forest creatures did night after night, all drawn to the ancient wooden phallus that violated the sky. Hunting wasps, sampling syconia, tracing a fractal path about the grove and the labyrinth that resembled so the seemingly random meanderings of rodents, deer, and fox, they would find frequent reward in the solemnity of a kiss, the desperate transientness of a wayward caress, all of which were but barely noticeable instants to the immortal dreaming eye.

"What a surprise to find you here," Palvinder Lal said, a broad,warm smile emblazoned on his handsome face, his strong hands clutching a stool and portable easel.

Kalya brushed her skirts and rose to her feet, snapping shut the taxonomical guide from which she'd been reading aloud. "Uncle, what a surprise to see you out here!"

"Is that so? How do you mean?"

"Well," Kalya explained, "you've been holed up in the house for a long time now. I was afraid you'd never come out to the gardens again."

"Or perhaps you were hoping I wouldn't!" He was still smiling, this time at Iskie, who had emerged from Yggdrasil's other side. Lal nodded toward the bottle of arak that lay alongside Iskie's books. "So that's where my private stock has got to."

Iskie chuckled amiably. "I use it as a biological preservative. I hope you don't mind."

"Of course not, Iskandar. My home is your home. And soon my home will be home to scores more!"

"The wedding?" Iskie asked.

"Yes, that's right." Lal grew suddenly grim, and beckoned Iskie to walk with him. No words slipped from Kalya's mouth, but her cheeks and forehead issued a torrent of objections. But Iskie did not hesitate, relaxing under Lal's avuncular embrace as the two of them strolled into the labyrinth.

"How are things, sir?" Iskie asked, a lilt of genuine concern in his voice.

"How do you mean?"

Iskie whispered, "Last time we spoke, you were disturbed by your uncle's death. Are you better?"

"Yes, thank you. Very kind of you for asking. One can never recover from losing a member of the family, of course. But we are all mature adults, yes? We go on. I have lost an uncle, but I have a son to whom I still have a duty. This is a country of emotional extremes, you know. We see much death here and much misery. Well, perhaps not my family, since we have considerable wealth compared to many others. But, in general, it's a common thing to see great joy and love existing simultaneously with great heartbreak and grief. I already have the grief. But my son's wedding will bring us much joy. You shall see."

"I'm sure it will," Iskie said. "And I'm very grateful to you for everything, for allowing me to stay here as long as I have and letting me get to know your family."

Lal stopped and faced Iskie, putting his hands on the shorter man's shoulders. "Iskandar, we all need family. Family is at the heart of the healthy human being. While you are a guest in my home, you are also family. And when you leave, I hope you will continue to think of us as family."

"Thanks," Iskie said, genuinely grateful.

"And as family, I have a request of you." Iskie tensed visibly. "Nothing too difficult, I assure you." Lal graced him with another of his magical grins, radiating charisma from every pore. "Our weddings are not typical Hindu fare. In fact, in many ways we Lals are not really Hindus. Sure, we have a pundit and a *mandap*—that's the structure we build for the wedding ceremony. But as we shall have the wedding here on the estate, it is not feasible to have the traditional arrival procession for the groom's party. You see?"

"Okay, sure," Iskie said, not fully understanding. "What would you like me to do?"

"Go with Subodh on a little trip for a few days, that's all. Are you a Christian? No, don't answer; it's not important. But in your ceremonies, you often have bachelor parties. When I was a student in London, I went to many! Make it a bachelor party if you'd like, just the two of you. Subodh doesn't have many other male friends. Just take him away for a couple of days, and bring him back on the morning of the wedding, early enough for us to dress him, of course."

Iskie was surprised. It was a simple request, but puzzling. "Of course. I'd be happy to. But what does that really have to do with Hindu tradition?"

Lal grinned again. "Nothing, I suppose. But the boy is getting on everyone's nerves, and it would be nice to be rid of him for a while." Lal chuckled, and Iskie joined in.

Iskie was silent for a moment. "Uncle," he said at last, "I don't really know about such things. But aren't Hindu weddings supposed to take place near the home of the bride, not the groom?"

Lal seemed to tongue the inside of his mouth in a fatigued, distant manner. Perhaps he had heard this particular question before. "We do things differently around here. I'm sure you've noticed." Iskie nodded, then turned to walk back to Kalya. But he was restrained by a firm and heavy hand on his shoulder. "Iskandar, one more thing."

"Yes?"

"I understand that you and Subodh have made special friends over in Omas village. No, I'm not upset. Boys will be boys. I was a boy once. Hard to believe? But Subodh is about to be married, and I can't have him dishonouring his wife."

Not when she's also a cousin, also family, Iskie mused. "So you'd like me to have a word with him?"

"Exactly. That's a good man." Lal once again put his arm around Iskie, and the two made their way back to Yggdrasil and Kalya. She had not moved since the two had departed, but still stood with arms crossed, watching them approach. Her expression was unreadable, though a hint of concern played across her features.

Iskie stood toe to toe with her, consciously fighting the reflex to touch her tenderly, feeling static charges pass between their clothing, smelling the scent of jasmine from her hair and the choir of morning kisses on her breath. For her part, Kalya gazed intently at Iskie's pink face, a hint of sorrow creasing her eyebrows. She made to touch his face, but resisted, the gesture resembling that of someone motioning to touch a photograph, to feel again something that has been lost. They turned in unison towards the house, stealing a final glance back at Palvinder Lal and his monstrous tree.

Lal's easel had been erected on the edge of the grove, in the sunlight. But it remained unused, its owner having drifted off elsewhere. Nearer to the great trunk, shrouded in Yggdrasil's shadow, yet beaten down by the midday sun, Lal bent by the roots and pulled from his clothing a metal container. He gingerly poured its contents into his left hand, weighing its dusty substance before sprinkling it upon the ground. Had they been nearer, the two would have seen Lal's eyes misting up, and heard his sobs of grief.

The memory of a nightmare struck Iskie then, that of an animated corpse tearing away the flesh from its own face. The image no longer terrified, but rather saddened him. For every terrible ghost is the product of love and tragedy. And that's never something to be scorned or feared.

The wind was picking up slightly and now carried more humidity. The birds did not chirp as much, and the morning slugs were fewer. The wasps still continued their timeless voyages from tree to tree, but were expending significantly more energy to do so. The wind, still slight compared to what was to come, drew long and blew hard. Beneath it all, the sleeping gods shivered, and the vortex of swirling lights, the elemental storm, flickered for a heartbeat, but was sustained by the loving return of one of their own, offered in silent tearful prayer by a grieving nephew, and lain in layered fashion at the base of the wooden phallus, unintentionally emulating the geological layering formed when the subcontinental stepchild had first collided with the mainland, creating India, waking the gods and fissuring the cosmic dream.

18

CHHATH

Kalya watched the villagers loping about slowly but purposefully. The men, bent under the weight of loads of wood and other items, would nod to her expressionlessly as they passed, and she would smile back weakly, conscious of her strangeness to them, her prim and sterile repose atop a polyester blanket upon the manicured estate lawn. The women walked by in groups, chittering joyously, gap-toothed grins reflecting the blinding sunlight in a scene that was heartbreaking in its romantic splendour. The women were unburdened, perhaps for the only time of the year, their regular back-breaking chores adopted by the eldest of their children during this very special time.

This was the first day of Chhath, a Hindu festival unique to Bihar. It would last four days, and would involve the consumption of sweet foods and the offering of consumable sacrifices to the god of the sun, Surya. The villagers, impoverished as many of them were, proudly bedecked themselves in their finest clothes, radiating incandescent vitality despite their weakened, fasting condition. For the most devout, the fast would be broken only at sundown when a feast of unsalted vegetarian foods would be laid out. The rice and coconut dishes and the deep-fried *puri*, when sprinkled with cane sugar, Kalya found particularly enticing. Though the Lals did not engage in any of the Chhath traditions, they would certainly take full advantage of its culinary attributes.

And on the third day of Chhath, when devotees from around the province would gather at the banks of the Ganges to engage in ritualistic bathing and perform further puja, the Lal family would wed its only son to Anjali, a princess of the clan. It was a timing insisted upon by the bride's religious parents and sanctified by the blessing of a guru. For at the moment of completion of the wedding rites, miles further south in the town of Gaya, the last vestiges of the dwindling cult of Surya would be completing their own Chhath rituals within the eight-hundred-year-old Sun Temple.

It must be so, the guru had insisted, for the wedding was mandated to occur in the lunar month of Kartik, on whose sixth day Chhath, which means six, was slated to begin. All was in accord, all part of the turning of the Great Wheel, all more fated than coincidental. All would be good.

Kalya absently licked her lips, tasting the lingering remains of Iskandar's departing kiss, and letting its flavour meld effortlessly with the aromas rising from the villagers' cooking. She had attended the festival only a couple of times before. Each time, she had been reminded of the region's ancientness, as if the village of Whell existed outside of time, not subject to the forces of global change or evolution. The recollection saddened her. Connections with the ancient are rare and valuable in this world. But to have them, it seemed, was also to deny the advantages of modernity. Those gap-toothed women enjoyed the simple comforts of their sweet foods more potently than she ever could, largely because they rarely had the opportunity to make and consume them.

She shook her head briskly to rouse herself from her introspection. This place, wonderful though it was, had a tendency to fray nerves and break hearts. A Westerner with the slightest sense of passion or romance could be easily seduced into one of three camps: the naive Orientalist, the distraught social justice crusader, or the phlegmatic bastard whose initial sympathies are stripped away by the unrelenting sensory onslaught. One thus had to acquire a special kind of emotional maturity to weather the storm of passions, to remain calm in one's own skin while continuing to seek growth. An impossible balance it was. Many had fallen from that highwire and had risen again either to hide behind colonial facades or to weep uncontrollably for the joyful tragedy that would eternally remain just beyond reach.

She rubbed her face, forcing her muscles to respond to the myriad touches of breeze, scent, and light, rose to her feet and gathered her blanket and reference books. Drawn by a wailing from within the heart, or perhaps by the smell of something less sweet than the desserts being prepared around her, she strolled down the dusty path into the thickness of the village. The sea of smiles that welcomed her was touching, its genuineness soothing in a world of fraudulence and superficiality. As always, children ran to her side, reaching up to touch her skirt or her hands, always beaming with the purest of infantile love, their tenderness seeping from every pore of their unwashed barefooted bodies.

With every step she retreated backwards in time towards the unseeable primal emotional fog, where to feel was never a complicated matter, never fraught with the dangers of betrayal or consequence. She breathed in the dewy day with melancholy calm, seeming to ingest sunlight with every inhalation, silently to exhale distrust and doubt with every sinking of her chest. She walked with purpose and rhythm, her feet alive with the borrowed joy of the children. One by one, they released her until gradually she walked alone out of the heart of Whell, away from the clamour of village activity. The sounds of life and family and commerce receded, and were replaced by the growing tonalities of squawking birds and monkeys, and by the ubiquitous buzz of flying insects.

She was once more at that special zone where the village terminated and the forest began. The mighty fig trees beckoned her inward, while the touchstones of human culture clanked distantly behind her, oblivious and unconcerned. It took some looking, but she located the partially camouflaged canopy that spanned the roots of one of the great trees, recognizing the thinly concealed campsite as a home of intransigence, a place of uneasy compromise between forest and settlement.

"Auntie," she cooed.

"Eh? Kalya? Dat you?" Eunice called back.

"Yes. May I come in?"

"Of course, child. Come, na." Kalya peeled back the canopy and sank comfortably into Eunice's tent. She felt the darkness creep about her, and endured the sudden assault of fungal odours and sickly heat. It was not entirely unpleasant. There was a thing here, a force resulting from the totality of presences. As objectionable as the odours might be, as disconcerting as the darkness and uncleanliness, and as weighty as the heat and humidity were, Eunice's abode was filled with a sparkling timelessness and pure sentiment, that of love.

Eunice's breathing was laboured, her sentences short and soft. But her voice still resonated against the darkness, like a disembodied omnipresence. "Happy Chhath, Kalya dear."

"Happy Chhath, Auntie," Kalya said, reaching to lay her hand atop Eunice's. It was wet and cool.

"What be dis, child?" Eunice unwrapped the item Kalya had placed in her hand. It was a piece of sweetened coconut folded inside a one-hundred rupee bill. "Me na take payment from you, child. Take it back, na."

"No, Auntie," Kalya said. "It's not payment. It's for Chhath. You must accept it."

Eunice chuckled softly. "What can me do fo' you, Kalya dear?"

"Nothing, Auntie," Kalya said. "I just wanted to say hello. I don't know when I'll be able to see you again." There was silence, but not emptiness. A cloud of contemplation filled the tent.

"Me see. What you readin'?" Eunice asked, presumably noticing Kalya's stack of books.

"Just some random books. This one is Gertrude Jobes's *Dictionary of Mythology*." Eunice issued a belly laugh, then began coughing most evilly. "What's so funny, Auntie?"

Eunice wheezed slightly, then spoke. "You big city people wan' know so much bout de ghost world. Stop read, na! *Feel*."

"I know, I know," Kalya said. "It's just interesting historically, is all. You know our big tree, Yggdrasil? It's named for Norse mythology. And trees are mentioned in mythologies of many cultures. Seems to be related to the Jacob's Ladder or the Indian rope trick—"

"Yes, yes, Kalya dear. All ladders to heaven. Dem got ting much much bigger dan trees now, right?"

"Well, yes. You mean buildings and towers?"

"Yes, me mean dat. And space ship and airplane and balloon and rocketship and satellite, dey all go much much higher dan tree."

"So?"

"Kalya dear, any dem people ever see heaven? No? Den why a tree can climb into heaven?"

Kalya shrugged, then realized that her gesture could not be seen in the darkness. "It's not the only thing I'm reading. I found a book on the history of Alexander the Great." She thought she could sense Eunice grinning in the blackness. "You know, because Iskie likes him so much."

"You is a good friend to de bug boy, Kalya dear. Is a good book?"

"Yes!" Kalya exclaimed. "It's all so weird. The Egyptians made Alexander into a deity. They associated him with Helios, the god of the sun!"

"Yes, me know," Eunice said in a disappointingly dismissive tone. "Look, Kalya dear. You find de story of how de Greek king tame he horse?"

"No, I don't think so."

"No matter," Eunice said. "You must remind it to de bug boy."

"Okay. I suppose he must know it. Why? What's so special about it?"

"Nevah you mind. Just remind he. Right?"

"Okay."

"And how 'bout dat book?" Eunice nudged the stained hardcover on the bottom of the pile.

Kalya grinned. "That's the book written by Subodh's professor. It's how Iskie and I met."

"Eh? Read me some."

Kalya opened *Insects of North and Middle India* to a familiar page and read aloud, struggling to make out the words in the tent's darkness.

> *Blastophaga psenes,* the symbiotic pollinator fig wasp, is an animal of great host specificity. To deviate for the moment from a strictly scientific reckoning, one might consider its life cycle in poetic terms. She is a player in a tragedy, an animal chased and

> threatened for the duration of her short violent life. Hers is also a fate reserved for the female of the species, while the male's role is more robotically simplistic, though surely less adventurous. She may never know the company of another of her species, except at birth and then again just before death. Her instinct, the result of millions of years of evolution, is to flee and oviposit, nothing more. Such single-mindedness of purpose is not without equal in the animal kingdom, but might be unique among insects with such specific symbiotic relationships with trees.

"Kalya, dear, why yuh choose dat passage?"

"I don't know, Auntie. Maybe because it's the least technical part of the book"

"Dat all?"

"No, I suppose not." She tried to change the subject. "Auntie, will you come to Subodh's wedding?"

Eunice reached forward and took Kalya's hands in her own. She was so close that Kalya could feel Eunice's breath on her face, and could sense the Guyanese woman's gaze poring over her. "Kalya," she said. "Life. . ." Her voice trailed off, her thought remaining unvocalized.

"Yes, Auntie?"

Eunice sighed. "Sometimes, Kalya dear, me wan' tell you so much 'bout de world. But what me know? Me just one old lady. What me got fo' say is dis. Just be, Kalya dear. Just be. Do what yuh feel is right. Go where yuh feel yuh must go. Yuh na got millions years evolution like de bug. Yuh na need da. Yuh got one heart. Listen to she, na." She leaned forward and kissed Kalya on the forehead, squeezing her hands meaningfully, then silently releasing them and sinking back into her corner with a dismissive and saddened silence.

Kalya breathed deeply of the clouds of fungal love before emerging from the black tent into the blinding white sunlight and fresh air. She fished for a cigarette, but had no fire. She felt a little bit older, and yearned anew to laugh aloud with the gap-toothed women of the village.

19

TAJ MAHAL

In July of 326 BCE, a violent thunderstorm whipped the river Hydaspes into a watery maelstrom. On the far side, the side beyond which lay the plush and wealthy lands of India, a mighty army readied itself. King Porus rode atop an elephant, the organic tanks of this era, confident of his invulnerability in the face of uncivilized Greek methods.

But Alexander, on the near side, would not be cowed. He burned all of the wagons of Persian booty that slowed him down, and dismissed many of his soldiers, choosing instead to reshape his forces with stealthy and swift Asian horsemen. That day they clashed, East and West. The Greeks had never before seen elephants, those frightening behemoths of impenetrable skin and ground-shaking roars. But their faith in their god-king was absolute, following unhesitatingly as Alexander led the charge into the Indian ranks.

In the battle that ensued, the demon horse Bucephalus was wounded and killed. Great Iskandar was grief-stricken, fighting on as a man possessed. The god-king and his beast had been as one since earliest youth, traversing the entire world inseparably, one offering forethought and will, the other bringing bestial might and focus. Their separation was a ripping asunder of joined tissues, and brought with it horrific pain and deafening wails. Much blood would anoint the soil upon which the Horse Temple would soon stand.

As fate had decreed, Alexander was master of this battle, no doubt channelling the god of war whose blood supposedly flowed in Alexander's veins, and focusing the bestial rage that lingered in the wake of Bucephalus's passing. Always waiting for an opportunity, the ancient invisible reptile whispered from the darkness into the god-king's ear, imploring vengeance. But Alexander's forebrain prevailed, allowing him to push his emotion aside and to silence, for the nonce, that jabbering, shadowed lizard. He spared Porus's life and allowed him to rule the Indian province as his vassal. Then he pushed on further south towards the Ganges. He believed that the holy Ganges flowed into Oceanus, that Earth-girdling sea. It was his path into the domain of the Titans, the land of the infinite dream.

Once more they were on a train together, watching the Gangetic plains stretch across the vista. This time Iskie was careful not to eat any of the morsels Subodh offered him. The rumble of the engine provided pink noise of narcotic quality and immunized him to the arrhythmic kicks of the small children in the seats behind them. As his eyelids drooped on occasion to shut out the expansive scenes of dusty sunset, movie stills of translucent romance would flash before his unseeing eye: the gentle curves of smooth brown skin, the ebullient fullness of hot red lips and the impenetrable thickness of a jungle of thick black hair, all coded with the signature of intoxicating jasmine. On his lips lingered the memory of morning kisses, chai flavoured with a hint of cigarette smoke.

To his right, slumped against the window, Subodh methodically fed himself long streams of fried plantain, blissfully unaware of the microbial battles being fought in his small intestine. His open eyes flickered in nystagmus, examining the landscape with unconscious focus. A lazy wrinkle meandered from the edge of his eye, spidering out to grasp the earliest quadrant of his left cheek. It was a sign of aging that was out of place on a face best known to cackle in puerile glee.

With intense examination, so easy here in an extended state of immobility, the elements of familial commonality could be made out to Iskie, those items of Lal physiognomy that, in total, constitute family resemblance. Subodh's general athletic physique, lean and lanky, was reminiscent of his father's towering form, while his rounder facial features were those of his mother. But there was something particular about the play between cheek and eyelash, a tremor or glint, a responsiveness to the slightest of breezes or gentlest of lights, that was mirrored in that flawless fabric of pulchritude, the face of Kalya Lal. Iskie's adoration of the female Lal overcame his distaste for Subodh's masculine demeanour. He lost himself in the illusion, drawn to a waking dream of togetherness, in which it was Kalya, not Subodh, who sat next to him. He straddled the thin line between love and obsession precariously, he realized. Therein lay both the beauty and the danger of his adventure.

With every moment, every rumble and jolt, they were propelled ever closer to Agra, the ancient Moghul city and home of the Taj Mahal, reportedly the world's greatest architectural testament to love. Iskie's hands felt dry. They lacked their usual tactile responsiveness and were stricken with a slight tetanus. He could see, smell, hear, taste and touch, but nothing more, the complement of his senses reduced to the banal five. A force compelled him to look again to Subodh, and he was met with a brilliant toothy grin. It emanated something akin to Palvinder Lal's incandescent disembodied charisma.

"Iskie, my man, this is the first time I've seen you completely and utterly sober in days! You didn't think to bring any of the good stuff?"

Iskie smiled absently and settled further into his seat. "Kalya wouldn't let me."

"Ohhh, the beast is tamed by the beauty. Such a tragically common tale."

"As I understand it, Subodh, you're about to be tamed by a beauty yourself."

Subodh chuckled dementedly, slurping back a plantain with deliberate noisiness. "I'll be tamed in name alone," he said. "But the beast shall remain free." He gestured to his anatomy in a vulgar manner.

"Very attractive," Iskie said.

"What's the matter with you, old man? Since you started getting it regular with my cousin you're all business. Remember Seema and Sonali? Remember how much fun we can have when you're more relaxed?"

"We'll have fun, don't you worry. That's why we're here."

"That's why we're on a train? Thanks, old man. But we both know we're here because my father wants me out of the way while he deals with Anjali's family."

"Anjali?" Iskie asked. "Your fiancee?"

Subodh made a sucking noise. "Oh yes. Sweet sweet sweet. Big and round in all the right places, just like Kalya."

"See? Your beast will indeed be tamed."

"Hey, Iskie," Subodh leaned into him, his face animated and lit by a scaly glow. "We should mix and match."

Iskie frowned and leaned away from Subodh. "What?"

"You know, old man. Kalya, Anjali. Mix and match. It's what we should have done with the other two, you know. You would have liked Sonali. Very creative."

Iskie repressed a shudder. "Kalya is your cousin. Remember?"

"Anjali is also my cousin, *na*?" Subodh swallowed, then licked his lips. "Do remember, Iskie, that you're the new player here. You've no idea what kind of history we Lal cousins have with each other. So many secrets left to tell, *na*? Such a mysterious place you must find this India." He gave a short chuckle.

Iskie sat in silent immovability for several heartbeats, the left corner of his upper lip turned up. He no longer resembled the sensual Tantric sculptures, as Professor Kumar had once noted, but rather the mocking depictions of foolishness and sinful excess made by the cults of Hanuman, the monkey god.

Subodh settled back against the window and regarded Iskie with a slit-eyed examining stare. "So, my old man, what shall we do in Agra?"

"I don't know, Subodh. You're getting married in a couple of days. What do you want to do?"

"Oh, you know what I want to do." He made another vulgar gesture, glancing over his shoulder briefly to see that no children were watching.

"Which reminds me of something your father asked me to mention to you," Iskie said.

"He wants me to keep it in the sheath. Yes, I get that message regularly. And yet he expects grandchildren. Such contradictions, such unfair contradictions."

"So," Iskie said, "what do you want to do in Agra? We'll be there in less than an hour."

"My man, we shall see the sights. The Taj is lovely this time of year." He pretended to sip from an imaginary teacup, pinky extended. "Then we shall have some dinner, perhaps retire to the smoking room for cigars and brandy, discuss the state of the world and empire and such, and wager on the cricket match and complain about the stock market. Then. . ." He leaned in close to Iskie. "Then I have a surprise for you."

The air was hot and sticky, a soup of vapours and fuels. Their bellies were stretched with copious amounts of limca and French fries and bubbled with a comfortable acidic reaction. Iskie had been surprised by his desperate need for American junk food. He had almost inhaled the fries, developing a craving for unsalted boiled eggs in the process. Subodh had watched in semi-silence, pausing between his own foraging to chuckle at Iskie's foreign voraciousness. Iskie's desire was for food of hardness and tactile substance. Indian food was wonderful, but it had a tendency towards mushiness, spiciness, and being overcooked. His tongue and esophagus rejoiced in gastric relief, sickening him somewhat, but sating a previously unidentified appetite. A good beef-steak, almost an impossibility in a largely Hindu nation, would be too much to hope for here, even in this overpriced hotel restaurant. But he could still fantasize about such a thing, its unseasoned barbecued simplicity requiring the full attention of his canines and incisors.

They had gone directly from the hotel restaurant to the Taj Mahal. It was a short bicycle-rickshaw ride, but impossibly circuitous by Iskie's reckoning. The street layout of downtown Agra, deliciously charming with a lingering Moghul flavour, was still a polluted Third World urban collision of styles, with dead ends and blind alleys, fragile houses bursting onto parking coves and the requisite gaggle of half-naked children and half-starved dogs. In the glow of the noon sun, it was a marvellous sight: a scene of thriving, throbbing twenty-first-century life constrained only by the infrastructure of a long-dead mediaeval empire.

The Taj Mahal complex itself was an anachronism, a museum of Muslim mores from the seventeenth century deposited deep in the heart of a modern Hindu hive. A sign at the entrance captured Iskie's imagination: *Offerings to the monument are prohibited.*

"Silly Hindus," Subodh quipped. "Always doing puja, even in a Muslim tomb!"

"Silly Hindus," Iskie replied. "Next thing you know, they'll be marrying their cousins." Subodh did not laugh, an absence of reaction that seemed to Iskie to be the deepest hypocrisy. But Iskie allowed himself to imagine a time before the government had sequestered the famous monument behind turnstiles and toll-keepers, a time when after a day's work in the fields the locals would stroll to this outlandish testament to love, and treat it like yet another gaudy temple. They would have burned incense and chanted prayers to the souls entombed within its finery. There was something both laughable and moving about such a scene.

The complex was larger than he had anticipated, with several enormous historical buildings bracketing the entrance to the causeway. He and Subodh stepped onto the path side by side, pausing for a moment as the sight of the monument struck their eyes. As the Taj Mahal was now a well-known icon reproduced in comic books, television shows, and postcards, the full impact of its virginal splendour was denied Iskie. He already knew of its precise dimensions, its storied past and blinding whiteness. Like an aged seductress, she nonetheless beckoned him forward with her shiny facade and promises of experienced tenderness.

They stumbled forward with matched cadence, paying no mind to the swarms of annoying tourists, each taking the same posed photos that had been taken millions of times before. This was a loop in time, wherein events reoccurred in perpetuity. The tourists grew indistinguishable from one another, gibbered on in equally indecipherable tongues, scolding ubiquitous children with the same timeless parental tones. The clicking of camera shutters resembled the noise of a thousand cicadas, serving to both comfort and numb Iskie's darting mind. "I need a drink," he said.

"Not here," Subodh said. "And not yet. Later, old man." They continued down the causeway, pausing about fifteen metres from the Taj Mahal. "You think maybe we should hold hands, lover?"

"No thanks, Subodh. I don't know where your hands have been."

"You know the story, Iskie?"

"Yes," Iskie replied. "Shah Jahan built the Taj Mahal as a monument and tomb for his wife Mumtaz. They're both buried here."

"You summarize in two sterile sentences the glories of a generation of Indians. That won't do."

"What do you want me to say? It's a monument to love? It's all been said before."

"Sure," Subodh said. "But you're the one who knows so much about Lenin. Why don't you talk about all the artists forced to toil for decades to complete it? How about the Persian artisans whose hands were cut off so that they couldn't make another? This is also a monument to cruelty and overwork."

"Why Subodh, I never knew you had any political thoughts at all." Iskie was serious, though his voice was reflexively tinged with sarcasm.

"I don't," Subodh spat. "But I'm no fan of people being forced to do anything. This to me is a monument to tyranny and slavery. There's no love here."

"Only obsession," Iskie added, completing the thought.

"How do you mean?"

"It's not love that causes you to bankrupt your nation for decades to build a tomb. It's obsession. That's not healthy. That's not something to celebrate."

"Then, Iskandar, for the first time in quite some time, it seems we can agree on something. You know what it reminds me of?"

"What?"

"Look at it! What does it look like to you?" Subodh grinned knowingly.

"I don't know." Iskie pondered. "A garlic bulb? A flower?"

"Right," Subodh said. "And what's a flower but a garden-variety pussy?"

"You're a man of few words, Subodh. It's a shame that all of those words are obscene."

"Like you don't see it. Don't look with your eyes, *gora*. Look with your lingam, your manhood." Subodh chuckled deviously. Iskie did not respond. Subodh smiled and slapped him on the back, turning him around, to face a striking rust-coloured mosque whose beauty was unappreciated by its proximity to the whorish Taj.

They sat on the floor of the mosque's entrance, soothed by its cool shade. The Taj Mahal could be seen through the teardrop entrance, occluded somewhat by intervening spires and the bodies of swarming tourists. The bustle was palpable, their detached sedation eerie for the locale and its emptiness. The occasional figure would stroll through the mosque. But Iskie only noticed the ones who were presumably Muslim women, identified by their garb, for the swath of flowing elegance their silhouettes cut against the well-lit entrances and exits. To his Western eyes, they were figures out of history, plucked from Europe's darkened past, but wandering the modernity of polluted Asia. It was another in a long list of his recent Orientalist sentiments, he realized, and it angered him for the naivety the tendency represented. Still, he found the thought pleasing, as if a drug had separated his mind from his body, allowing him to float above this complex of cultural and temporal collisions. Arak would have given him greater insight, he thought. The moonshine was a kind of magic, it seemed, allowing him to distinguish anachronisms from real temporal displacements. He missed it. And for the very first time in a lifetime of regular drinking, he craved the stuff.

"Can we go get that drink now?" Iskie asked Subodh. "Any chance of finding some arak down here?"

"No," Subodh said, never taking his eyes off of the blinding Taj. "You do realize that 'arak' is the general word for moonshine in most of the northern states? But the stuff you've been drinking is special. It's made only in our village, out of items grown locally." He seemed to brighten. "You know, I've been thinking of mass-producing it. Start a whole new family business. What you think, old man?"

"I think your father would be pleased," Iskie said, and meant it. "He wants you to be a businessman."

"Yes, he does. With Anjali's contacts, I could do it, too! And you know the best part?"

"What?"

"It means I could supply you with the stuff well after you've gone!"

Iskie smiled amiably, but a shadow darkened his features. When would he be gone? It was a surprisingly uncomfortable thought, one that tightened his chest and constricted his breath. Movement was his mantra. His ease with travel had taken him around the world and would continue to shift him through adventures and environments. Inconstant stimuli kept his brain active, he felt, allowed him to cogitate on matters of worldly and timeless importance. Movement kept him from wallowing in the emotional morasses to which more sedentary people eventually fell victim. Travel was the method by which Alexandrian Destiny effected its will and lured its subjects from frightful hiding and hermetic safety. Yet the thought of immobile restfulness now soothed him, presenting itself to his mind as the inchoate comforts of brown jasmine-scented skin.

He stood and wandered to the rear of the mosque, towards the dribbling Yamuna River. Across the river, he could see yet another ancient structure, a rust-coloured spired behemoth that stood at guard over the historic site. "What's that?"

"That's the Lal Qila," Subodh said. "The red fort."

"Isn't that supposed to be in Delhi?"

"We have red forts all over this country. It's like an epidemic. But that one's special. Shah Jahan's son Aurangzeb had him imprisoned there after he took over the empire in a coup."

"And why was that again?"

"You said it yourself, Iskie. Shah Jahan had nearly bankrupted the country building this thing, this Taj. And I suppose Aurangzeb was cruel. He took the empire, and put his father there for the rest of his life, never allowing him to visit the Taj, only to look at it from across the river."

Iskie grunted. "Then it's not just a monument to obsession. It's a monument to treachery."

"Love, obsession, treachery, cunts. It's all the same. Can we go now?"

20

The Waking Dream

Kingfisher beer was an excellent brand. However, a bottle sold for the equivalent of a labourer's daily wage. No wonder moonshine was so common. Still, a professionally processed lager was golden joy to a throat that had been scorched for days by a screech fermented from unknown vegetables by village amateurs. Iskie guzzled his third bottle with relish, and decided with a characteristic Diamandi sense of abstruse responsibility that he would end it there. He selected a cigar from the box before him, sniffing its length in mock sophistication.

"You are an odd one, old man," Subodh remarked.

"If I am the odd one, then that would make you the even one. And I certainly would not characterize you as even, not in any sense."

"Beer really flattens your sense of humour, doesn't it? I think the harder stuff does better things for your personality." Subodh never paused in his munching of papadam. Perhaps the food fueled his tongue. "You're a fascinating drunk, old man. But you should beware.

Charming and witty young drunks often grow into blithering, pathetic old winos."

"And you should treat your elders with more respect, young man." Iskie countered, biting off the end of the cigar.

"Elder? Iskie, I'm only a year or two younger than you."

"Yes, but I have crossed a special age threshold that you will soon come to know. I am at that age when exercise can be both a life-saving necessity and a life-threatening feat. When exerted, my body simultaneously cries out, Thank you! and Fuck you!"

"Sounds more like your sex life. Oh, and don't you object! My room is only a couple of doors down from yours. I've heard much in the wee hours these past days."

"So that was you with your ear to my door? I thought it was horny old Tenali mistaking my room for yours."

"Oh! You wound me, sir!"

Iskie leaned close to Subodh, bathing him in foul beer breath. "You know, Kalya thinks you're gay."

"She's mistaken, of course," Subodh said. "She only thinks it because I enjoy fucking blokes."

"I see." Iskie sucked on his cigar, not noticing or caring that it wasn't lit. "I shall convey to her the error of her assumption."

Subodh stood up and beckoned Iskie to follow. "I've paid the bill," he said. "We have to go somewhere now."

"This is your bachelor party. I'm supposed to pay the bill."

"It's father's money. Don't worry. Let's go." He took Iskie by the upper arm and pulled him out of the restaurant and onto the street. The full moon was high in the sky now, illuminating the void and dusty slum streets. At the end of the sloped bricked road, a spire of the glorious Taj Mahal reflected in the moonlight. It was a marvellous sight, one right out of a storybook. The beer welled in Iskie's stomach into an enormous belch, and he found himself giggling foolishly. A staid part of his mind found an instant to remark on the shame of wasting a perfect romantic setting on drunken schoolboy antics.

Subodh dragged him along the labyrinthine stony streets and shooed away emboldened stray dogs as he marched. After what seemed to Iskie to be hours, they stopped before a shoddy concrete building with a dim kerosene lamp in the window. Subodh rapped twice on the door, and it creaked open, revealing a damp and dark hallway and a narrow concrete stairwell. "Just a couple of hours," Subodh said to the kerosene lamp. The lamp spoke back in Hindi, and it and Subodh launched into an indecipherable Vedic quarrel, culminating in Subodh's relinquishment of a sheaf of rupees. A fat brown hand emerged from behind the lamp and brushed the money into a drawer. Subodh and Iskie then stumbled down the hall and into a room.

The cubicle was barely large enough for its single bed and small table, illuminated only by a flickering stub of a candle. Iskie collapsed onto the bed, feeling his head clear somewhat. His tolerance for beer had dwindled, it seems, but his renowned alcoholic resistance was steadily reasserting itself, slowly pumping his forebrain clear of toxins. Subodh shut the door quickly and bent over the table, his face a study of tight focus. He fished some items from his pocket and bent to work.

Iskie leaned closer to watch. "Iskandar," Subodh asked, "do you like all women?"

"What do you mean?"

"You like white women, black women, Indian women, Chinese women?"

"Yes, of course. A fat boy like me can't afford to be picky."

"I had pegged you as a connoisseur of expensive imports." He never looked up from his work, his hands busily unwrapping foils and rolling papers.

"I am, of course, a man of sophisticated tastes." This time it was Iskie who drank from an imaginary teacup, pinky extended.

"And among white women," Subodh continued, "do you like both brunettes and blondes?"

"Like so many of my breed," Iskie said, remembering that this was, after all, a bachelor party of sorts, "I must admit to an inexplicable appetite for blondes." The quiet part of his mind took a brief moment to consider the evolutionary basis of that response, noting the association between blonde hair and youth in women. He pushed such thoughts aside, uncharacteristically content to sit upon his intellect and let the base world phase in and out of focus.

"Then, my friend, allow me to introduce to you my personal

favourite: the Lebanese blonde." Subodh bowed and, with a theatrical fluorish, produced a fresh joint.

Iskie accepted it and laughed. He took the candle and lit the joint, sucking deeply from it. Not usually one for the inhaled delights, his lungs objected fiercely. But the beer had primed his autonomic system well, allowing him to easily suppress the coughs. He soon lost track of how many tokes he had taken, and indeed how many joints Subodh had rolled, sinking into a delicious bath of tingly numbness.

"Hey," Subodh said. "Let's go to the roof. It's a fabulous view." Iskie nodded assent and allowed himself to roll off the bed and to his feet. The duo floated in puerile delight, then gleefully danced up the narrow stairwell, emerging onto a flat and dusty rooftop. There were several other bodies huddled in various states, but the two paid them no notice. Instead, their senses were unwaveringly focused upon the glowing Taj, whose reflective brilliance was near to blinding.

The ancient jewels and marbles that constituted the Taj Mahal's body, lugged from all parts of the Persian world, had a certain luminous value unmeasured by their weight or purity. The mineral-encrusted edifice seemed to absorb moonlight and blast it back out again, rising out of the urban slum like a kind of celestial temple afloat on a black ocean. It was a heart-stopping sight that would no doubt inspire both poets and thieves. Here, it was reserved for addicts and derelicts.

"Quite a beautiful monument to obsession and treachery, wouldn't you say?" Subodh asked.

"Obsession and treachery bring out the best in people, I guess."

"But you don't find it romantic, Iskandar?"

"Are you coming on to me, Subodh? You know I'm not your type. I'm not man enough."

"Perhaps not," Subodh chuckled. "But I think your breasts are quite lovely."

Iskie batted his eyelashes and pretended to adjust his bosoms. "By the way," Iskie added, in sudden seriousness. "This was a good surprise. Thanks. But again, I'm supposed to be surprising *you*. This is *your* bachelor party!"

"Old man, if I were really a Hindu I'd explain to you that we don't have bachelor parties. Instead, I'm going to tell you to fuck off and relax.

Also, this wasn't *the* surprise." Iskie looked at him hard. Subodh raised his right arm and beckoned to a group of huddled figures in the corner of the rooftop. They were four in number. They rose to their feet and scampered over to where Iskie and Subodh sat, holding their ragged hip-hugging red saris to their shapely bodies.

As they neared, their features became better lit by the ghostly Taj light. The three smaller figures beamed with childlike faces, slitted eyes, and light skin. To Iskie they looked Nepalese and no more than teenagers. But they exuded a definite sexual sense, concealing and revealing their physical features with practised seductive precision, playing the male libido like a stringed instrument, compelling sympathetic vibrations with their own sensual tonalities.

The fourth was taller and rather mysterious—even, it seemed to Iskie, a bit ominous. Her face remained partially concealed behind the pallu that folded up from her sari. Her gestures seemed overwrought, as if a pronounced femininity was forced to compensate for an unfeminine form. The word *hijra* came to Iskie's mind, and he knew it described a kind of Indian transsexual or eunuch. But the *hijra* did not travel or associate with real women, did they?

"Good evening, ladies," Subodh said to them. The tall woman and one of the others sat next to Subodh, caressing his arms, back, and shoulders.

"Hello, mister," they cooed in unison, their soft voices thickly accented and highly pitched, their words almost drowned in girlish giggles.

"Iskie," Subodh said, "Aren't you going to say hello to the ladies? I'm sorry, I couldn't find a blonde on short notice."

Iskie burped up a bolus of hashish smoke tinted with the malty smell of Kingfisher. The two standing girls emitted slight childish laughs. "Hello, ladies," Iskie said, the intoxicants having eroded his reflexive hesitancy. They sat down next to him, touching him in the same way that the others were massaging Subodh. It felt wonderful. His brain was softened by a duality of substances. His limbs were fatigued from a day of sightseeing. His stomach was sated. His body rejoiced in the attentions of sensual young women. And his optic nerves were held in rapture by a sight of architectural cosmic transcendence. It had all the trappings of a dream. In that moment, he was once again Iskandar of the lunar dreamscape, held in static suspension above a world chained to the wheel of unrelenting time.

But it wasn't a dream. The slight breeze that occasionally chilled him, the gibbous moon whose movement across the night sky indicated the deliberate passage of time, and the occasional bubbling in his restless stomach were all proof of that.

Iskie glanced to his side. Subodh was engaged in a furious and sloppy kiss with the tall one, her face still concealed from Iskie's view. The smaller woman had her right hand inside Subodh's shirt, its business unseen but not unimaginable.

He looked back to his own women, taking the time to appreciate them up close. They were indistinguishable from each other, sharing the features of millions of their brethren. Their high cheekbones, unchipped teeth and raven-black hair were clear indications of youth. But there were signs of hardship on their skin, rips in their clothing, calluses on their bare feet. Still, their undulating movements, full lips, and dancing eyes played his manhood expertly, stirring within him great remorseless desire.

One of them closed her Oriental eyes and leaned into him, dropping to drag the tip of her tongue along his neckline. The other reached under his shirt and caressed his torso, teasing manual explorations further south. Someone took his hand and placed it on her breast; he was unsure who. It was soft and supple, its nipple hardening instantly.

The one on his left whispered something in his ear in a language he did not understand. Iskie found it thrilling. Then she said, in a gentle low moan, "What is your name?" Iskie didn't respond, overwhelmed as he was by sensory inputs. "What's your name?" she cooed again, aspirating the words so that they stroked his aural canal. Maybe they required a name to personalize the exchange, to make it less clinical. Again, he did not answer.

The one on the right began to nibble gently on the rim of his ear, breathing heavily and loudly. "What do you want me to do? What's your name?" she breathed, sending shivers up his spine. "*Who are you?*" Slowly, Iskie glanced back to Subodh. His lips were still engaged with those of the tall woman, his head cradled in her hands, while the smaller one tended to other parts of his form. The tall woman locked her unblinking eyes on Iskie's, though her body remained focused on Subodh. A chill rippled over Iskie's skin. He sprang to his feet.

"What's wrong?" Subodh demanded, pushing away the smaller woman, but remaining reclined in the tall one's arms.

"Nothing. This isn't for me. You can stay. I'll meet you back at the hotel."

"So much for your adventure, *na*?" Subodh said. "Suit yourself." He dismissed Iskie with a wave and buried his face in the tall woman's bosom.

Iskie walked back to the stairwell, allowing himself a glance back. All five bodies writhed as if they were one dying beast, or a monster in the pangs of childbirth. The other figures on the rooftop, still huddled in immobility, paid the scene no notice. But Iskie felt watched by the radiant face of the unavoidable Taj, and by the prickling glare of his own imagined elemental. He jogged down the steps and hurried past the kerosene lamp, emerging hurriedly onto the chilly, black, run-down street, his brain still afloat, suspended in a chemical soup.

Gone was the warming glow of the imposing monument, blocked out by the squalid buildings around him. Even the streetlights were all extinguished, plunging Iskie into utter blackness, save for the stars, the moon, and the occasional kerosene lamp in the windows of the uninviting hovels. Uncharacteristically for Agra, the temperature had dropped noticeably, and Iskie regretted not having worn long pants and a long-sleeved shirt. But the toxins in his veins would protect him from that sort of discomfort for some time yet. Unfortunately, they also shielded him from fully rational thought and complete control over his muscles.

He stumbled along the cobbled road, trying to identify a direction. Everything looked the same, streets merging with alleys and snaking through one miniature shantytown after another. But there were no people out, only the occasional scamper of rats and the nearby howls of stray dogs. There were sounds of human life, though: couples bickering in hushed whispers and the occasional colicky cough. He saw a promising light from a door jamb, and cautiously entered the structure, rapping gently on the door as he pushed it open. Inside, a family was gathering its things, cleaning pots and folding blankets. The husband shouted at him in Hindi and moved towards the door brusquely, a look of violence in his eyes. Iskie scrambled back onto the street, just as the door slammed shut and a deadlock slid into place.

He would not find his way out of this maze in the darkness, he knew. He looked about desperately, trying to find his way back to the concrete building in which he had left Subodh and the prostitutes. But even that location was lost to him. His watch showed two o'clock in the morning. There would be people out again in three or four hours, maybe even some English speakers. He made his way into a corner of the street, a place that seemed somewhat dry and warm. Perhaps he could wait out both the night and his inebriation. He sank to the ground and huddled in the darkness, drawing his knees up to his chest in a comforting foetal position.

In his immobility, the sensory stillness of his environment became more pronounced. The occasional chitters of human interaction had vanished now. And the sparse moonlight did not filter down to his location. There was no sound, not even the familiar buzz of insects. Only his nose was alive, assaulted by the stench of refuse and decay. His heart slowed and his breathing shallowed. The effects of his earlier chemical indulgence reasserted itself then, numbing his mind yet again, allowing his eyes to slip from perfect focus to a gaze about one-billionth of a degree behind common reality.

Arak would have made this ordeal tolerable. Instead, he fought a sense of nauseating fear that boiled from his loins up through his stomach, threatening to grip his throat with the iron fist of irrational paranoia. And in the shadows beyond him, where the interplay of filtered moonbeams and ambient light shifted spectra through differing degrees of grey, a familiar figure of interplexing light began to take shape. It seemed at home in such a foul-smelling vermin-infested place as this. As always, it sat as his mirror, silently watching him.

His drug-addled imagination formed the light show into a figure, man-sized and hunched. But from the shadows there emerged neither a man nor a ghost, but a dog of mixed breed. It was thin and sinewy, stricken with sores and scars, and baring its teeth with obvious unpleasant intent. Its growling approach was neither cautious nor fearful, but rather deliberately aggressive. Iskie rose to his feet and backed away from the corner, hoping the dog only desired his place. But as he moved away, the animal followed, stalking him.

Iskie turned and walked slowly down the street, looking back on occasion to check on the dog. It was no longer snarling, but still followed him, growling lowly. Iskie navigated wildly, turning onto streets and alleys at random. Still, the dog followed, and it was soon joined by several others, each more mangy and desperate than the last. Soon, an entire pack was following him, keeping about six metres to his rear. He was careful not to turn onto a street that was too wide, lest the animals find room enough to flank him.

There were still some hours before dawn and Iskie was growing weary. He stopped to rest, but the dogs kept ambling towards him. Then they exposed their teeth and began to approach him more stealthily, each struggling to find a flank along the narrow alleyway. Iskie bolted. He ran with all the lingering strength in his addled limbs, leaping piles of rubbish and scaling small fences along the way. The dogs kept chasing, easily overcoming those same obstacles, and now carelessly baring their teeth with fury. Iskie's body began to fail him, a sharp pain erupting from an ankle, a dull ache constricting his lungs.

His mind found surprising clarity, the effort of his adrenal glands having overwhelmed the toxins that had dulled and wearied his nerves. But his body was spent, starved for warmth, rest, and fluids. He stumbled into an awkward limp, moving ever forward as the dogs became more brazen. Professor Kumar had once described the autonomic nervous system as embodying the Four F's: feeding, fighting, fleeing and … mating. The memory caused Iskie's strained face to briefly relax in a smile, and an epiphany struck him. To dwell upon an innocuous memory in a time of genuine physical distress was to deny the grip of reptilian autonomy, to function free of the constraints of the immediate biological survival imperative. Perhaps, he wondered, this was what overcame doomed mountain climbers before they lay down to succumb to the cold. Perhaps in those final moments of life, after hours of a desperate return to the evolutionary hub, wrought with panic and adrenaline, such people were indeed graced with the essence of evolved humanity, the quiet considered recollection of a life lived.

Ignoring his limp, he stood proudly before the dogs. He marched towards them, mouth seamed and eyes bright with fire. The dogs continued to snarl, but they did not approach. He continued to march, forcing his strained ligaments to endure the pain, and waded through the filthy swarm of animals. They did not attack, and neither did they part for him, but merely watched impotently as he penetrated their ranks and continued on through the maze of streets, leaving them behind in their dumb bewilderment.

In his mind, Iskie had shown Alexandrian courage. His was the kind of pluck that inspired men to lead the charge over enemy ramparts, as the Greek king had been famous for doing. Iskie recalled a story of how when Alexander's men had grown weary of the many battles, their king had pushed them once more from their barges onto the Indian shore to loot and pillage. On one side of a wall waited the local warriors, armed to the teeth. On the other side, Alexander's men implored their master to let them return to the river. The god-king himself stood atop the wall, burning with solar intensity. Faced with the choice of escaping with his men or leaping headlong and alone into the enemy, he did not falter. He jumped alone into the melee, his sword's blade a dancing jewel under the Indian sun. For love of their king, the Greeks tore down the wall and fought to wrest Alexander's battered body from enemy hands. Alexander was feared mortally wounded, but he would heal weeks later, having shown his men that true courage springs from love, and that the frailty of the flesh is unimportant against such a revelation.

Iskie was red with self-satisfaction, his jaw as rigid as that of a mythic hero. He was puffed up and grand, expanded taut into a shell of spirited heroic brazenness. Yet a hollowness lingered, the same that had plagued him all day. After all, Alexander himself had not been sustained solely by deeds and voyages, but also by softer sentiments.

Some minutes later, guided only by his own sense of intent, Iskie emerged onto a major street that was nonetheless still abandoned. A sole motorized rickshaw puttputted towards him, a taxi driver on his way home. Iskie flagged him down and paid double to be returned to his hotel. His head hurt, his clothes were torn, his shins were bruised, and one ankle strained. Eunice would be proud.

21

A Binding

On the third day of Chhath, devotees stay indoors preparing more offerings. It is typically a joyous time in the household, when all the family members are engaged in a task that will result in the production of delicious foods to be consumed either by living mouths or by annihilating fire. The rising of the sun on the following day is anticipated with great delight, its arrival signalling the flowing of the benedictions of the god Surya, and a reminder that with each turn of the Great Wheel, the world is scrubbed anew and is prepared for a new beginning.

On this third day, in the villages of Whell and Omas, the preparations were identical to those of centuries past. The adherence to festival rites was a responsibility of joyful solemnity. Of course, it was dabbed here and there with touches of the modern: the occasional transistor radio blaring Bollywood film songs to the men grinding grain, or the Adidas running shoes worn by the children of some of the better-off villagers. But the flavour of the day was unmistakably one of timelessness. Thus was its charm. Thus was its power. All was primed for the rites that would pass in the evening and involved the offering of the foodstuffs to the fire god Agni. And that, in turn, was in preparation for the morning of the fourth and final day.

On the elevated plateau overlooking the heart of Whell, related work was underway. Workers had finished constructing a wood and bamboo *mandap* the night before, their labours lit by candles in elephant-shaped earthenware pots that were further signatures of Chhath festivity. In the morning, while devotees had dutifully ignored the rising sun, women of the wealthiest clan had lovingly graced the boxlike structure with garlands and ribbons. Within this flimsy cage a wedding would occur.

As the hours passed, their numbers grew. The estate became a humming hive. The currents of spirited conversation ebbed and flowed with the variability of temperature throughout the humid day. There was also an assault of colour. The men were decked out in fine cotton suits or finely embroidered undyed kurtas, while the women were universally clad in all manner of saris, from the regal Rajasthani purple to the more garish and brightly coloured northern styles. Weaving through the throngs were the ubiquitous streams of skinny children, seeming to course through the pockets of adults like insects following a complex but purposeful trajectory.

As the sun climbed to its apex in the sky, the crowd quieted. In its midst, two patriarchs met and embraced. Words were spoken and mutated rites performed, though neither man seemed comfortable with or knowledgeable about them. A hooded figure was led to the flowered structure, her head bent in mock submissiveness, her features concealed by clothing and jewellery of gold, jade, and taupe. As this all happened beneath Yggdrasil's Methuselah eye, the scene was one of civilized sylvan perfection: the artifice of human beauty caressed by the natural.

It was then that Iskandar awoke from a deep sleep, rising from his bed after what was supposed to have been a very brief respite. The train had crawled in at dawn, met by an Ambassador sedan driven by the man of silhouettes, Tenali. A spent and toxic Subodh, who had been spirited away to be bathed, dressed, and scented, left Iskie alone to curl up in his bed, grateful for a few moments of silence and stillness. Awake once more, he now absorbed the emptiness of the estate and recognized the urgency of his station. Someone had laid out a princely outfit for him, an embroidered kurta and pyjama of the softest silk. Melting into the crowd without incident, he quickly assembled himself and eased outside onto the lawn.

He wiped the sleep from his eyes and let the scene wash over him. The multitude of Lal faces was baffling, each familiar yet foreign. He felt the press of many eyes on his back. But that, of course, was a familiar sensation to him, one he easily ignored. Instead, he focused his energies on trying to see the happenings within the *mandap*. It seemed that Subodh had completed his procession, the *bharat*, for there he sat crowned with a kingly turban and veil, his eyes to the ground while a holy man muttered endlessly next to him.

Iskie considered briefly the events that had brought him to this point, the signposts of Alexandrian Destiny, the elements of his adventure. The pursuit of wasps, themselves driven by a kind of oneness of divine will, had ameliorated his already fluid decision-making process and brought him to this curious vale of passions and flavours. The pages of a book, torn by a woman of whom he conceived best as a formless, scented warmth and light, had pointed his direction. It was a strange and decidedly unorthodox route to this, the observance of an ancient rite of familial binding and presumed love, a rite of definitive permanence. And Iskie felt again the hollowness that had bitten him in Agra. It chilled him and caused him to breathe more heavily. He tried to slip back behind his eyes into his special realm of scientific dispassion, but found that he could not linger there. Dispassion offered him no comfort. *Why am I so unsettled?* But no ready response was forthcoming, except unconvincing hand-waving arguments about hangovers and fatigue.

Iskie cast his eyes about. To his further discomfort, he caught sight of Seema and Sonali crouched in a distant corner, surrounded by a clique of fresh-faced boys. He averted his gaze instinctively, but found, to his greater horror, that he was seated directly before an even more unwelcome sight. Professor Pradeep Kumar nodded to Iskie across the rows of bobbing black heads, a friendly smile dancing on his lips. Next to Kumar, Goran Damjanovic seemed to convulse in a silent belly laugh, no doubt preoccupied with another untranslatable Slavic joke. Iskie nodded in response, and quietly shuffled back towards the far edge of the grove.

He knew his destination then. His hollowness was filled with a seeping warmth and contentment. He knew its name and sang it joyfully to himself.

Abruptly, large groups of people stood and began milling about and speaking in loud whispers, though the couple remained locked in their bamboo prison. Iskie found himself suddenly shaking hands with strangers and trying to learn innumerable and unpronounceable Indian names. Without warning, the party of Seema and Sonali and their two courtiers appeared before him, smiling coldly while clutching the fringes of their saris to their bodices. Iskie tried to turn away, but caught sight of Kumar approaching from another direction. He returned his attention to the glittering young women.

"Iskandar," Seema sang, "you look like you want to run away!"

"Yes, Iskie," Sonali said giggling. "We don't bite. Well, maybe Seema would. But you know that already." The two of them laughed aloud and were quickly shushed by one of their beaming boys.

"I'm Rajesh Dhir," the hushing boy said. He was shiny and wiry, diminutive, and with thinning hair. But he was bursting with vitality and dangerous intelligence. "And you are the famous Diamandi, the white bug chaser. We've heard reports of the white ghost in the woods. Glad to know it's just you!"

"I'm a little too fat to be a good ghost," Iskie answered, with no humour in his voice.

"Iskie," Sonali said, "why are you trying to run away?"

"Oh, he's looking for Kalya," Seema added. "Aren't you, Iskie?" Her eyes slitted somewhat. But it could have been Iskie's imagination.

"Where is she?" Iskie asked.

"If Subodh weren't getting married, I bet we'd find them both in his bedroom right now," Dhir exclaimed. Iskie shot him a hard look. "Come on, man. These Lal cousins are notorious! Especially that Subodh. I don't know how he's going to stick to one woman now." The other boy, silent and unnamed, just smiled and nodded.

"He's going to have to wait another day," Seema said. The others looked to her questioningly. "Didn't you hear? My mother says that Anjali will be spending the night in the village while Subodh stays in the big house. And it's going to be that way until they go away together tomorrow night. She says Subodh's mother can't stand the idea of her son sleeping with anyone under her own roof!"

Sonali restrained a sputtering laugh. "She must be deluding herself!"

"Look," Iskie said. "I'd like to find Kalya. Have you seen her?"

"She's the cousin from America, right?" Dhir asked. "Yes, I think I saw her and the tall pointy servant go down that path earlier." Dhir pointed beyond the labyrinth to the path that extended past the grove into the village. Iskie nodded his thanks and went off.

"Iskandar!" Seema called back. "We're all staying in one of the guest houses over there. Come by later tonight!" She blew him a kiss and the four of them exploded in laughter. Iskie hurried along.

The laughter receded behind him as he descended into the village. Its dirt paths had been swept clean, each home at its manicured best. Those whose stations were not lofty enough to warrant an invitation to the wedding lingered in comfortable groups, exchanging holiday pleasantries. To Iskie, they offered wide grins and genial nods, the children waving frantically.

He continued along the path, its route deliberately circuitous. In a typical moment of random focus, he considered the ancientness of his steps, the fact that villagers had walked these same paths for centuries if not millennia. The subdued extravagance above and behind him was a taste of the New World in this web of pervasive oldness. In many ways, with every step he was descending into the past.

With no sign of Kalya in the heart of the village, his destination became clear. He quickened his pace and soon emerged onto the pine-needle-strewn clearing that marked the border between village and forest—Eunice's domain. There, instead of a coyly draped canopy, he saw a raging fire, its smoke having somehow remained undetected from within the village. A lone dark figure tended the fire, while a second sat further in the distance, looking on with glazed and immobile features.

"Kalya?" he asked, bursting with a need to hold her near, the hollowness now completely expunged from his questing heart.

"Iskie?"

He sat next to her and slipped his hand into hers. He reached over and dabbed the tears on her face. "What is this?"

"A cremation," she answered.

Iskie's face paled. "Eunice?" he asked. Kalya nodded. "When? How?"

Kalya did not answer at once, nor did she turn to look at Iskie. Instead, her gaze was transfixed on the flames, her attention on the attendant odours and shapes. Against her will, she recalled the funeral pyre of her Ajee so many years ago. Both women had brought her repeatedly to the edge of the forest, had given her cause to flirt with the untamed fringe of nature. "She had been dying for a while, Iskie. Pancreatic cancer, I think. It finally happened the day you left for Agra. She wanted to be cremated the same time as Subodh's wedding." Iskie shot her a look of bewilderment. "I don't know why. Something about love and death being necessarily linked."

They sat in silence for some time, watching Tenali feed the rising flames with wood and kerosene. The sun was low on the horizon now, and the fire crackled in lively contrast to the motionless canvas of darkening forest.

"I don't understand," Iskie said suddenly. "She told me I could see her one more time."

Kalya looked to him with a disappointed frown clawing her features. She withdrew from him somewhat, denying him her warmth. "Iskie, she was just an old woman. It's not like she really knew the future."

"I know, I know. But she said—"

"Just be quiet, Iskie. You didn't know her. I did. I think I may have been the only one."

Iskie nodded, abashed. He took a deep breath, then draped his arm over her, pulling her closer. "I'll come to your room tonight. I'll make you forget all this. . ." She pushed him away and froze him with a penetrating stare.

"Look what Subodh has done to you!" she spat. "Already thinking with your crotch, just like the rest of them. I really don't want to look at you right now. Just go away."

Iskie leapt to his feet. "Look, that's not what I meant. I'm trying to comfort you." He sighed, then nodded and began backing away. A touch of the chilling emptiness nipped him then, but he willed it away, confident that the warmth would soon return. In the meantime, he would find his own comfort in a bottle of arak. He had missed its odd herbal flavour, its mind-expanding properties. Casting a final glance at both the holy fire and the grieving girl, he trudged back towards the village. In the distance, animals howled among the trees, and the full moon began its ascent from beneath the jagged horizon.

22

ARAK

The great wheel turned and night dropped its starry fabric upon the world. As predicted, a glorious full moon presided over this tropical vale, showering the straggling wedding celebrants with the gentlest of light, constraining the world of colour to a handful of hues but a universe of moods. Like those nights so many years ago when the Lal children would camp by the grove with their Ajee, this evening saw the dance of dry leaves tossed in a kind of ghostly cotillion, a mystic quadrille to summon the unseen things. Descending darkness brought its own palette of shades, and an anaglyph of ethereality was slowly drawn.

On the Lal estate, conversation among the lingering drunkards was loud but sporadic, punctuated here and there by the slapping of a knee or an explosion of heartfelt laughter. Soon, even these raucous few tired of revelry and made their stumbling way to the guest houses reserved for them in the village below. Quieter sounds emanated from the blackness. A symphony of crickets emerged from the background of the natural soundscape, setting an irregular rhythm for the arrival of bolder sounds.

Monkeys and owls joined the chorus, while the braying of domesticated village beasts rose in a solo before subsiding to the undifferentiated background.

The moonlight shone down upon Yggdrasil from an acute angle, altering its pouncing form to resemble instead the outstretched arms of a grandfather. Yggdrasil was the conductor of this strange concert and beckoned the buzzing things and grunting beasts to sing in their own musical way. The bats, though silent, danced frenetically to this environmental orchestration, fluttered against the starfield, and wove through the forest and grove. They soared to breathe and then dove to chase the female fig wasps who, it seemed, never slept.

Had any of the celebrants remained, they might have chanced to glimpse the orange flash of a timid predator prancing on the fringes of the grove. The forest fox trod lightly upon the bed of pine needles, licking the moisture from the air and smelling the coming monsoons. In the unearthly twinkle of moonlight, passing soundlessly and timelessly, she appeared as a ghost flickering between the trees.

Taking no notice of the natural treasures that presented themselves to him, a pink-skinned young man sauntered lazily past the grove and through the labyrinth. He did not notice the parade of dung beetles, the shamelessness of frolicking grouse or even the passage of a lone mongoose on the hunt for a cold slithering thing. Iskandar, making his way to the Lal estate, entered the house from the servants' entrance where workers were cleaning up as silently as they could. Smoothly, he snatched the last bottle of arak from the pantry and continued on walking to his room, intent on numbing his brain and soothing his thoughts.

He fell backward onto his bed, in his mind plummeting through the lunar dreamscape, over that conceptual cliff that had stultified so many dreamers. He pressed the bottle to his lips and drank deeply, enjoying the sensation of the vegetative bitterness slipping through his throat. As he swallowed, the ceiling opened up once more, and he pictured himself floating to the sky. But the ground had also opened, and a vortex on the other side of the world sucked him back down to Earth. The two forces were balanced, he felt, keeping him unsuspended but weightless. Such was the magic of arak.

His thoughts began to fragment, to lose that tethered tautness that formed his intellect, but that usually prevented him from deviating too far from the conventional. He continued to drink, sipping now as a baby would suckle from a teat. He closed his eyes, and disjointed movie frames presented themselves to his idle brain. They were awash with abstractness, smeared water colours that so resembled a squashed insect. He traced the streaks with his mind's eye, imagining them to be the trail of Alexander's march from Pella to India, then seeing instead the flight trajectory of a female fig wasp. A smile crept onto his lips: he must remember one day to intoxicate a wasp and see if it still remembered, or cared for, its singular mission. Or would that be cruel?

The dream earlier that afternoon, during his brief nap before the wedding, had been a sudden one awash with the usual bright colours and subsonic hums. Perhaps weddings had been on his mind, for his unconscious had brought him images of Olympia, Alexander's mother, on the day of her wedding to Philip of Macedon. What kind of man has dreams of lesser known historical figures? he asked himself wordlessly. *A man who wishes to find meaning*, came the soundless reply, echoing across the dreamscape in a familiar voice that was not his own. In the dream, Olympia had been dressed in what Iskie imagined to be ancient Hellenic wedding garb, but what had truly resembled modern Indian dress: sheer red fabric wrapped loosely about the hips and bosom. About her had danced an aura of devious play, witchery and revelry, though the gravity of contemplative intelligence had marked the features of her middle-aged face. Olympia had been a Dionysian, a heretic, not unlike Eunice.

Eunice's name lingered with him for a while, like a fading whisper. He pushed it down towards his subconscious. Eunice was dead. What would she herself have said about this? *The only cause of death is life, bug boy*, came another reply, this time in his own voice, sounding ridiculous with its fake Caribbean accent.

He breathed deeply and slowly, feeling with every breath greater intoxication grip his body. In the reddish blackness of his closed eyes and the silence of the room, he lost all sense of the passage of time. His breathing became a cadence to mark off the passing moments. The inhalations and exhalations became fewer and more widely spaced. He yearned to slip in between them, to pry apart the kernels of sequentiality and rest in the timeless space in between. Therein would lie true peace and understanding, with all roles and motivations laid out to be appraised and acknowledged, with vital context readily apparent to those willing to see. He held the moments in stasis.

In between the kernels he found that place of eternal stillness. It lulled his mind, but sang to his heart, causing ripples of formless emotion to wash along his spine: love, regret, self-pity, desire, rage. A formless glut of feeling, it was, seeking shape within his body, seeking purchase once more on the roughly trodden path of happenstance and sequentiality.

He opened his eyes. The room was dark, with only the traces of moonlight seeping in from the shuttered window. He could smell immobility and ancientness. Mixed in with them was a more earthly odour, one of rotting flesh. It grew in potency, seeming to swirl and coalesce. It took form in the corner of the room, presenting itself as planes of interplexing light, mere angular reflections of soft moonlight.

Feeling sluggish, as though he were swimming in glycerin, he pulled himself to a sitting position. The thing in the corner was similarly distorted, the way dim light appeared in murky water. He knew the wall was mere metres away, but sensed it to be much farther. He sat in awkward stillness, stealthy in the dark, but aware of his aloneness with a thing of disgusting beauty and questionable existence. If he looked directly upon it, it shifted from being. If he looked away, it appeared again in his periphery, taunting him to appreciate it fully. In sobriety, this would have been maddening. Or not happening at all.

Unable to take his eyes off the thing, he saw it take form and stand, no longer glittering but dull and ragged. He smelled its potency, an eons-old bacterial feast brewed in a fungal stew. Like a plane of light, it slipped through the cracks of his door and into the hallway. Iskie followed, not noticing if he, too, flattened his body and slid through the crevices, or whether he simply opened the door and walked through.

The house was silent and perfectly dark. The only light suffused from the walls, as if stored from years of human warmth. Iskie could not feel the floor beneath his feet, nor see his hand before his face. But he could smell his quarry. It stood to his side, moving ever slowly down the hall. He followed, tuning his peripheral vision to appreciate the thing that led him, willing it to appear as a man.

Iskie stumbled along, oddly feeling little fear—feeling little of anything anymore, really. He reached out to the wall and felt an angular object. It was the framed passage from Tennyson's *The Lady of Shalott.* He used it to steady himself, his memory settling on a passage from the poem: "But in her web she still delights/ To weave the mirror's magic sights." Staying close to the wall, he moved forward, following the odour and struggling to perceive the luminous being he had willed to human form. His brain swam and the world spun.

He came upon a door frame. It was Kalya's room, he realized. The door was open, and a crack of moonlight from the bedroom window revealed the bed to be empty. He lingered for a moment. The figure turned back to him, drawn by his immobility.

The moments slipped in viscous fluidity, time having slowed and thickened. Every cell in Iskie's body was lit with a microscopic flame. The face of the apparition was gradually revealed to him, sharpening in focus as it neared, but visible only peripherally. He held his breath for an instant, his energies directed entirely to the absorption of the vision that angled before him. He looked upon it as fully as his sideways glance would allow, appreciating for the first time in his life the thing that had watched him since childhood. It was a robust and ancient form, with black pupils atop black irises, oily pools that drew him in. His sideways perception would not permit the whole body to be seen, but the face could be sensed in pieces and patches, though only as partly imagined shards of suspended light. It had no ears, but it possessed a bridgeless animalistic nose that now seemed to breathe in long gasping wretches. Its mouth was a bestial gash afflicted with chipped and bloodied canine teeth, tools for ripping and tearing. And its cheeks. . .on either side of its face, were fresh scratch marks, open and bloodied.

Iskie gasped. *Bucephalus?*

It turned and continued to move silently down the hallway. Iskie struggled to maintain his perception, to gather whether it was more than the random interplay of reflected moonlight. He followed, stepping cautiously in the blackness, battling his drunkenness while keeping close to the hallway wall. He came upon another door, Subodh's room. The door was unlocked, but noises could be heard from within. He gingerly pushed open the door and peered in.

Subodh lay atop the bed, writhing in delight, struggling to remain silent. Atop him sat a voluptuous brown figure of soft curves and long hair. Her head turned slightly. The moonlight played strangely on the sliver of her face, enhancing her eyes' appearance of reflectivity. As recognition washed over him, Iskie's jaw quivered and his heart weakened. "*Kalya*," he wept.

The kernels of time flowed again, though now he was trapped between them, unable to act or react. He stood in drowning senselessness, feeling his eyes well with tears and his ears deafened by the rush of his own blood. On the nape of his neck he felt a foul breath, an ancient wet thing whispering words he could not make out. Bucephalus lingered a moment longer, then continued down the hallway. Iskie followed, staggering now from the shortness of his breath and the torrent of unfiltered despair that threatened to overcome him.

A door was opened and he stumbled through it. He was outdoors, no longer aware of the path he was to follow. There was no longer any sight or smell of Bucephalus, only the night's embrace. The air on Iskie's skin felt ancient, though the sounds of life from the night-blackened trees were vital and fresh. The peculiar odour of evening grass, pollens, and spores percolated in the darkness, assaulted his subconscious, and drove him to further distraction, away from the transient focus that had gripped him to this point. He kept trudging along the walk-up and down into the village, with every step becoming more enveloped by the wild night.

The moonlight flooded his world and he sensed his true alonenes. Sniffing back tears, he kept walking, gripping his scalp in an effort to wring sobriety back into his head. Once he tripped and fell, tearing the knees of his expensive pyjama. Bloodied and bowed, unable to think coherently, and discomforted by a strange pressure in his sinuses, he stumbled aimlessly, a pale-skinned beggar.

"What have we here?" he heard someone remark. "It's the white ghost, I think. The *gora bhut*. Come to suck milk from our goats? Or just to scare the children and seduce the women?" Laughter.

"But why does the white ghost haunt these woods? Plenty Indian ghosts here already."

"Maybe the brown ones need a *sahib* to keep them in line, eh?" More laughter. "But look, he's bloody! Maybe he isn't playing the ghost tonight, but rather the beast or the knave."

"Come now, friends. Let us not be rude to our spirit visitor. Is it right that we make assumptions of him? Let's simply ask him. Iskandar, who are you this night? Are you the lover, the seeker, the beast, the ghost, or the knave? Who are you?"

Iskie, squinting at the four figures, managed to stand straight and wipe his face clean. "Rajesh Dhir?" he asked. "Is that you?"

"Yes, old man," Dhir said with Subodh's schoolboy familiarity. "Fall down, did we?"

A girl threw her arms about Iskie and held him to her. He did not resist, and was comforted by her warmth. He allowed himself to sag, sinking into her torso, but repressed his tears. "Poor Iskandar," Seema said, stroking his hair and face. "Kalya broke your heart, didn't she."

"Serves him right," Sonali sneered, the head of the unnamed silent boy resting in her lap. She swayed a little, knocking over one of the several empty liquor bottles that were arrayed on the tree stump.

"No one deserves a broken heart," Seema said. "Especially not our white ghost. He is supposed to be the one to break hearts, like he broke mine." She pulled Iskie's face towards her own until their noses touched, and he could detect the stench of alcohol upon her breath. "But I forgive you, Iskie, because I knew I'd have you back." She pressed her lips to his, tasting deeply of his tears and dread.

Iskie reclined into the embrace, taking hold of Seema's head and shoulders and kissing her with abandon. Her lips were bitter, tainted with a residue of rum and cigarette smoke, but they were warm and willing. His tongue probed the wetness of her mouth, his lips revelling in the springy tenderness of her flesh, the welcome calm of her scent and her soft voice. He lingered for some time, afraid to let go lest the coldness of the night snatch him once more and infuse his body and will with the dead wetness that he sensed was all about him.

Still, Iskie found that he could not feel. Maybe it was the arak, which dulled his senses in order to lend him perception of a different sort. Or maybe it was an innate failing on his part, an intrinsic inability to act from genuine raw passion. A part of him screamed in rationalization: his feelings for Kalya, his Roxanne, had been illusory after all, a fantasy fixation not bred from true familiarity. Another part pleaded to return to the dreamscape wherein the world was as he willed it, with the forces of nature and the egos of gods bent to service his fantasies. And with the dissolution of the dream, he would flee. Back to Kumar's hill station. Or back to Canada. Eunice had said that his story began in India. But it didn't have to end here.

He pulled himself from Seema's lips, abashed at the ease with which he had sunk to their comfort. He held her face in his hands and drew her gaze into his black eyes, silently pleading with her to read his heart. "No," he mouthed to her. "No. I'm sorry. I cannot."

Surprisingly, Seema laughed. "I know that, Iskie. But it was nice to taste you again." From over Seema's shoulder, Iskie sensed a dark glare. A man of silhouettes, bearing wood and empty gas canisters, stared at him in silence, his deliberate tread towards the estate slowing.

"Tenali!" The servant's glowering expression reached deeply into Iskie's mind, searing him with a special kind of shame. He was reminded of Kalya's words: *Tenali's eyes are my eyes*. Surely, his shame was unwarranted. But emotions are not meant to follow the rules of reason. They are a magical fog of both benign and vicious potential, true poisons of the intellect. He watched Tenali's back vanish in the distance, as if through the wrong end of a telescope.

"Iskandar," Rajesh Dhir said foppishly, "if you're not going to kiss our dear Seema, might I have her back? We were enjoying a dance before you arrived, you know." Dhir took Seema's hand and pulled her to him. "First Kalya interrupts us, then moments later Iskandar barges in, and now that nasty servant tramps by. Could these woods be any less private?" There was more annoying drunken laughter.

"Kalya?" Iskie spun to face Dhir. "She was here just before me?"

"Sure, man! She said she came from a funeral. Strange girl. She was off to get something to eat in the pantry."

"Then who's in the house with Subodh?"

Dhir almost fell over, he was laughing so hard. "His wife, of course!"

23

TIME TO FLEE

The memory of the poem on the wall lingered. "Thro' the noises of the night/ She floated down to Camelot." It was a dreamy phrase, eliciting within him reflection and remorse. But he had been wakened from the dream, and Tennyson's words were now cold and sterile.

He found her finishing a quick meal of dal and rice in the pantry. The servants had magically vanished and true stillness had overcome the house. The spoor of Tenali remained, however. Iskie felt the silhouette man's eyes on his face and shoulders, like strong fingers pointing and pressing. She cleaned her plate with a swipe of her right hand, wiping it on her skirt. She rose and left.

"Wait," Iskie said. "Where are you going?"

She didn't look back. "To my room," she answered. "I have to pack."

"Are you leaving?"

"Yes," she said, without emotion. "I've just decided. It's almost sunrise. Tenali will drive me to the train station at first light. I'm going to Delhi, then flying home." She kept walking, and Iskie followed.

His heart bubbled in his throat. "I have to tell you something," he said.

"I know. Tenali saw."

"You have to understand. . ."

She pierced him with a look, then whispered, "Keep your voice down. Come to my room." Iskie's face hardened, and he perceived the gradual subsidence of his most recent chemical augmentation. He followed her sheepishly into her room, not even taking notice of Subodh's tightly shut door or the crooked picture frame on the hallway wall.

Kalya said nothing, but simply took a large suitcase down from a shelf and placed it on her bed. Her room was almost bare, and she began to pack her few belongings in a rushed though passionless manner.

"You have to understand," Iskie began. "I thought—"

"It doesn't matter what you thought," Kalya interrupted, never pausing in her task. "Your first instinct was to run to that girl. What does that say about you? Or about what I mean to you?"

Iskie deposited himself on the bed and clutched his scalp, pressing his fingers until it hurt. "I'm sorry, Kalya. I'm sorry. Don't leave. Please, let's just talk about it a little."

Kalya sighed. "Don't plead, Iskie. Look, I'm mad at you right now, but it will fade. The bigger question is, What am I doing here? This is not my home, and my vacation is over. It's just time for me to go."

"How can you say that? Where will you go?"

She arched her back and pressed her hands against the base of her neck, as if forcing back a thought. "Oh, Iskie. When I was a little girl in Montreal, I got to come here to visit a couple of times. My fondest memories are of the times I spent with my Ajee, my grandmother."

"You told me about those times."

"Yes, I know. Back then, the stories she told me about this place, and about our family's history, seemed to make this village a sort of fantasy home. You see? There is a connection, but I never let myself forget that it was a fantasy. I never let myself forget that so many of Ajee's stories were also fantasies. Reality is never as interesting as fantasy, and it's never as easy. But in the end, it's always more enduring. This was never my real home. I always knew that I was just hiding out here, just resting. And now I've got to go home. There isn't much left for me here."

Iskie felt punched in the chest. "What will Auntie and Uncle say?"

She chuckled softly. "Trust me, they'll be relieved. They won't know I've left until well into the day. Oh, they'll openly lament losing me, but, privately they'll be happy that I'm not their responsibility any longer. They've been expecting this for a while."

"Kalya, this is my fault. I shouldn't be the cause of you leaving. I should be the one who leaves. Or neither of us should leave. Not yet!"

Kalya continued her packing, her face a portrait of determined solemnity. "It's nobody's fault, Iskie. Well, maybe it's a little your fault. But it's still time for me to go. I only wish. . ."

"What? You wish what?"

She sighed, then glimpsed herself in the vanity mirror on the dressing case. She lingered on the image for a while, curiously slow to recognize her own face. Her features were taut and tensed, her skin flush with the heat of the night, and her eyes alive, straining to peer through into the future. Hers was a wild expression, she felt, almost feral. It was a disturbing sight, reflecting panic in the quiver of her jowls, and simpleness in the unblinking openness of her eyes. She repressed a brief urge to flee from the reflection, to run off into the forest night. "I only wish I could have trusted you," she said, at last tearing her eyes from her reflection and feeling tempted now to leave without even packing. "Or that you had trusted me."

"Tell me how to change your mind!"

She bent over him and held his face in her hands. "You can't. Please don't try."

He watched her pack in silence, noting the scent and dimension of every item of clothing, every folded Indian print. She placed a sheaf of papers in the suitcase, then paused, picked an envelope and handed it to Iskie.

"Here," she said. "Something to remember me by. It's one of the letters Neil wrote to me. It may sound cruel of me now, but I want you to know the true voice of treachery. Neil's a master of it. Never become like him. Or like Subodh. Iskie, there's still hope for you."

He took the letter joylessly. "Kalya, there's something else I need to tell you about. Tonight, I think I saw Bucephalus."

She stopped for a moment. "Really? Oh, Iskie. You drink so much bloody arak, is it a wonder you have hallucinations? I wish I'd never introduced you to the stuff. It's not magic and it doesn't give you any special kind of perception. I think the sooner you stop looking for meaning where there isn't any, the sooner you'll find some real meaning. Don't you agree?"

"Is that what Eunice told you?"

Kalya was silent for a moment. "Iskie, Eunice told me to tell you one last thing. She told me to remind you of how Alexander tamed his horse. Do you know that story?"

"Yes, I think so," Iskie answered distantly. He slowly recalled the tale. "King Philip had purchased Bucephalus when Alexander was still a boy. But the horse was too headstrong to tame. So Philip was going to destroy it. Alexander asked his father to be given the horse if he could prove he could master it. All Alexander did was to turn the horse's head to face the sun, so it couldn't see its own shadow. It seems it was being spooked by the shadow the whole time."

Kalya smirked. "Spooked by shadows. Pretty poignant, eh?"

"Yeah, maybe, if you fill it with allegory. I always thought it was a stupid story."

"A stupid story? But you love everything about Alexander!"

"Do I?" Iskie's breathing grew shallower, and he found himself clenching and unclenching his fists. "I'm supposed to be his reincarnation, right?" He tried to laugh, but coughed instead. "But Alexander's Roxanne didn't leave him, did she?"

"No, Iskie. She was murdered, remember?"

"I'm not Alexander, Kalya. I know that. It was just a game."

"No it wasn't, Iskie." She shoved the last of her things into the case, then began changing her clothes in front of him. "You're fearless like Alexander. You're brilliant like him, and a bit ruthless and immoral like him, too. And like Alexander, you keep inventing meaning in things, making things seem more important and grand than they need to be—filling them with allegory, if you will." She fixed him with a good hard stare. "You're already pretty damned meaningful and impressive, Iskie. You don't need to create more importance. Because when you do, and when you rationalize it all with Fate and Destiny, you risk losing those things that might actually be truly important."

Iskie grinned a little through his sorrow. Kalya peered at him curiously as she kicked off her slippers and tied on her runners. A memory of words spoken in a Caribbean accent stoked his smile. *Yuh don' need pretend to search fo' God, when all you wan' be one kiss. It okay. It human.* He chuckled some more, but the tears continued to well.

"And Iskie," she said soberly, "maybe what you think you feel for me. . . maybe you invented that, too."

Iskie looked at her in horror, then shook his head vigorously. "No!"

"I wonder," Kalya said, "who Alexander loved and trusted more, the horse or his Roxanne. I guess we'll never know." She zipped up her suitcase and stood up with finality. Then she bent low and kissed Iskie on the forehead, letting her lips linger for a moment. She pressed her eyes shut, forcing back the world for a few seconds longer, revelling one last time in restful hiding. Time to wake, time to flee. "Goodbye, my Alexander," she sang, casting a final glance at her reflection in the mirror. And she was gone, leaving Iskie, wet, dishevelled and bloody-kneed, to stare at the walls of her empty room and long in vain to be cast once more into the dream.

24

REGRET

It was the fourth and final day of Chhath. Most of the revelry had come to an end, but the sunrise proved the pinnacle of the festival, the point at which the devotees of Surya dabbed their foreheads with benedictive dyes and sang age-old songs of renewal. An Ambassador sedan sped away to the train station, its passenger curled up in the back seat clutching her suitcase and willing herself not to feel regret. Meanwhile, the new groom rose from his bed to walk down the path into the village where his new bride had miraculously reappeared in her guest house. They enjoyed a meal together for the first time as husband and wife, watched dutifully by representatives from both families which were now, after all, the same family.

After this relaxed ceremonial obligation, guests gradually vanished into the morning and returned to their lives of variable fascination and depth. Some went to their homes, others lingered on the estate, while still others took to exploring the forest and its many curiosities. The hour before noon saw one particular gathering, that of a Himalayan professor and his friend with the parents of the groom, the four drawn to the oddly calming complexity of the Victorian labyrinth.

"The maze is one of the more nauseating of artistic archetypes," Goran pronounced.

"How so?" Palvinder Lal asked. Professor Kumar closed his eyes and shook his head, fearing the tactlessness to come.

"Every teenage boy draws one on the back of his grammar notebook. Thinks it is so complicated and important. Just silly swirls. It is the art of children," Goran said proudly.

"Mr. Damjanovic," Mrs Lal said, "Palvinder's great-great-great-grandfather designed this maze."

Goran scowled. "Then he must have been a teenage boy when he did it."

Kumar stepped in. "Actually, the labyrinth is a mathematical goldmine. Your ancestor chose well to adopt its design. Things in a maze are never as they seem. Much like the rest of this property, really."

"How so?" Mrs Lal asked.

"Take the pine needles on the ground," Kumar continued. "Many would say that they're an indication of decay. Pine needles sometimes turn to acid, you see. But they also retain moisture and keep the soil healthy and fertile. An undisciplined eye would see only the darkness, while a truly open eye would see both the dark and the light. You get my meaning?"

Goran rolled his eyes. "You are a good entomologist, Pradeep, but a truly shitty poet and philosopher. Stick with your strengths."

"Well, there's more," Kumar said. "I surveyed much of this region for my book. Goran, did you know that the army of Alexander the Great once rested by that big tree? To some, it's a major historical site. You probably would not have guessed that."

"No, I would not," Goran said, winking at the Lals. "Because everyone knows Alexander never made it into Bihar. I am an artist, Pradeep, which means I am closer to being a historian than would be an entomologist. Wouldn't you agree? But I will grant you that Bihar was probably home to the historic Buddha at one point. He was famous for sitting by trees. Maybe he sat by that one. Alexander, Buddha. . . is all the same. Famous dead men who sit like stumps. Makes for boring stories and truly horrible art."

Mrs Lal smiled. Palvinder opened up his easel and unrolled the canvas. On it was his sketch of a man's face contorted in agony, the flesh of his cheeks scratched away by his own hands. "Mr. Damjanovic—"

"Please, call me Goran."

"All right. Goran. You're in the arts?"

"In the arts, of the arts, for the arts. But what is art in this day? I fart after tea, some say it is art. My gallery does not hang farts, though. Don't know how." The Lals frowned, but offered no other reaction. Kumar laughed nervously.

"Perhaps," Palvinder Lal said, "you can give me your opinion of this piece." He gestured to his sketch on the easel.

Goran glanced at it cursorily. "Piece of crap. I would not buy it." The Lals remained expressionless. Kumar massaged his forehead. "But I like the expression on the face. Reminds me of Munsch."

Palvinder's spirits were buoyed some. "Really? What do you think the expression says?"

"It says regret," Goran offered. "Terrible regret when it's too late. Like maybe this man lost much money betting on a worthless Indian cricket team. I like that the exact moment of greatest regret is captured in a static manner, like a movie still. Otherwise, it is still crap."

Lal said, "What if I tell you he's in the last moments of his life?" His wife placed a hand on his shoulder.

"Well, then his regret has to do with love. What else can it be? He has a son, maybe, with whom he has not reconciled." Goran paused and frowned. "No, that is not it. This is not a man of great outward passion, at least not most of his life, only now at the end. He has puttered his whole life on that ridiculous Hindu duty—dharma—or trying to fight and dominate, only to realize too late that all he wanted was a little love." Goran looked Kumar squarely in the eye. "Or he was a scientist who thought his work was more important than it was, he got a swelled head, and now it explodes."

Kumar suddenly brightened. "Look who comes! Iskandar!" Iskie shuffled toward them, freshly showered and shaved, carrying a pack of things, but offering very little in the way of expression.

"We've not formally met," Goran said to Iskie. "But maybe you've seen me visiting Pradeep in the lab. He speaks often of you."

"Yes, yes," Kumar said. "We've both been reading your thesis proposal, Iskie. Very interesting. I've been expounding your virtues as a philosopher among entomologists. Please, give us a taste. Tell us about the spiritual plight of the fig wasp, about the 'reversal of the sexual archetype,' as you put it. Something about 'the feminine in blind pursuit of the masculine, in stark opposition to the tradition of the biological imperative.'"

"Jesus Christ," Goran groaned under his breath.

Iskie smiled. "Maybe," he said. "Maybe I misspoke. Or overspoke, if that's a word. Maybe it's just a bug trying to find a place to lay its eggs, living a simple unconcerned life, the poor little bastard. Now, if you excuse me." He nodded genially to the Lals and walked on in the direction of Yggdrasil's grove.

To Iskie's shrinking back, Palvinder Lal said, "There goes a romantic figure. He's a boy of many passions and deep intellect. Ripe for misadventure and heartbreak, I should think."

"Oh, he's not a romantic figure," Kumar said dryly, his words coated with a thin film of anger. "He's a tragic figure."

"How so?" Lal asked.

"To know so much about the world, yet to know so little about the world. Now, that's a tragedy."

Goran rolled his eyes. "No, Pradeep. The real tragedy is that you insist on trying to sound poetic when you just haven't got it in you. Come, let us have lunch."

25

CODA

Iskie sat at Yggdrasil's feet, playing with the almost empty bottle of arak, refusing to sip from it. The sun was at its peak now, and a terror of black clouds nipped at its edges. The great rains had come at last. The blazing full moon of the previous night had left no record of its intensity, having been swallowed in whole and in silence by the percolating sky. He let his mind slip over the past few days and hours, resting comfortably at points of pleasure and curiosity. He wound the tape of memory to the point of greatest calm earlier the night before, when the particles of time had been stilled and apprehended, held aloft for the spaces in between to be inspected.

Positioned in that remembered stasis, he formed himself in the corner of his room and squatted to watch his own drunken body sit up on the bed and squint at him. A being of light and imagination, he slid through the door and down the hall, drawn to the outside. Behind him, his self followed, stumbling in disgusting intoxication.

He watched as his body opened the door to Subodh's room and his eyes glazed over. He went back to himself, whispered in his own ear, "Things aren't as they seem. Trust her. Walk away." But he could not be heard, his helpfulness mistaken for monstrous inhuman gurgling. So instead he walked on into the night, dissolved for good into the embracing black forest and melded comfortably with the symphony of sound and the feral odours that circulated timelessly and cyclically.

In the here and now, he poured the contents of the bottle onto Yggdrasil's roots, imagining a drunken sleeping god at the Earth's core, then imagining again that this was only a tree, albeit an old tree, understanding at last that the world was whatever he made of it. His memory of Kalya shone in his inner eye, bright as the sun. He looked upon her remembered image unblinkingly, refusing to be seduced and spooked by shadows without form and substance, and refusing to give them shape and solidity.

In his mind, Kalya's parting words echoed: "Iskie, there's still hope for you." He fingered the envelope in his pocket, the one on which was so plainly printed Kalya Lal's Montreal address. And a boyish smile danced anew on his yogic lips and in his bright eyes.

ACKNOWLEDGMENTS

As with everything else in my life, my literary inspiration flows from my wonderful parents, Sursati and Walter Deonandan. It is their experiences, teachings, and perspective which truly reside at the heart of my writings.

Divine Elemental began as two short stories written in Guatemala while visiting my eldest sister, Kalowatie. My cousin Sandy Vishnu stood over my shoulder at several points, her presence challenging me to craft a more layered and intriguing narrative. A more unlikely muse I cannot imagine, but I am nonetheless grateful.

Helping the novel to evolve were several individuals who gen-erously read the manuscript at various stages and provided brutal but welcome feedback. They are: Adam Stevens, Barbra Sniderman, Julia Lenardon, Justine Whelan, Kristine O'Brien, Lauren Greenwald, Mary Ann Gorcsi, Sejal Patel, Sneh Aurora, Sue Kelly and Tine De Marez. Tine also volunteered her photographic suppleness and finesse for the author portrait. A special thanks goes to Linda Morra, not only for poring over initial drafts of the completed manuscript, but also for providing invaluable expert editorial guidance.

Final editing was done by Charles Anthony Stuart, who did a splendid professional job. David Drummond managed to evoke almost all of the story's many disparate themes with his clever and eye-catching cover art. And of course, this book would not be in print were it not for the keen eye (and excellent literary taste) of my publisher, Ms Nurjehan Aziz.

The naming of fictional characters is a task I try to enjoy as much as possible. For those who care about such things, the character "Neil Falter" was a wedding present to Neil Klar and Laura-Beth Falter, while "Rajesh Dhir" was the fulfilment of a promise made to Dhir's namesake. Iskie's surname, meanwhile, was derived from the name of my old friend Diamando Diamantakos. "Lal" was chosen for its Sanskrit meaning, "beloved one." The name of the fictional author "Jan Birbalsingh" was taken from Frank Birbalsingh, a Guyanese Canadian scholar whose surname I find delightfully curious. Lastly, while studying in India in 1996, it seemed to me that all my professors were named "Pradeep Kumar." In those days, reference was commonly made to the various Pradeeps Kumar who would grace our lecture halls in turn.

Lastly, the tale of Tomamu Nomei was adapted from a very old Japanese ghost story.

Generous funding was provided by grants from The Canada Council for the Arts, The Ontario Arts Council, and The Toronto Arts Council.

RAYWAT DEONANDAN was born in Guyana and makes his home in Toronto. He is the author of *Sweet Like Saltwater* (TSAR, 1999), which won the Guyana Prize for Best First Work.